EVERYMAN, I will go with thee,

and be thy guide,

In thy most need to go by thy side

SNORRI STURLUSON

Born in Iceland, 1178. Law-speaker of
the General Assembly, 1215–18, 1222–31.
In Norway 1218–20, 1237–9. Accused of
treason by the Norwegian king and murdered by a political enemy in 1241.

SNORRI STURLUSON

Heimskringla

PART ONE

The Olaf Sagas

IN TWO VOLUMES · VOLUME TWO

TRANSLATED BY
SAMUEL LAING

REVISED WITH AN INTRODUCTION
AND NOTES BY
JACQUELINE SIMPSON, M.A.

DENT: LONDON
EVERYMAN'S LIBRARY
DUTTON: NEW YORK

© *Editing and Introduction*
J. M. Dent & Sons Ltd, 1964

All rights reserved
Printed in Great Britain by
Redwood Press Limited
Trowbridge, Wiltshire
for
J. M. DENT & SONS LTD
Aldine House · Bedford Street · London
First included in Everyman's Library 1914
Revised edition 1964
Reprinted 1973

No. 722   ISBN (if a hardback) 0 460 00722 x
No. 1722   ISBN (if a paperback) 0 460 01722 5

CONTENTS

SAGA OF KING OLAF (HARALDSSON) THE SAINT

CHAPTER XCVIII. OF OLAF KING OF NORWAY, AFTER THE MEETING.—After the events now related Olaf returned with his people to Viken. He went first to Tunsberg, and remained there a short time, and then proceeded to the north of the country. In harvest time he sailed north to Drontheim, and had winter provision laid in there, and remained there all winter. Olaf Haraldsson was now sole and supreme king of Norway, and the whole of that sovereignty, as Harald Haarfager had possessed it, and had the advantage over that monarch of being the only king in the land. By a peaceful agreement he had also recovered that part of the country which Olaf the Swedish king had before occupied; and that part of the country which the Danish king had got he retook by force, and ruled over it as elsewhere in the country. The Danish king Canute ruled at that time both over Denmark and England; but he himself was in England for the most part, and set chiefs over the country in Denmark, without at that time making any claim upon Norway.

CHAPTER XCIX. HISTORY OF THE EARLS OF ORKNEY [995]. —It is related that in the days of Harald Haarfager the king of Norway, the islands of Orkney, which before had been only a resort for vikings, were settled. The first earl in the Orkney Islands was called Sigurd, who was a son of Eystein Glumra, and brother of Ragnvald earl of Möre. After Sigurd his son Guttorm was earl for one year. After him Torf Einar, a son of Rognvald, took the earldom, and was long earl, and was a man of great power. Halfdan Haaleg, a son of Harald Haarfager, assaulted Torf Einar, and drove him from the Orkney Islands; but Einar came back and killed Halfdan in the island Ronaldshay. Thereafter King Harald came with an army to the Orkney Islands. Einar fled to Scotland, and King Harald made the people of the Orkney Islands give up their udal properties, and hold them under oath from him. Thereafter the king and earl were reconciled, so that the earl became the king's man, and took the country as a fief from him; but that it should pay no scatt or feu duty, as it was at that time much plundered by vikings. The earl paid the king sixty marks of gold; and then King Harald went to plunder in Scotland, as related in the "Glim Drapa."[1] After Torf Einar, his sons Arnkel, Erlend, and Thorfin Hausakliff ruled over these lands. In their days came Eric Bloodyaxe from Norway, and subdued these earls. Arnkel and Erlend fell in a war expedition; but Thorfinn ruled the country long, and became an old man. His sons were Arnfinn, Haavard, Lödver, Liot, and Skule. Their mother was Grelaud, a daughter of Earl Dungad of Caithness. Her mother was Groa, a daughter of Thorstein Raude. In the latter days of Earl Thorfinn came Eric Bloodyaxe's sons, who had fled from Earl Hakon out of Norway, and committed great excesses in Orkney. Earl Thorfinn died on a bed of sickness, and his sons after him ruled over the country, and there are many stories concerning them. Lödver lived the longest of them, and ruled alone over this country. His son was Sigurd the Thick, who took the earldom after him, and became a powerful man and a great warrior. In his days came Olaf Trygvesson from his viking expedition in the Western ocean, with his troops, landed in Orkney, and took Earl Sigurd prisoner in South Ronaldshay, where he lay with one ship. King Olaf allowed the earl to ransom his life by letting himself be baptized, adopting the true faith, becoming his man, and introducing Christianity into all the Orkney Islands. As a hostage, King Olaf took his son, who was called Hund, or the Whelp. Then Olaf went to Norway, and became king; and Hund was several years with King Olaf in Norway, and died there. After his death Earl Sigurd showed no obedience or fealty to King Olaf. He married a daughter of the Scottish king Malcolm,[2] and their son was called Thorfinn. Earl Sigurd had besides older sons; namely, Sumarlid, Bruse, and Einar Rangmund. Four or five years after Olaf Trygvesson's fall Earl Sigurd went to Ireland, leaving his eldest sons to rule the country, and sending Thorfinn to his mother's father the Scottish king. On this expedition Earl Sigurd fell in Brian's battle.[3] When the news was received in

---

[1] By Thorbjorn Hornklove; see *Sagas of the Norse Kings*, pp. 56 ff.
[2] Malcolm II, King of Scotland, 1005-34.
[3] *i.e.* the battle of Clontarf, which was on 23rd April 1014—not 1004 or 1005, as Snorri reckons. It was fought between Brian Boru, High King of Ireland, and an alliance of Norse and Irish led by the viking king of Dublin, Sigtrygg Silky-Beard. The most elaborate and colourful account

Orkney the brothers Sumarlid, Bruse, and Einar were chosen
earls, and the country was divided into three parts among them.
Thorfinn Sigurdsson was five years old when Earl Sigurd fell.
When the Scottish king heard of the earl's death he gave his
relation Thorfinn Caithness and Sutherland, with the title of
earl, and appointed good men to rule the land for him.   Earl
Thorfinn was ripe in all ways as soon as he was grown up: he
was stout and strong, but ugly; and as soon as he was a grown
man it was easy to see that he was a severe and cruel, but a very
clever man.   So says Arnor, the earl's scald [1]:—

> " Under the rim of heaven no other,
> So young in years as Einar's brother,
> In battle had a braver hand,
> Or stouter, to defend the land."

CHAPTER C. OF THE EARLS EINAR AND BRUSE.—The brothers
Einar and Bruse were very unlike in disposition.   Bruse was a
soft-minded, peaceable man,—sociable, eloquent, and of good
understanding.   Einar was obstinate, taciturn, and dull;
but ambitious, greedy of money, and withal a great warrior.
Sumarlid, the eldest of the brothers, was in disposition like
Bruse, and lived not long, but died in his bed.   After his death
Thorfinn claimed his share of the Orkney Islands.   Einar
replied, that Thorfinn had the dominions which their father
Sigurd had possessed, namely, Caithness and Sutherland, which
he insisted were much larger than a third part of Orkney; therefore he would not consent to Thorfinn's having any share.
Bruse, on the other hand, was willing, he said, to divide with
him.   " I do not desire," he said, " more than the third part
of the land, and which of right belongs to me."   Then Einar
took possession of two parts of the country, by which he became
a powerful man, surrounded by many followers.   He was often
in summer out on marauding expeditions, and called out great
numbers of the people to join him; but it went always un-
pleasantly with the division of the booty made on his viking
cruises.   Then the bonders grew weary of all these burdens;
but Earl Einar held fast by them with severity, calling in all
services laid upon the people, and allowing no opposition from
any man; for he was excessively proud and overbearing.   And

of it in Icelandic is in *Njál's Saga*, chaps. cliv–vii; the chief Irish source
is *The War of the Gaedhil with the Gaill.*

[1] More correctly, " poet of the earls " (*jarlaskáld*), for both Earl Thorfinn
and Earl Rognvald of Orkney were his patrons.   He also wrote in praise of
King Magnus the Good and King Harald the Stern.

now there came dearth and scarcity in his lands, in consequence of the services and money outlay exacted from the bonders; while in the part of the country belonging to Bruse there were seasons of abundance, and a peaceful life for the bonders. He was well liked.

CHAPTER CI. OF THORKEL AAMUNDSSON.—There was a rich and powerful man who was called Aamund, who dwelt in Rossay [1] at Sandwick, in Laupandanes. His son, called Thorkel, was one of the ablest men in the islands. Aamund was a man of the best understanding, and most respected in Orkney. One spring Earl Einar proclaimed a levy for an expedition, as usual. The bonders murmured greatly against it, and applied to Aamund, with the entreaty that he would intercede with the earl for them. He replied, that the earl was not a man who would listen to other people, and insisted that it was of no use to make any entreaty to the earl about it. " As things now stand, there is a good understanding between me and the earl; but, in my opinion, there would be much danger of our quarrelling, on account of our different dispositions and views on both sides; therefore I will have nothing to do with it." They then applied to Thorkel, who was also very loath to interfere; but promised at last to do so, in consequence of the great entreaty of the people. Aamund thought he had given his promise too hastily. Now when the earl held a Thing, Thorkel spoke on account of the people, and entreated the earl to spare the people from such heavy burdens, recounting their necessitous condition. The earl replies favourably, saying that he would take Thorkel's advice. " I had intended to go out from the country with six ships, but now I will only take three with me; but thou must not come again, Thorkel, with any such request." The bonders thanked Thorkel for his assistance, and the earl set out on a viking cruise, and came back in autumn. The spring after the earl made the same levy as usual, and held a Thing with the bonders. Then Thorkel again made a speech, in which he entreated the earl to spare the people. The earl now was angry, and said the lot of the bonders should be made worse in consequence of his intercession; and worked himself up into such a rage that he vowed they should not both come next

[1] Krossay, or Rossay, is Pomona, or the Mainland (Meginland)—the principal island of the Orkneys ; and Laupandanes is apparently the western part of the island, in which the farm of Sandwick and parish of the same name are situated. Sandwick was undoubtedly the residence of Aamund, and is now known by the same name—Sandwick.

spring to the Thing in a whole skin. Then the Thing was closed. When Aamund heard what the earl and Thorkel had said at the Thing, he told Thorkel to leave the country, and he went over to Caithness to Earl Thorfinn. Thorkel was afterwards a long time there, and brought up the earl in his youth, and was on that account called Thorkel the Fosterer; and he became a very celebrated man.

CHAPTER CII. THE AGREEMENT OF THE EARLS.—There were many powerful men who fled from their udal properties in Orkney on account of Earl Einar's violence, and the most fled over to Caithness to Earl Thorfinn; but some fled from the Orkney Islands to Norway, and some to other countries. When Earl Thorfinn was grown up he sent a message to his brother Einar, and demanded the part of the dominion which he thought belonged to him in Orkney; namely, a third of the islands. Einar was nowise inclined to diminish his possessions. When Thorfinn found this he collected a war-force in Caithness, and proceeded to the islands. As soon as Earl Einar heard of this he collected people, and resolved to defend his country. Earl Bruse also collected men, and went out to meet them, and bring about some agreement between them. An agreement was at last concluded, that Thorfinn should have a third part of the islands as of right belonging to him, but that Bruse and Einar should lay their two parts together, and Einar alone should rule over them; but, if the one died before the other, the longest liver should inherit the whole. This agreement did not seem just, as Bruse had a son called Ragnvald, but Einar had no son. Earl Thorfinn set men to rule over his land in Orkney, but he himself was generally in Caithness. Earl Einar was generally on viking expeditions to Ireland, Scotland, and Bretland.[1]

CHAPTER CIII. EYVIND URARHORN'S MURDER [1018-19-20].—One summer that Earl Einar marauded in Ireland, he fought in Ulfreksfjord [2] with the Irish king Konofogor, as has been related before [p. 199], and suffered there a great defeat. The summer after this Eyvind Urarhorn was coming from the west from Ireland, intending to go to Norway; but the weather was boisterous, and the current against him, so he ran into Osmundswall,[3] and lay there wind-bound for some time. When

[1] *i.e.* Wales.
[2] Lough Larne.
[3] Osmundswall (*Ásmundarvágr*) is a harbour on the peninsula of Walls on the island of Hoy (*vide* p. 46, note 3).

Earl Einar heard of this, he hastened thither with many people, took Eyvind prisoner, and ordered him to be put to death; but spared the lives of most of his people. In autumn they proceeded to Norway to King Olaf, and told him Eyvind was killed. The king said little about it, but one could see that he considered it a great and vexatious loss; for he did not usually say much if anything turned out contrary to his wishes. Earl Thorfinn sent Thorkel Fosterer to the islands to gather in his scatt. Now as Einar gave Thorkel the greatest blame for the dispute in which Thorfinn had made claim to the islands, Thorkel came suddenly back to Caithness from Orkney, and told Earl Thorfinn that he had learnt that Earl Einar would have murdered him if his friends and relations had not given him notice to escape. " Now," says he, " it is come so far between the earl and me, that either something decisive between us must take place if we meet, or I must remove to such a distance that his power will not reach me." The earl encouraged Thorkel much to go east to Norway to King Olaf. " Thou wilt be highly respected," says he, " wherever thou comest among honourable men; and I know so well thy disposition and the earl's that it will not be long before ye each have sword out." Thereupon Thorkel made himself ready, and proceeded in autumn to Norway, and then to King Olaf, with whom he stayed the whole winter, and was in high favour. The king often entered into conversation with him, and he thought, what was true, that Thorkel was a high-minded man of good understanding. In his conversations with Thorkel, the king found a great difference in his description of the two earls; for Thorkel was a great friend of Earl Thorfinn, but had much to say against Einar. Early in spring the king sent a ship west over the sea to Earl Thorfinn, with the invitation to come east and visit him in Norway. The earl did not decline the invitation, for it was accompanied by assurances of friendship.

CHAPTER CIV. EARL EINAR'S MURDER.—Earl Thorfinn went east to Norway, and came to King Olaf, from whom he received a kind reception, and stayed till late in the summer. When he was preparing to return westwards again, King Olaf made him a present of a large and fully-rigged long-ship. Thorkel the Fosterer joined company with the earl, who gave him the ship which he brought with him from the West. The king and the earl took leave of each other tenderly. In autumn Earl Thorfinn came to Orkney, and when Earl Einar heard of it he

went on board his ships with a numerous band of men. Earl
Bruse came up to his two brothers, and endeavoured to mediate
between them, and a peace was concluded and confirmed by
oath. Thorkel Fosterer was to be in peace and friendship with
Earl Einar; and it was agreed that each of them should give a
feast to the other, and that the earl should first be Thorkel's
guest at Sandwick. When the earl came to the feast he was
entertained in the best manner; but the earl was not cheerful.
There was a great room, in which there were doors at each end.
The day the earl should depart Thorkel was to accompany him
to the other feast; and Thorkel sent men before, who should
examine the road they had to travel that day. The spies came
back and said to Thorkel they had discovered three ambushes.
" And we think," said they, " there is deceit on foot." When
Thorkel heard this he lengthened out his preparations for the
journey, and gathered people about him. The earl told him to
get ready, as it was time to be on horseback. Thorkel answered,
that he had many things to put in order first, and went out and
in frequently. There was a fire upon the floor. At last he went
in at one door, followed by an Iceland man from Eastfjord,
called Halvard, who locked the door after him. Thorkel went
in between the fire and the place where the earl was sitting. The
earl asked, " Art thou ready at last, Thorkel? "

Thorkel answers, " Now I am ready; " and struck the earl
upon the head so that he fell upon the floor.

Then said the Icelander, " I see you are all far too slow-witted
to drag the earl out of the fire; " and took an axe, which he set
under the earl's neck, and put him upright on the bench. Thorkel
and his two comrades then went in all haste out of the other
door opposite to that by which they went in, and Thorkel's men
were standing without fully armed. The earl's men now went
in, and took hold of the earl. He was already dead, so nobody
thought of avenging him: and also the whole was done so
quickly; for nobody expected such a deed from Thorkel, and
all supposed that there really was, as before related, a friendship
fixed between the earl and Thorkel. The most who were within
were unarmed, and they were partly Thorkel's good friends;
and to this may be added, that fate had decreed a longer life
to Thorkel. When Thorkel came out, he had not fewer men
with him than the earl's troop. Thorkel went to his ship, and
the earl's men went their way. The same day Thorkel sailed
out eastwards into the sea. This happened after winter; but
he came safely to Norway, went as fast as he could to Olaf, and

was well received by him. The king expressed his satisfaction at this deed, and Thorkel was with him all winter.

CHAPTER CV. AGREEMENT BETWEEN KING OLAF AND EARL BRUSE.—After Earl Einar's fall Bruse took the part of the country which he had possessed; for it was known to many men on what conditions Einar and Bruse had entered into a partnership. Although Thorfinn thought it would be more just that each of them had half of the islands, Bruse retained the two-thirds of the country that winter. In spring, however, Thorfinn produced his claim, and demanded the half of the country; but Bruse would not consent. They held Things and meetings about the business; and although their friends endeavoured to settle it, Thorfinn would not be content with less than the half of the islands, and insisted that Bruse, with his disposition, would have enough even with a third part. Bruse replies, "When I took my heritage after my father I was well satisfied with a third part of the country, and there was nobody to dispute it with me; and now I have succeeded to another third in heritage after my brother, according to a lawful agreement between us; and although I am not powerful enough to maintain a feud against thee, my brother, I will seek some other way, rather than willingly renounce my property." With this their meeting ended. But Bruse saw that he had no strength to contend against Thorfinn, because Thorfinn had both a greater dominion, and also could have aid from his mother's brother, the Scottish king. He resolved, therefore, to go out of the country; and he went eastward to King Olaf, and had with him his son Ragnvald, then ten years old. When the earl came to the king he was well received. The earl now declared his errand, and told the king the circumstances of the whole dispute between him and his brother, and asked help to defend his kingdom of Orkney, promising, in return, the fullest friendship towards King Olaf. In his answer, the king began with showing how Harald Haarfager had appropriated to himself all udal rights in Orkney, and that the earls, since that time, have constantly held the country as a fief, not as their udal property. "As a sufficient proof of which," said he, "when Eric Bloodyaxe and his sons were in Orkney the earls were subject to them; and also when my relation Olaf Trygvesson came there thy father, Earl Sigurd, became his man. Now I have taken heritage after King Olaf, and I will give thee the condition to become my man, and then I will give thee the islands as a fief; and we shall try if I cannot give thee aid that will be more to the purpose than Thorfinn can get from the Scottish king. If thou wilt not accept of these terms, then will I win back my udal property there in the West, as our forefathers and relations of old possessed it."

The earl carefully considered this speech, laid it before his friends, and demanded their advice if he should agree to it, and enter into such terms with King Olaf and become his vassal. "But I do not see what my lot will be at my departure if I say No; for the king has clearly enough declared his claim upon Orkney; and from his great power, and our being in his hands, it is easy for him to make our destiny what he pleases."

Although the earl saw that there was much to be considered for and against it, he chose the condition to deliver himself and his dominion into the king's power. Thereupon the king took the earl's power, and the government over all the earl's lands, and the earl became his vassal under oath of fealty.

CHAPTER CVI. THE EARL'S AGREEMENT TO THE KING'S TERMS.—Thorfinn the earl heard that his brother Bruse had gone east to King Olaf to seek support from him; but as Thorfinn had been on a visit to King Olaf before, and had concluded a friendship with him, he thought his case would stand well with the king, and that many would support it; but he believed that many more would do so if he went there himself. Earl Thorfinn resolved, therefore, to go east himself without delay; and he thought there would be so little difference between the time of his arrival and Bruse's, that Bruse's errand could not be accomplished before he came to King Olaf. But it went otherwise than Earl Thorfinn had expected; for when he came to the king the agreement between the king and Bruse was already concluded and settled, and Earl Thorfinn did not know a word about Bruse's having surrendered his udal domains until he came to King Olaf. As soon as Earl Thorfinn and King Olaf met, the king made the same demand upon the kingdom of Orkney that he had done to Earl Bruse, and required that Thorfinn should voluntarily deliver over to the king that part of the country which he had possessed hitherto. The earl answered in a friendly and respectful way, that the king's friendship lay near to his heart: "And if you think, sire, that my help against other chiefs can be of use, you have already every claim to it; but I cannot be your vassal for service, as I am an earl of the Scottish king, and owe fealty to him."

As the king found that the earl, by his answer, declined fulfilling the demand he had made, he said, " Earl, if thou wilt not become my vassal, there is another condition; namely, that I will place over the Orkney Islands the man I please, and require thy oath that thou wilt make no claim upon these lands, but allow the man I place over them to sit in peace. If thou wilt not accept of either of these conditions, he who is to rule over these lands may expect hostility from thee, and thou must not think it strange then, if pride were to meet with a fall."

The earl begged of the king some time to consider the matter. The king did so, and gave the earl time to take the counsel of his friends on the choosing one or other of these conditions. Then the earl requested a delay until next summer, that he might go over the sea to the West, for his proper counsellors were all at home, and he himself was but a child in respect of age; but the king required that he should now make his election of one or other of the conditions. Thorkel Fosterer was then with the king, and he privately sent a person to Earl Thorfinn, and told him, whatever his intentions might be, not to think of leaving Olaf without being reconciled with him, as he stood entirely in Olaf's power. From such hints the earl saw there was no other way than to let the king have his own will. It was no doubt a hard condition to have no hope of ever regaining his paternal heritage, and moreover to bind himself by oath to allow those to enjoy in peace his domain who had no hereditary right to it: but seeing it was uncertain how he could get away, he resolved to submit to the king and become his vassal, as Bruse had done. The king observed that Thorfinn was more high-minded, and less disposed to suffer subjection than Bruse, and therefore he trusted less to Thorfinn than to Bruse; and he considered also that Thorfinn would trust to the aid of the Scottish king, if he broke the agreement. The king also had discernment enough to perceive that Bruse, although slow to enter into an agreement, would promise nothing but what he intended to keep; but as to Thorfinn, when he had once made up his mind he went readily into every proposal, and made no attempt to obtain any alteration of the king's first conditions: therefore the king had his suspicions that the earl would infringe the agreement.

CHAPTER CVII. EARL THORFINN'S DEPARTURE, AND RECONCILIATION WITH THORKEL. — When the king had carefully considered the whole matter by himself, he ordered the signal to sound for a General Thing, to which he called in the earls.

Then said the king, " I will now make known to the public
our agreement with the Orkney earls. They have now acknowledged my right of property to Orkney and Shetland, and have
both become my vassals, all which they have confirmed by oath;
and now I will invest them with these lands as a fief: namely,
Bruse with one third part, and Thorfinn with one third, as they
formerly enjoyed them; but the other third, which Einar
Rangmund had, I adjudge as fallen to my domain, because he
killed Eyvind Urarhorn, my court-man, partner, and dear friend;
and that part of the land I will manage as I think proper. I
have also, my earls, to tell you it is my pleasure that ye enter
into an agreement with Thorkel Aamundsson for the murder
of your brother Einar; for I will take that business, if ye agree
thereto, within my own jurisdiction." The earls agreed to
this, as to everything else that the king proposed. Thorkel
came forward, and surrendered to the king's judgment of the
case, and the Thing concluded. King Olaf awarded as great a
penalty for Earl Einar's murder as for three lendermen; but
as Einar himself was the cause of the act, one third of the mulct
fell to the ground. Thereafter Earl Thorfinn asked the king's
leave to depart, and as soon as he obtained it made ready for
sea with all speed. It happened one day, when all was ready
for the voyage, the earl sat in his ship drinking; and Thorkel
Aamundsson came unexpectedly to him, laid his head upon the
earl's knee, and bade him do with him what he pleased. The
earl asked why he did so. " We are, you know, reconciled men,
according to the king's decision; so stand up, Thorkel."

Thorkel replied, " The agreement which the king made as
between me and Bruse stands good; but what regards the
agreement with thee thou alone must determine. Although
the king made conditions for my property and safe residence in
Orkney, yet I know so well thy disposition that there is no going
to the islands for me, unless I go there in peace with thee, Earl
Thorfinn; and therefore I am willing to promise never to return
to Orkney, whatever the king may desire."

The earl remained silent; and first, after a long pause, he
said, " If thou wilt rather, Thorkel, that I shall judge between
us than trust to the king's judgment, then let the beginning of
our reconciliation be, that you go with me to the Orkney Islands,
live with me, and never leave me but with my will, and be
bound to defend my land, and execute all that I want done, as
long as we both are in life."

Thorkel replies, "This shall be entirely at thy pleasure, Earl, as well as everything else in my power." Then Thorkel went on, and solemnly ratified this agreement. The earl said he would talk afterwards about the mulct of money, but took Thorkel's oath upon the conditions. Thorkel immediately made ready to accompany the earl on his voyage. The earl set off as soon as all was ready, and never again were King Olaf and Thorfinn together.

CHAPTER CVIII. EARL BRUSE'S DEPARTURE.—Earl Bruse remained behind, and took his time to get ready. Before his departure the king sent for him, and said, " It appears to me, Earl, that in thee I have a man on the west side of the sea on whose fidelity I can depend; therefore I intend to give thee the two parts of the country which thou formerly hadst to rule over; for I will not that thou shouldst be a less powerful man after entering into my service than before: but I will secure thy fidelity by keeping thy son Ragnvald with me. I see well enough that with two parts of the country and my help, thou wilt be able to defend what is thy own against thy brother Thorfinn." Bruse was thankful for getting two thirds instead of one third of the country, and soon after he set out, and came about autumn to Orkney; but Ragnvald, Bruse's son, remained behind in the East with King Olaf. Ragnvald was one of the handsomest men that could be seen,—his hair long, and yellow as silk; and he soon grew up, stout and tall, and he was a very able superb man, both of great understanding and polite manners. He was long with King Olaf. Ottar Svarte speaks of these affairs in the poem he composed about King Olaf:—

> " From Shetland, far off in the cold North sea,
> Come chiefs who desire to be subject to thee:
> No king so well known for his will, and his might,
> To defend his own people from scaith or unright.
> These isles of the West 'midst the ocean's wild roar,
> Scarcely heard the voice of their sovereign before:
> Our bravest of sovereigns before could scarce bring
> These islesmen so proud to acknowledge their king."

CHAPTER CIX. OF THE EARLS THORFINN AND BRUSE.— The brothers Thorfinn and Bruse came west to Orkney; and Bruse took the two parts of the country under his rule, and Thorfinn the third part. Thorfinn was usually in Caithness and elsewhere in Scotland; but placed men of his own over the islands. It was left to Bruse alone to defend the islands, which at that time were severely scourged by vikings; for the Northmen and Danes went much on viking cruises in the West sea, and frequently touched at Orkney on the way to or from the West, and plundered, and took provisions and cattle from the coast. Bruse often complained of his brother Thorfinn, that he made no equipment of war for the defence of Orkney and Shetland, yet levied his share of the scatt and duties. Then Thorfinn offered to him to exchange, and that Bruse should have one third and Thorfinn two thirds of the land, but should undertake the defence of the land for the whole. Although this exchange did not take place immediately, it is related in the Saga of the Earls [1] that it was agreed upon at last; and that Thorfinn had two parts, and Bruse only one, when Canute the Great subdued Norway, and King Olaf fled the country. Earl Thorfinn Sigurdsson has been the ablest earl of these islands, and has had the greatest dominion of all the Orkney earls; for he had under him Orkney, Shetland, and the Hebrides, besides very great possessions in Scotland and Ireland. Arnor, the earl's scald, tells of his possessions:—

> " From Thurso-skerry to Dublin,
> All people hold with good Thorfinn—
> All peoples love his sway,
> And the generous chief obey."

Thorfinn was a very great warrior. He came to the earldom at five years of age, ruled more than sixty years,[2] and died in his bed about the last days of Harald Sigurdsson (about 1066). But Bruse died in the days of Canute the Great, a short time after the fall of Saint Olaf (after 1033).

CHAPTER CX. OF HAREK OF THIOTTO [1019].—Now, as two stories are proceeding together, we shall return to that which we left,—at King Olaf Haraldson having concluded peace with King Olaf the Swedish king, and having the same summer gone north to Drontheim [p. 218]. He had then been king in Norway five years. In harvest time he prepared to take his winter residence at Nidaros, and he remained all winter there. Thorkel the Fosterer, Aamund's son, as before related [p. 224], was all that winter with him. King Olaf inquired very carefully how it stood with Christianity throughout the land, and learnt that it was not observed at all to the north of Halogaland, and was far from being observed as it should be in Naumedal,

---

[1] *i.e.* the text now reconstructed under the name of *The Orkneyinga Saga* (translated by A. B. Taylor, 1938); this source was much used by Snorri.

[2] This is a mistake for fifty, caused by reckoning Thorfinn's earldom from the death of his father Sigurd (*vide* pp. 219–20).

and the interior of Drontheim. There was a man by name
Harek, a son of Eyvind Skaldaspiller,[1] who dwelt in an island
called Thiotto in Halogaland. Eyvind had not been a rich
man, but was of high family and high mind. In Thiotto, at
first, there dwelt many small bonders; but Harek began with
buying a farm not very large, and lived on it, and in a few years
he had got all the bonders that were there before out of the
way; so that he had the whole island, and built a large head-
mansion. He soon became very rich; for he was a very prudent
man, and very successful. He had long been greatly respected
by the chiefs, and being related to the kings of Norway, had
been raised by them to high dignities. Harek's father's mother,
Gunhild, was a daughter of Earl Halfdan, and of Ingeborg,
Harald Haarfager's daughter. At the time the circumstance
happened which we are going to relate he was somewhat advanced
in years. Harek was the most respected man in Halogaland,
and for a long time had the Lapland trade, and did the king's
business in Lapland,[2] sometimes alone, sometimes with others
joined to him. He had not himself been to wait on King Olaf,
but messages had passed between them, and all was on the most
friendly footing. This winter that Olaf was in Nidaros, messengers passed between the king and Harek of Thiotto. Then
the king made it known that he intended going north to Halogaland, and as far north as the land's end; but the people of
Halogaland expected no good from this expedition.

CHAPTER CXI. OF THE PEOPLE OF HALOGALAND [1020].—
Olaf rigged out five ships in spring, and had with him about
300 men. When he was ready for sea he set out northwards
along the land; and when he came to Naumedal district he
summoned the bonders to a Thing, and at every Thing was
accepted as king. He also made the laws to be read there as
elsewhere, by which the people are commanded to observe
Christianity; and he threatened every man with loss of life, and
limbs, and property, who would not subject himself to Christian
law. He inflicted severe punishments on many men, great as
well as small, and left no district until the people had consented
to adopt the holy faith. The most of the men of power and
of the great bonders made feasts for the king, and so he proceeded
all the way north to Halogaland. Harek of Thiotto also made

---

[1] A notable tenth-century poet (see *Sagas of the Norse Kings*, pp. 104 ff.).
[2] The sole right to trade with the Lapps (Finns) and collect their tribute
of furs to the Norwegian king—a very valuable monopoly.

a feast for the king, at which there was a great multitude of guests, and the feast was very splendid. Harek was made lenderman, and got the same privileges he had enjoyed under the former chiefs of the country.

CHAPTER CXII. OF AASMUND GRANKELSSON.—There was a man called Grankel, or Granketel, who was a rich bonder, and at this time rather advanced in age. In his youth he had been on viking cruises, and had been a powerful fighter; for he possessed great readiness in all sorts of bodily exercises. His son Aasmund was equal to his father in all these, and in some, indeed, he excelled him. There were many who said that with respect to comeliness, strength, and bodily expertness, he might be considered the third remarkably distinguished for these that Norway had ever produced. The first was Hakon Athelstan's foster-son; the second, Olaf Trygvesson. Grankel invited King Olaf to a feast, which was very magnificent; and at parting Grankel presented the king with many honourable gifts and tokens of friendship. The king invited Aasmund, with many persuasions, to follow him; and as Aasmund could not decline the honours offered him, he got ready to travel with the king, became his man, and stood in high favour with him. The king remained in Halogaland the greater part of the summer, went to all the Things, and baptized all the people. Thore Hund dwelt at that time in the island Biarkö.[1] He was the most powerful man in the North, and also became one of Olaf's lendermen. Many sons of great bonders resolved also to follow King Olaf from Halogaland. Towards the end of summer King Olaf left the North, and sailed back to Drontheim, and landed at Nidaros,[2] where he passed the winter. It was then that Thorkel the Fosterer came from the West from Orkney, after killing Einar Rangmund, as before related [p. 224]. This autumn corn was dear in Drontheim, after a long course of good seasons, and the farther north the dearer was the corn; but there was corn enough in the East country, and in the Uplands, and it was of great help to the people of Drontheim that many had old corn remaining beside them.

CHAPTER CXIII. OF THE SACRIFICES OF THE DRONTHEIM PEOPLE.—In autumn the news was brought to King Olaf that the bonders had had a great feast on the first winter-day's eve,

---

[1] A farm and island north-east of Hindöen in the county of Tromsö.
[2] The town of Trondhjem.

at which there was a numerous attendance and much drinking; and it was told the king that all the remembrance-cups to the Æser, or old gods, were blessed according to the old heathen forms; and it was added, that cattle and horses had been slain, and the altars sprinkled with their blood, and the sacrifices accompanied with the prayer that was made to obtain good seasons. It was also reported that all men saw clearly that the gods were offended at the Halogaland people turning Christian. Now when the king heard this news he sent men into the Drontheim country, and ordered several bonders, whose names he gave, to appear before him. There was a man called Olve of Egge, so called after his farm on which he lived. He was powerful, of great family, and the head-man of those who on behalf of the bonders appeared before the king. Now, when they came to the king, he told them these accusations; to which Olve, on behalf of the bonders, replied, that they had had no other feasts that harvest than their usual entertainments, and social meetings, and friendly drinking parties. "But as to what may have been told you of the words which may have fallen from us Drontheim people in our drinking parties, men of understanding would take good care not to use such language; but I cannot hinder drunken or foolish people's talk." Olve was a man of clever speech, and bold in what he said, and defended the bonders against such accusations. In the end, the king said the people of the interior of Drontheim must themselves give the best testimony to their being in the right faith. The bonders got leave to return home, and set off as soon as they were ready.

CHAPTER CXIV. OF THE SACRIFICES BY THE PEOPLE OF THE INTERIOR OF THE DRONTHEIM DISTRICT [1021].—Afterwards, when winter was advanced, it was told the king that the people of the interior of Drontheim had assembled in great number at Mære, and that there was a great sacrifice in the middle of winter, at which they sacrificed offerings for peace and a good season. Now when the king knew this on good authority to be true, he sent men and messages into the interior, and summoned the bonders whom he thought of most understanding into the town. The bonders held a council among themselves about this message; and all those who had been upon the same occasion in the beginning of winter were now very unwilling to make the journey. Olve, however, at the desire of all the bonders, undertook to go on that journey. When he came to the town

he went immediately before the king, and they talked together.
The king made the same accusations against the bonders, that
they had held a mid-winter sacrifice. Olve replies, that this
accusation against the bonders was false. " We had," said he,
" Yule feasts and drinking feasts wide around in the districts;
and the bonders do not prepare their feasts so sparingly, sire,
that there is not much left over, which people consume long
afterwards. At Mære there is a great farm, with a large house
on it, and a great neighbourhood all around it, and it is the
great delight of the people to drink many together in company." The king said little in reply, but looked angry, as
he thought he knew the truth of the matter better than it
was now represented. He ordered the bonders to return
home. " I shall some time or other," says he, " come to the
truth of what you are now concealing, and in such a way that
ye shall not be able to contradict it. But, however that may be,
do not try such things again." The bonders returned home,
and told the result of their journey, and that the king was
altogether enraged.

CHAPTER CXV. MURDER OF OLVE OF EGGE. — At Easter
(2nd April 1021) the king held a feast, to which he had invited
many of the townspeople as well as bonders. After Easter he
ordered his ships to be launched into the water, oars and tackle
to be put on board, decks to be laid in the ships, and tilts [1] and
rigging to be set up, and to be laid ready for sea at the piers.
Immediately after Easter he sent men into Værdal. There was
a man called Thorald, who was the king's bailiff, and who
managed the king's farm there at Haug; [2] and to him the king
sent a message to come to him as quickly as possible. Thorald
did not decline the journey, but went immediately to the town
with the messenger. The king called him in, and in a private
conversation asked him what truth there was in what had been
told him of the principles and living of the people of the interior
of Drontheim, and if it really was so that they practised sacrifices
to heathen gods. " I will," says the king, " that thou declare
to me the things as they are, and as thou knowest to be true;
for it is thy duty to tell me the truth, being my man."

Thorald replies, " Sire, I will first tell you that I have brought
here to the town my two children, my wife, and all my loose

[1] The ships appear to have been decked fore and aft only; and in the
middle, where the rowers sat, to have had tilts or tents set up at night to
sleep under.

[2] In the west of Værdalen between Værdalsören and Stiklestad.

property that I could take with me, and if thou desirest to know the truth it shall be told according to thy command; but if I declare it, thou must take care of me and mine."

The king replies, " Say only what is true on what I ask thee, and I will take care that no evil befall thee."

Then said Thorald, " If I must say the truth, king, as it is, I must declare that in the interior of the Drontheim land almost all the people are heathen in faith, although some of them are baptized. It is their custom to offer sacrifice in autumn for a good winter, a second at mid-winter, and a third in summer. In this the people of Eynar, Sparbu, Værdal, and Skogn partake. There are twelve men who preside over these sacrifice-feasts, and in spring it is Olve who has to get the feast in order, and he is now busy transporting to Mære everything needful for it."

Now when the king had got to the truth with a certainty, he ordered the signal to be sounded for his men to assemble, and for the men-at-arms to go on board ship. He appointed men to steer the ships, and leaders for the people, and ordered how the people should be divided among the vessels. All was got ready in haste, and with five ships and 300 men he steered up the fjord. The wind was favourable, the ships sailed briskly before it, and nobody could have thought that the king would be so soon there. The king came in the night time to Mære,[1] and immediately surrounded the house with a ring of armed men. Olve was taken, and the king ordered him to be put to death, and many other men besides. Then the king took all the provision for the feast, and had it brought to his ships; and also all the goods, both furniture, clothes, and valuables, which the people had brought there, and divided the booty among his men. The king also let all the bonders he thought had the greatest part in the business be plundered by his men-at-arms. Some were taken prisoners and laid in irons, some ran away, and many were robbed of their goods. Thereafter the bonders were summoned to a Thing; but because he had taken many powerful men prisoners, and held them in his power, their friends and relations resolved to promise obedience to the king, so that there was no insurrection against the king on this occasion. He thus brought the whole people back to the right faith, gave them teachers, and built and consecrated churches. The king sentenced Olve to be *ugild*,[2] and all that he possessed was adjudged to the

---

[1] Mære is now a large mound in Inderöen, near the head of the Drontheim fjord, in the district called Sparbu.

[2] *Úgildr*, " without right of atonement "; *i.e.* the king retrospectively outlawed Olve for treason, so no atonement need be paid for his death.

king; and of the men he judged the most guilty, some he ordered to be executed, some he maimed, some he drove out of the country, and took fines from others. The king then returned to Nidaros.

CHAPTER CXVI. OF THE SONS OF ARNE.—There was a man called Arne Armodsson, who was married to Thora, Thorstein Galge's daughter. Their children were Kalf, Finn, Thorberg, Aamund, Kolbiorn, Arnbiorn, and Arne. Their daughter, who was called Ragnhild, was married to Harek of Thiotto. Arne was a lenderman, powerful, and of ability, and a great friend of King Olaf. At that time his sons Kalf and Finn were with the king, and in great favour. The wife whom Olve of Egge¹ had left was young and handsome, of great family, and rich, so that he who got her might be considered to have made an excellent marriage; and her land was in the gift of the king. She and Olve had two sons, who were still in infancy. Kalf Arneson begged of the king that he would give him to wife the widow of Olve; and out of friendship the king agreed to it, and with her he got all the property Olve had possessed. The king at the same time made him his lenderman, and gave him an office in the interior of the Drontheim country. Kalf became a great chief, and was a man of very great understanding.

CHAPTER CXVII. KING OLAF'S JOURNEY TO THE UPLANDS [1021].—When King Olaf had been seven years in Norway the earls Thorfinn and Bruse came to him, as before related [p. 229], in the summer, from Orkney, and he became master of their land. The same summer Olaf went to North and South Möre, and in autumn to Raumsdal. He left his ships there, and came to the Uplands, and to Lessö.² Here he laid hold of all the best men, and forced them, both at Lessö and Dovre, either to receive Christianity or suffer death, or else, if they could, flee to escape. After they received Christianity, the king took their sons in his hands as hostages for their fidelity. The king stayed several nights at a farm in Lessö called Bover,³ where he placed priests. Then he proceeded over Orkedal⁴ and Ljardal, and

---

¹ Egge, the estate of Olve, whose murder is related in the preceding chapter, is the farm of Egge, near Stenkjær, at the head of the Trondhjem fjord.
² Lesje and Lesjeskogen.
³ Properly *Bæjar*, *i.e.* Bö, at the east end of Lesje-vand.
⁴ A mistaken emendation of the manuscript reading *Orudal*; the right emendation is " Lorudal " (modern Lordalen), a lateral valley to Lesje.

came down from the Uplands at a place called Stafabreka.
There a river runs along the valley, called the Otta, and a
beautiful hamlet, by name Loar (now Lom), lies on both sides
of the river, and the king could see far down over the whole
neighbourhood. " A pity it is," said the king, " so beautiful
a hamlet should be burnt." And he proceeded down the valley
with his people, and was all night on a farm called Næs. The
king took his lodging in a loft, where he slept himself; and it
stands to the present day,[1] without anything in it having been
altered since. The king was five days there, and summoned by
message-token the people to a Thing, both for the districts of
Vaage, Loar, and Hedal; and gave out the message along with
the token, that they must either receive Christianity and give
their sons as hostages, or see their habitations burnt. They
came before the king, and submitted to his pleasure; but some
fled south down the valley.

CHAPTER CXVIII. THE STORY OF DALE GUDBRAND.—There
was a man called Dale Gudbrand, who was like a king in the
valley (Gudbrandsdal), but was only herse [2] in title. Sigvat
the scald compared him for wealth and landed property to
Erling Skialgsson. Sigvat sang thus concerning Erling:—

> " I know but one who can compare
> With Erling for broad lands and gear—
> Gudbrand is he, whose wide domains
> Are most like where some small king reigns.
> These two great bonders, I would say,
> Equal each other every way.
> He lies who says that he can find
> One by the other left behind."

Gudbrand had a son, who is here spoken of. Now when
Gudbrand received the tidings that King Olaf was come to Loar,
and obliged people to accept Christianity, he sent out a message-
token,[3] and summoned all the men in the valley to meet him at
a farm called Hundthorp.[4] All came, so that the number could
not be told; for there is a lake [5] in the neighbourhood called

---

[1] The house on this farm of Næs in which King Olaf lodged is said to
have stood till 1830 when it was removed to Ekre and rebuilt.

[2] *Hersir*, title of certain hereditary leaders in some parts of Norway; it
probably originally implied military command (cf. *herr*, " army "), but
was of lower rank than a *jarl* (earl).

[3] *i.e.* an arrow sent to all men of a district as summons; *cf.* p. 144.

[4] A farm by the river Laagen in Gudbrandsdal; there are several mounds
about it, on one of which is a huge standing-stone in honour of St. Olaf.

[5] Not a lake but a mere expansion of the river Laagen.

Laugen, so that people could come to the place both by land and by water. There Gudbrand held a Thing with them, and said, " A man is come to Loar who is called Olaf, and will force upon us another faith than what we had before, and will break in pieces all our gods. He says that he has a much greater and more powerful god; and it is wonderful that the earth does not burst asunder under him, or that our god lets him go about unpunished when he dares to talk such things. I know this for certain that if we carry Thor, who has always stood by us, out of our temple that is standing upon this farm, Olaf's god will melt away, and he and his men be made nothing so soon as Thor looks upon them." Then the bonders all shouted as one person that Olaf should never get away with life if he came to them; and they thought he would never dare to come farther south through the valley. They chose out 700 men to go northwards to Breden, to watch his movements. The leader of this band was Gudbrand's son, eighteen years of age, and with him were many other men of importance. When they came to a farm called Hof [1] they heard of the king; and they remained three nights there. People streamed to them from all parts, from Lessö, Loar, and Vaage, who did not wish to receive Christianity. The king and Bishop Sigurd fixed teachers in Loar and in Vaage. From thence they went round Urgorost, [2] and came down into the valley at Usvold, [3] where they stayed all night, and heard the news that a great force of men were assembled against them. The bonders who were in Breden heard also of the king's arrival, and prepared for battle. As soon as the king arose in the morning he put on his armour, and went southwards over Suwold, [4] and did not halt until he came to Breden, where he saw a great army ready for battle. Then the king drew up his troops, rode himself at the head of them, and began a speech to the bonders, in which he invited them to adopt Christianity. They replied, " We shall give thee something else to do to-day than to be mocking us; " and raised a general shout, striking also upon their shields with their weapons. Then the king's men ran forward and threw their spears; but the bonders turned round instantly and fled, so that only few men remained behind. Gudbrand's son was taken prisoner; but the king gave him his life, and took him with him. The king was four days here.

---

[1] Hof of Breden.
[2] The manuscripts read *Ugurost*; this should be emended to *Vágarost* (modern Rosta), a stretch of road between Vaage and Sel.
[3] Manuscript reading *Úsu*; emend to Sel.
[4] Manuscript reading *Súvollum* amend to *Silvollum*, modern Selvoldene.

Then the king said to Gudbrand's son, " Go home now to thy father, and tell him I expect to be with him soon."

He went accordingly, and told his father the news, that they had fallen in with the king, and fought with him; but that their whole army, in the very beginning, took flight. " I was taken prisoner," said he, " but the king gave me my life and liberty, and told me to say to thee that he will soon be here. And now we have not 200 men of the force we raised against him; therefore I advise thee, father, not to give battle to that man."

Says Gudbrand, " It is easy to see that all courage has left thee, and it was an unlucky hour ye went out to the field. Thy proceeding will live long in the remembrance of people, and I see that thy fastening thy faith on the folly that man is going about with has brought upon thee and thy men so great a disgrace."

But the night after, Gudbrand dreamt that there came to him a man surrounded by light, who brought great terror with him, and said to him, " Thy son made no glorious expedition against King Olaf; but still less honour wilt thou gather for thyself by holding a battle with him. Thou with all thy people wilt fall; wolves will drag thee, and all thine, away; ravens will tear thee in stripes." At this dreadful vision he was much afraid, and tells it to Thord Istromaga,[1] who was chief over the valley. He replies, " The very same vision came to me." In the morning they ordered the signal to sound for a Thing, and said that it appeared to them advisable to hold a Thing with the man who had come from the north with this new teaching, to know if there was any truth in it. Gudbrand then said to his son, " Go thou, and twelve men with thee, to the king who gave thee thy life." He went straightway, and found the king at a farm called Lidstad,[2] and laid before him their errand; namely, that the bonders would hold a Thing with him, and make a truce between them and him. The king was content; and they bound themselves by faith and law mutually to hold the peace so long as the Thing lasted. After this was settled the men returned to Gudbrand and Thord, and told them there was made a firm agreement for a truce. The king, after the battle with the son of Gudbrand, had proceeded to Lidstad, and remained there for five days: afterwards he went out to meet the bonders, and hold a Thing with them. On that day there

[1] *i.e.* " Big-Belly "; this is Thord Guttormsson of Steig (*vide* p. 265).
[2] Now Listad above the church of Söndre Fron. The Thing-place was at Hundorp and the Temple of Thor at Hore.

fell a heavy rain. When the Thing was seated, the king stood up and said that the people in Lessö, Loar, and Vaage had received Christianity, broken down their houses of sacrifice, and believed now in the true God who had made heaven and earth and knows all things.

Thereupon the king sat down, and Gudbrand replies, " We know nothing of him whom thou speakest about. Dost thou call him God, whom neither thou nor any one else can see? But we have a god who can be seen every day, although he is not out to-day, because the weather is wet, and he will appear to thee terrible and very grand; and I expect that fear will mix with your very blood when he comes into the Thing. But since thou sayest thy God is so great, let him make it so that to-morrow we have a cloudy day but without rain, and then let us meet again."

The king accordingly returned home to his lodging, taking Gudbrand's son as a hostage; but he gave them a man as hostage in exchange. In the evening the king asked Gudbrand's son what like their god was. He replied, that he bore the likeness of Thor; had a hammer in his hand; was of great size, but hollow within; and had a high stand, upon which he stood when he was out. "Neither gold nor silver are wanting about him, and every day he receives four cakes of bread, besides meat." They then went to bed, but the king watched all night in prayer. When day dawned the king went to mass, then to table, and from thence to the Thing. The weather was such as Gudbrand desired. Now the bishop stood up in his chasuble, with bishop's mitre upon his head, and bishop's staff in his hands. He spoke to the bonders of the true faith, told the many wonderful acts of God, and concluded his speech well.

Thord Istromaga replies, " Many things we are told of by this horned man [1] with the staff in his hand crooked at the top like a ram's horn; but since ye say, comrades, that your god is so powerful, and can do so many wonders, tell him to make it clear sunshine to-morrow forenoon, and then we shall meet here again, and do one of two things,—either agree with you about this business, or fight you." And they separated for the day.

CHAPTER CXIX. DALE GUDBRAND IS BAPTIZED.—There was a man with King Olaf called Kolbein Sterki (the Strong), who came from a family in the Fjords district. Usually he was so equipt that he was girt with a sword, and besides carried

[1] Alluding to the bishop's mitre.

a great stake, otherwise called a club, in his hands. The king told Kolbein to stand nearest to him in the morning; and gave orders to his people to go down in the night to where the ships of the bonders lay and bore holes in them, and to set loose their horses on the farms where they were: all which was done. Now the king was in prayer all the night, beseeching God of his goodness and mercy to release him from evil. When mass was ended, and morning was grey, the king went to the Thing. When he came there some bonders had already arrived, and they saw a great crowd coming along, and bearing among them a huge man's image glancing with gold and silver. When the bonders who were at the Thing saw it they started up, and bowed themselves down before the ugly idol. Thereupon it was set down upon the Thing-field; and on the one side of it sat the bonders, and on the other the king and his people.

Then Dale Gudbrand stood up, and said, "Where now, king, is thy god? I think he will now carry his head lower; and neither thou, nor the man with the horn whom ye call bishop, and sits there beside thee, are so bold to-day as on the former days; for now our god, who rules over all, is come, and looks on you with an angry eye: and now I see well enough that ye are terrified, and scarcely dare to raise your eyes. Throw away now all your opposition, and believe in the god who has all your fate in his hands." And so he concluded his speech.

The king now whispers to Kolbein Sterki, without the bonders perceiving it, "If it come so in the course of my speech that the bonders look another way than towards their idol, strike him as hard as thou canst with thy club."

The king then stood up and spoke. "Much hast thou talked to us this morning, and greatly hast thou wondered that thou canst not see our God; but we expect that he will soon come to us. Thou wouldst frighten us with thy god, who is both blind and deaf, and can neither save himself nor others, and cannot even move about without being carried; but now I expect it will be but a short time before he mets his fate: for turn your eyes towards the east,—behold our God advancing in great light."

The sun was rising, and all turned to look. At that moment Kolbein gave their god a stroke, so that the idol burst asunder; and there ran out of it mice as big almost as cats, and reptiles, and adders. The bonders were so terrified that some fled to their ships; but when they pushed out from shore they filled with water, and could not get away. Others ran for their horses, but could not find them. The king then ordered the bonders to be called together, saying he wanted to speak with them; on which the bonders came back, and the Thing was again seated.

The king rose up and said, " I do not understand what your noise and running mean. Ye see yourselves what your god can do,—the idol ye adorned with gold and silver, and brought meat and provisions to. Ye see now that the protecting powers who used it were the mice and adders, reptiles and paddocks; and they do ill who trust to such, and will not abandon this folly. Take now your gold and ornaments that are lying strewed about on the grass, and give them to your wives and daughters; but never hang them hereafter upon stock or stone. Here are now two conditions between us to choose upon,—either accept Christianity, or fight this very day; and the victory be to them to whom the God we worship gives it."

Then Dale Gudbrand stood up and said, " We have sustained great damage upon our god; but since he will not help us, we will believe in the God thou believest in."

Then all received Christianity. The bishop baptized Gudbrand and his son. King Olaf and Bishop Sigurd left behind them teachers, and they who met as enemies parted as friends; and Gudbrand built a church in the valley.[1]

CHAPTER CXX. HEDEMARK BAPTIZED [1022].—King Olaf proceeded from thence to Hedemark, and baptized there; for when he once had carried away their kings as prisoners, he had not ventured himself, after such a deed, to go far into the country with few people at that time, but a small part of Hedemark was baptized; but the king did not desist from his expedition before he had introduced Christianity over all Hedemark, consecrated churches, and placed teachers. He then went to Hadeland and Thoten, improving the customs of the people, and persisting until all the country was baptized. He then went to Ringerike, where also all people went over to Christianity. The people of Raumarike then heard that Olaf intended coming to them, and they gathered a great force. They said among themselves that the journey Olaf had made among them the last time was not to be forgotten, and he should never proceed so again. The king, notwithstanding, prepared for the journey. Now when the king went up into Raumarike

[1] The church stood at Listad until 1787 when it was removed to where the church of Söndre Fron now is.

with his forces, the multitude of bonders came against him at a river called Nittia;[1] and the bonders had a strong army and began the battle as soon as they met; but they soon fell short, and took to flight. They were forced by this battle into a better disposition, and immediately received Christianity; and the king scoured the whole district, and did not leave it until all the people were made Christians. He then went east to Solör, and baptized that neighbourhood. The scald Ottar Black[2] came to him there, and begged to be received among his men. Olaf the Swedish king had died the winter before, and Onund, the son of Olaf, was now the sole king over all Sweden. King Olaf returned, when the winter was far advanced, to Raumarike. There he assembled a numerous Thing, at a place where the Eidsvold Things have since been held. He made a law, that the Upland people should resort to this Thing, and that Eidsvold laws should be good through all the districts of the Uplands, and wide around in other quarters, which also has taken place. As spring was advancing, he rigged his ships, and went by sea to Tunsberg. He remained there during the spring, and whilst the town was most frequented, and goods from other countries were brought to the town for sale. There had been a good year in Viken, and tolerable as far north as Stad; but it was a very dear time all to the north.

CHAPTER CXXI. RECONCILIATION OF THE KING AND EINAR TAMBARSKELVE.—In spring King Olaf sent a message west to Agder, and north all the way to Hordaland and Rogaland, prohibiting the exporting or selling of corn, malt, or meal; adding, that he, as usual, would come there with his people in guest-quarters. The message went round all the districts; but the king remained in Viken all summer, and went east to the boundary of the country. Einar Tambarskelve had been with the Swedish king Olaf since the death of his relation Earl Swend, and had, as the king's man, received great fiefs from him. Now that the king was dead, Einar had a great desire to come into friendly agreement with Olaf; and the same spring messages passed between them about it. While the king was lying in the Gotha river, Einar Tambarskelve came there with some men; and after treating about an agreement, it was settled that Einar should go north to Drontheim, and there take possession of all the lands and property which Bergliot had received in dower. Thereupon Einar took his way north; but the king

---

[1] The river Nit in Nittedal (Nedre Romerike).   [2] *Vide* p. 172.

remained behind in Viken, and remained long in Sarpsborg in autumn, and during the first part of winter.

CHAPTER CXXII. RECONCILIATION OF THE KING AND ERLING SKIALGSSON [1022].—Erling Skialgsson held his dominion so that all north from Sogn Lake, and east to the Naze, the bonders stood under him; and although he had much smaller royal fiefs than formerly, still so great a dread of him prevailed that nobody dared to do anything against his will, so that the king thought his power too great. There was a man called Aslak Fitiaskalle, who was powerful, and of high birth. Erling's father Skialg, and Aslak's father Askel, were first cousins. Aslak was a great friend of King Olaf, and the king settled him in South Hordaland, where he gave him a great fief, and great income, and ordered him in no respect to give way to Erling. But this came to nothing when the king was not in the neighbourhood; for then Erling would reign as he used to do, and was not more humble because Aslak would thrust himself forward as his equal. At last the strife went so far that Aslak could not keep his place, but hastened to King Olaf, and told him the circumstances between him and Erling. The king told Aslak to remain with him until he should meet Erling; and sent a message to Erling that he should come to him in spring at Tunsberg. When they all arrived there they held a meeting, at which the king said to him, "It is told me concerning thy government, Erling, that no man from Sogn Lake to the Naze can enjoy his freedom for thee; although there are many men there who consider themselves born to udal rights, and have their privileges like others born as they are. Now, here is your relation Aslak, who appears to have suffered great inconvenience from your conduct; and I do not know whether he himself is in fault, or whether he suffers because I have placed him to defend what is mine; and although I name him, there are many others who have brought the same complaint before us, both among those who are king's officials in our districts, and among the bailiffs who have our farms to manage, and are obliged to entertain me and my people."

Erling replies to this, "I will answer at once. I deny altogether that I have ever injured Aslak, or any one else, for being in your service; but this I will not deny, that it is now as it has long been, that each of us relations will willingly be greater than the other: and, moreover, I freely acknowledge that I am ready to bow my neck to thee, King Olaf; but it is more difficult for me to stoop before one who is of slave descent in all his generation, although he is now your bailiff, or before others who are but equal to him in descent, although you bestow honours on them."

Now the friends of both interfered, and entreated that they would be reconciled; saying, that the king never could have such powerful aid as from Erling, "if he was your friend entirely." On the other hand, they represent to Erling that he should give in to the king; for if he was in friendship with the king, it would be easy to do with all the others what he pleased. The meeting accordingly ended so that Erling should retain the fiefs he formerly had, and every complaint the king had against Erling should be dropped; but Skialg, Erling's son, should come to the king, and remain in his power. Then Aslak returned to his dominions, and the two were in some sort reconciled. Erling returned home also to his domains and followed his own way of ruling them.

CHAPTER CXXIII. HERE BEGINS THE STORY OF ASBIORN SELSBANE [1022].—There was a man called Sigurd Thoreson, a brother of Thore Hund of Biark Island. Sigurd was married to Sigrid Skialg's daughter, a sister of Erling. Their son, called Asbiorn, became as he grew up a very able man. Sigurd dwelt at Aumd, in Thrandeness,[1] and was a very rich and respected man. He had not gone into the king's service; and Thore in so far had attained higher dignity than his brother, that he was the king's lenderman. But at home, on his farm, Sigurd stood in no respect behind his brother in splendour and magnificence. As long as heathenism prevailed, Sigurd usually had three sacrifices every year: one on winter-night's eve, one on mid-winter's eve, and the third in summer. Although he had adopted Christianity, he continued the same custom with his feasts: he had, namely, a great friendly entertainment at harvest time; a Yule feast in winter, to which he invited many; the third feast he had about Easter, to which also he invited many guests. He continued this fashion as long as he lived. Sigurd died on a bed of sickness when Asbiorn was eighteen years old. He was the only heir of his father, and he followed his father's custom of holding three festivals every year.. Soon after Asbiorn came to his heritage the course of seasons began to grow worse, and the corn harvests of the people to fail; but Asbiorn held his usual feasts, and helped himself by having old

[1] Now called Trondenes or Trones; it is in Hindö, not in Ömd (Aumd).

corn, and an old provision laid up of all that was useful. But
when one year had passed and another came, and the crops were
no better than the year before, Sigrid wished that some if not
all of the feasts should be given up. That Asbiorn would not
consent to, but went round in harvest among his friends buying
corn where he could get it, and some he received in presents.
He thus kept his feasts this winter also; but the spring after
people got but little seed into the ground, for they had to buy
the seed-corn. Then Sigrid spoke of diminishing the number
of their house-servants. That Asbiorn would not consent to,
but held by the old fashion of the house in all things. In
summer it appeared again that there would be a bad year for
corn; and to this came the report from the south that King
Olaf prohibited all export of corn, malt, or meal from the
southern to the northern parts of the country. Then Asbiorn
perceived that it would be difficult to procure what was necessary for a housekeeping, and resolved to put into the water a
vessel for carrying goods which he had, and which was large
enough to go to sea with. The ship was good, all that belonged
to her was of the best, and in the sails were stripes of cloth of
various colours. Asbiorn made himself ready for a voyage,
and put to sea with twenty men. They sailed from the north
in summer; and nothing is told of their voyage until one day,
about the time the days begin to shorten, they came to Karmtsund, and landed at Augvaldsness. Up in the island Karmt
there is a large farm not far from the sea, and a large house
upon it called Augvaldsness, which was a king's house, with an
excellent farm, which Thore Sel, who was the king's bailiff, had
under his management. Thore was a man of low birth, but had
swung himself up in the world as an active man; and he was
polite in speech, showy in clothes, and fond of distinction, and
not apt to give way to others, in which he was supported by the
favour of the king. He was besides quick in speech, straight-
forward, and free in conversation. Asbiorn, with his company,
brought up there for the night; and in the morning, when it
was light, Thore went down to the vessel with some men and
inquired who commanded the splendid ship. Asbiorn named
his own and his father's name. Thore asks where the voyage
was intended for, and what was the errand.

Asbiorn replies, that he wanted to buy corn and malt; saying,
as was true, that it was a very dear time north in the country.
" But we are told that here the seasons are good; and wilt thou,
farmer, sell us corn? I see that here are great corn stacks,

and it would be very convenient if we had not to travel farther."

Thore replies, " I will give thee the information that thou needst not go farther to buy corn, or travel about here in Rogaland; for I can tell thee that thou must turn about, and not travel farther, for the king forbids carrying corn out of this to the north of the country. Sail back again, Halogalander, for that will be thy safest course."

Asbiorn replies, " If it be so, bonder, as thou sayest, that we can get no corn here to buy, I will, notwithstanding, go forward upon my errand, and visit my family in Sole, and see my relation Erling's habitation."

Thore:—" How near is thy relationship to Erling? "

Asbiorn:—" My mother is his sister."

Thore:—" It may be that I have spoken heedlessly, if so be that thou art sister's son of the Rogalanders' king."

Thereupon Asbiorn and his crew struck their tents, and turned the ship to sea. Thore called after them, " A good voyage, and come here again on your way back." Asbiorn promised to do so, sailed away, and came in the evening to Jœderen. Asbiorn went on shore with ten men; the other ten men watched the ship. When Asbiorn came to the house he was very well received, and Erling was very glad to see him, placed him beside himself, and asked him all the news in the north of the country. Asbiorn concealed nothing of his business from him; and Erling said it happened unfortunately that the king had just forbidden the sale of corn. " And I know no man here," says he, " who has courage to break the king's order, and I find it difficult to keep well with the king, so many are trying to break our friendship."

Asbiorn replies, " It is late before we learn the truth. In my childhood I was taught that my mother was free-born throughout her whole descent, and that Erling of Sole was her boldest relation; and now I hear thee say that thou hast not the freedom, for the king's slaves here in Jœderen, to do with thy own corn what thou pleasest."

Erling looked at him, smiled through his teeth, and said, " Ye Halogalanders know less of the king's power than we do here; but a bold man thou mayst be at home in thy conversation. Let us now drink, my friend, and we shall see to-morrow what can be done in thy business."

They did so, and were very merry all the evening. The following day Erling and Asbiorn talked over the matter again;

and Erling said, " I have found out a way for you to purchase corn, Asbiorn. It is the same thing to you whoever is the seller." He answered that he did not care of whom he bought the corn, if he got a good right to his purchase. Erling said, " It appears to me probably that my slaves have quite as much corn as you require to buy; and they are not subject to law, or land regulation, like other men." Asbiorn agreed to the proposal. The slaves were now spoken to about the purchase, and they brought forward corn and malt, which they sold to Asbiorn, so that he loaded his vessel with what he wanted. When he was ready for sea Erling followed him on the road, made him presents of friendship, and they took a kind farewell of each other. Asbiorn got a good breeze, landed in the evening at Karmtsund, near to Augvaldsness, and remained there for the night. Thore Sel had heard of Asbiorn's voyage, and also that his vessel was deeply laden. Thore summoned people to him in the night, so that before daylight he had sixty men; and with these he went against Asbiorn as soon as it was light, and went out to the ship just as Asbiorn and his men were putting on their clothes. Asbiorn saluted Thore, and Thore asked what kind of goods Asbiorn had in the vessel.

He replied, " Corn and malt."

Thore said, " Then Erling is doing as he usually does, and despising the king's orders, and is unwearied in opposing him in all things, insomuch that it is wonderful the king suffers it."

Thore went on scolding in this way, and when he was silent Asbiorn said that Erling's slaves had owned the corn.

Thore replied hastily, that he did not regard Erling's tricks. " And now, Asbiorn, there is no help for it: ye must either go on shore, or we will throw you overboard; for we will not be troubled with you while we are discharging the cargo."

Asbiorn saw that he had not men enough to resist Thore; therefore he and his people landed, and Thore took the whole cargo out of the vessel. When the vessel was discharged Thore went through the ship, and observed, " The Halogalanders have good sails: take the old sail of our vessel and give it them; it is good enough for those who are sailing in a light vessel." Thus the sails were exchanged. When this was done Asbiorn and his comrades sailed away north along the coast, and did not stop until they reached home early in winter. This expedition was talked of far and wide, and Asbiorn had no trouble that winter in making feasts at home. Thore Hund invited Asbiorn and his mother, and also all whom they pleased to take along with

them, to a Yule feast; but Asbiorn sat at home, and would not
travel, and it was to be seen that Thore thought Asbiorn
despised his invitation, since he would not come. Thore
scoffed much at Asbiorn's voyage. "Now," said he, "it is
evident that Asbiorn makes a great difference in his respect
towards his relations; for in summer he took the greatest
trouble to visit his relation Erling in Jœderen, and now will
not take the trouble to come to me in the next house. I don't
know if he thinks there may be a Thore Sel in his way upon every
holm." Such words, and the like sarcasms, Asbiorn heard of;
and very ill satisfied he was with his voyage, which had thus
made him a laughing-stock to the country, and he remained at
home all winter, and went to no feasts.

CHAPTER CXXIV. ASBIORN KILLS THORE [1023].—Asbiorn
had a long-ship standing in the naust [1] (boat-house); it was
a snekke (cutter) of twenty benches; and after Candlemas (2nd
February) he had the vessel put in the water, brought out all
his furniture, and rigged her out. He then summoned to him
his friends and people, so that he had nearly ninety men all well
armed. When he was ready for sea, and got a wind, he sailed
south along the coast; but as the wind did not suit, they
advanced but slowly. When they came farther south they
steered outside the rocks, outside the usual ships' channel,
keeping to sea as much as it was possible to do so. Nothing is
related of his voyage before the fifth day of Easter [2] (25th April),
when, about evening, they came on the outside of Karmt Island.
This island is so shaped that it is very long, but not broad at its
widest part; and outside it lies the usual ships' channel. It is
thickly inhabited; but where the island is exposed to the ocean
great tracts of it are uncultivated. Asbiorn and his men
landed at a place in the island that was uninhabited. After
they had set up their ship-tents Asbiorn said, "Now ye must
remain here and wait for me. I will go on land in the isle,
and spy what news there may be which we know nothing of."
Asbiorn had on mean clothes, a broad-brimmed hat, a fork in
his hand, but had girt on his sword under his clothes. He went
up to the land, and in through the island; and when he came
upon a hillock, from which he could see the house on Augvalds-

---

[1] *Naust.* The word Naust is in common use still in the Orkney Isles for a
dock for a small boat excavated in the shore-bank.
[2] *i.e.* the Thursday after Easter Sunday. The sermon referred to on
p. 252 would be that of Good Friday.

ness, and on as far as Karmt Sound, he saw people in all quarters flocking together by land and by sea, and all going up to the house of Augvaldsness. This seemed to him extraordinary; and therefore he went up quietly to a house close by, in which servants were cooking meat. From their conversation he discovered immediately that King Olaf had come there to a feast, and that he had just sat down to table. Asbiorn turned then to the feasting-room, and when he came into the ante-room one was going in and another coming out; but nobody took notice of him. The hall-door was open, and he saw that Thore Sel stood before the table of the high seat. It was getting late in the evening, and Asbiorn heard people ask Thore what had taken place between him and Asbiorn; and Thore had a long story about it, in which he evidently departed from the truth. Among other things he heard a man say, "How did Asbiorn behave when you discharged his vessel?" Thore replied, "When we were taking out the cargo he bore it tolerably, but not well; and when we took the sail from him he wept." When Asbiorn heard this he suddenly drew his sword, rushed into the hall, and cut at Thore. The stroke took him in the neck, so that the head fell upon the table before the king, and the body at his feet, and the table-cloth was soiled with blood from top to bottom. The king ordered him to be seized and taken out. This was done. They laid hands on Asbiorn, and took him from the hall. The table-furniture and table-cloths were removed, and also Thore's corpse, and all the blood wiped up. The king was enraged to the highest; but remained quiet in speech, as he always was when in anger.

CHAPTER CXXV. OF SKIALG, THE SON OF ERLING SKIALGS-SON.—Skialg Erlingsson stood up, went before the king, and said, "Now may it go, as it often does, that every case will admit of alleviation. I will pay thee the mulct for the bloodshed on account of this man, so that he may retain life and limbs. All the rest determine and do, king, according to thy pleasure."

The king replies, "Is it not a matter of death, Skialg, that a man break the Easter peace; and in the next place that he kills a man in the king's lodging; and in the third that he makes my feet his execution-block, although that may appear a small matter to thee and thy father?"

Skialg replies, "It is ill done, king, in as far as it displeases thee; but the deed is, otherwise, done excellently well. But if the deed appear to thee so important, and be so contrary to thy will, yet may I expect something for my services from thee; and certainly there are many who will say that thou didst well."

The king replies, " Although thou hast made me greatly indebted to thee, Skialg, for thy services, yet I will not for thy sake break the law, or cast away my own dignity."

Then Skialg turned round, and went out of the hall. Twelve men who had come with Skialg all followed him. and many others went out with him. Skialg said to Thorarin Nefiolfsson, " If thou wilt have me for a friend, take care that this man be not killed before Sunday." Thereupon Skialg and his men set off, took a rowing boat which he had, and rowed south as fast as they could, and came to Jœderen with the first glimpse of morning. They went up instantly to the house, and to the loft in which Erling slept. Skialg rushed so hard against the door that it burst asunder at the nails. Erling and the others who were within started up. He was in one spring upon his legs, grasped his shield and sword, and rushed to the door, demanding who was there. Skialg names himself, and begs him to open the door. Erling replies, " It was most likely to be thee who hast behaved so foolishly; or is there any one who is pursuing thee? " Thereupon the door was unlocked. Then said Skialg, " Although it appears to thee that I am so hasty, I suppose our relation Asbiorn will not think my proceedings too quick; for he sits in chains there in the north at Augvaldsness, and it would be but manly to hasten back and stand by him." The father and son then had a conversation together, and Skialg related the whole circumstances of Thore Sel's murder.

CHAPTER CXXVI. OF THORARIN NEFIOLFSSON.—King Olaf took his seat again when everything in the hall was put in order, and was enraged beyond measure. He asked how it was with the murderer. He was answered, that he was outside in the gallery under guard.

The king says, " Why is he not put to death? "

Thorarin Nefiolfsson replies, " Sire, would you not call it murder to kill a man in the night-time? "

The king answers, " Put him in irons then and kill him in the morning."

Then Asbiorn was laid in chains, and locked up in a house for the night. The day after the king heard matins sung, and then went to the Thing, where he sat till high mass. As he

was going to mass he said to Thorarin, " Is not the sun high
enough now in the heavens that your friend Asbiorn may be
hanged ? "

Thorarin bowed before the king, and said, " Sire, it was said
by Bishop Sigurd on Friday last, that the King who has all
things in his power had to endure great temptation of spirit;
and blessed is he who rather imitates him, than those who
condemned the man to death, or those who caused his slaughter.
It is nòt long till to-morrow, and that is a working day."

The king looked at him, and said, " Thou must take care then
that he is not put to death to-day; but take him under thy
charge, and know for certain that thy own life shall answer for it
if he escape in any way."

Then the king went away. Thorarin went also to where
Asbiorn lay in irons, took off his chains, and brought him
to a small room, where he had meat and drink set before
him, and told him what the king had determined in case Asbiorn
ran away. Asbiorn replies, that Thorarin need not be afraid
of him. Thorarin sat a long while with him during the day,
and slept there all night. On Saturday the king arose and went
to attend matins, and from thence he went to the Thing, where
a great many bonders were assembled, who had many complaints to be determined. The king sat there long in the day,
and it was late before the people went to high mass. Thereafter
the king went to table. When he had got meat he sat drinking
for a while, so that the tables were not removed. Thorarin
went out to the priest who had the church under his care, and
gave him two marks of silver to ring in the Sabbath as soon as
the king's table was taken away. When the king had drunk
as much as he wished the tables were removed. Then said the
king, that it was now the time for the slaves to go to the murderer
and put him to death. In the same moment the bell ràng in
the Sabbath.

Then Thorarin went before the king, and said, " The Sabbath-
peace this man must have, although he has done evil."

The king said, " Do thou take care, Thorarin, that he do not
escape."

The king then went to the church, and attended the nones
service,[1] and Thorarin sat the whole day with Asbiorn. On
Sunday the bishop visited Asbiorn, confessed him, and gave
him leave [2] to hear high mass. Thorarin then went to the king,

[1] In Norwegian church law, the Sabbath began on the Saturday at nones
(3 p.m.).
[2] Otherwise, being guilty of murder, he could not enter a church.

and asked him to appoint men to guard the murderer. " I will now," he said, " be free of this charge." The king thanked him for his care, and ordered men to watch over Asbiorn who was again laid in chains. When the people went to high mass Asbiorn was led to the church, and he stood outside of the church with his guard; but the king and all the people stood in the church at mass.

CHAPTER CXXVII. ERLING'S RECONCILIATION WITH KING OLAF.—Now we must again take up our story where we left it [p. 251],—that Erling and his son Skialg held a council on this affair, and according to the resolution of Erling, and of Skialg and his other sons, it was determined to assemble a force and send out message-tokens. A great multitude of people accordingly came together. They got ready with all speed, rigged their ships, and when they reckoned upon their force they found they had nearly 1500 [1] men. With this war-force they set off, and came on Sunday to Augvaldsness on Karmt Island. They went straight up to the house with all the men, and arrived just as the Gospel reading was finished. They went directly to the church, took Asbiorn, and broke off his chains. At the tumult and clash of arms all who were outside of the church ran into it; but they who were in the church looked all towards them, except the king, who stood still, without looking around him. Erling and his sons drew up their men on each side of the path which led from the church to the hall, and Erling with his sons stood next to the hall. When high mass was finished the king went immediately out of the church, and first went through the open space between the ranks drawn up, and then his retinue, man by man; and as he came to the door Erling placed himself before the door, bowed to the king, and saluted him. The king saluted him in return, and prayed God to help him. Erling took up the word first, and said, " My relation Asbiorn, it is reported to me, has been guilty of misdemeanour, king; and it is a great one, if he has done anything that incurs your displeasure. Now I am come to entreat for him peace, and such penalties as you yourself may determine; but that thereby he redeem life and limb, and his remaining here in his native land."

The king replies, " It appears to me, Erling, that thou thinkest the case of Asbiorn is now in thy own power, and I do not therefore know why thou speakest now as if thou wouldst offer terms

[1] i.e. 1800.

for him. I think thou hast drawn together these forces because thou art determined to settle what is between us."

Erling replies, "Thou only, king, shalt determine, and determine so that we shall be reconciled."

The king:—"Thinkest thou, Erling, to make me afraid? and art thou come here in such force with that expectation? No, that shall not be; and if that be thy thought, I must in no way turn and fly."

Erling replies, "Thou hast no occasion to remind me how often I have come to meet thee with fewer men than thou hadst. But now I shall not conceal what lies in my mind, namely, that it is my will that we now enter into a reconciliation; for otherwise I expect we shall never meet again." Erling was then as red as blood in the face.

Now Bishop Sigurd came forward to the king and said, "Sire, I entreat you on God Almighty's account to be reconciled with Erling according to his offer,—that the man shall retain life and limb, but that thou shalt determine according to thy pleasure all the other conditions."

The king replies, "You will determine."

Then said the bishop, "Erling, do thou give security for Asbiorn, such as the king thinks sufficient, and then let Asbiorn receive promise of peace from the king, and leave all in his power."

Erling gave a surety to the king on his part, which he accepted.

Thereupon Asbiorn received his life and safety, and delivered himself into the king's power, and kissed his hand.

Erling then withdrew with his forces, without exchanging salutation with the king; and the king went into the hall, followed by Asbiorn. The king thereafter made known the terms of reconciliation to be these:—" In the first place, Asbiorn, thou must submit to the law of the land, which commands that the man who kills a servant of the king must undertake his service, if the king will. Now I will that thou shalt undertake the office of bailiff which Thore Sel had, and manage my estate here in Augvaldsness." Asbiorn replies, that it should be according to the king's will; " but I must first go home to my farm, and put things in order there." The king was satisfied with this, and proceeded to another guest-quarter. Asbiorn made himself ready with his comrades, who all kept themselves concealed in a quiet creek during the time Asbiorn was away from them. They had had their spies out to learn how it went with him, and would not depart without having some certain news of him.

CHAPTER CXXVIII. OF THORE HUND AND ASBIORN SELS-
BANE.—Asbiorn then set out on his voyage, and about spring
got home to his farm. After this exploit he was always called
Asbiorn Selsbane.[1] Asbiorn had not been long at home before
he and his relation Thore met and conversed together, and
Thore asked Asbiorn particularly all about his journey, and
about all the circumstances which had happened in the course
of it. Asbiorn told everything as it had taken place.

Then said Thore, " Thou thinkest that thou hast well rubbed
out the disgrace of having been plundered in last harvest."

" I think so," replies Asbiorn; " and what is thy opinion,
uncle?"

" That I will soon tell thee," said Thore. " Thy first expedition to the south of the country was indeed very disgraceful,
and that disgrace has been redeemed; but this expedition is
both a disgrace to thee and to thy family, if it end in thy becoming the king's slave, and being put on a footing with that worst
of men, Thore Sel. Show that thou art manly enough to sit
here on thy own property, and we thy relations shall so support
thee that thou wilt never more come into such trouble."

Asbiorn found this advice much to his mind; and before they
parted it was firmly determined that Asbiorn should remain on
his farm, and not go back to the king or enter into his service.
And he did so, and sat quietly at home on his farm.

CHAPTER CXXIX. KING OLAF BAPTIZES VOSS AND VALDERS
DISTRICTS [1023].—After King Olaf and Erling Skialgsson had
this meeting at Augvaldsness, new differences arose between
them, and increased so much that they ended in perfect enmity.
In spring the king proceeded to guest-quarters in Hordaland,
and went up also to Voss, because he heard there was but little of
the true faith among the people there. He held a Thing with the
bonders at a place called Vang,[2] and a number of bonders came
to it fully armed. The king ordered them to adopt Christianity;
but they challenged him to battle, and it proceeded so far that
the men were drawn up on both sides. But when it came to the
point such a fear entered into the blood of the bonders that none
would advance or command, and they chose the part which was
most to their advantage; namely, to obey the king and receive
Christianity: and before the king left them they were all
baptized. One day it happened that the king was riding on his

---

[1] The bane or destroyer of Thore Sel.
[2] Vossevangen on the railway between Bergen and Christiania.

way a singing of psalms, and when he came right opposite some hills[1] he halted and said, " Man after man shall relate these my words, that I think it not advisable for any king of Norway to travel hereafter between these hills." And it is a saying among the people that the most kings since that time have avoided it. The king proceeded to Osterfjord, and came to his ships, with which he went north to Sogn, and had his living in guest-quarters there in summer: when autumn approached he turned in towards the Fjords district, and went from thence to Valders, where the people were still heathen. The king hastened up to the lake in Valders,[2] came unexpectedly on the bonders, seized their vessels, and went on board of them with all his men. He then sent out message-tokens, and appointed a Thing so near the lake that he could use the vessels if he found he required them. The bonders resorted to the Thing in a great and well-armed host; and when he commanded them to accept Christianity the bonders shouted against him, told him to be silent, and made a great uproar and clashing of weapons. But when the king saw that they would not listen to what he would teach them, and also that they had too great a force to contend with, he turned his discourse, and asked if there were people at the Thing who had disputes with each other which they wished him to settle. It was soon found by the conversation of the bonders that they had many quarrels among themselves, although they had all joined in speaking against Christianity. When the bonders began to set forth their own cases, each endeavoured to get some upon his side to support him, and this lasted the whole day long until evening, when the Thing was concluded. When the bonders had heard that the king had travelled to Valders, and was come into their neighbourhood, they had sent out message-tokens summoning the free and the unfree to meet in arms, and with this force they advanced against the king: so that the neighbourhood all around was left without people. When the Thing was concluded the bonders still remained assembled; and when the king observed this he went on board his ships, rowed in the night right across the water, landed in the country there, and began to plunder and burn. The day after the king's men rowed from one point of land to another, and over all the king ordered the habitations to be set on fire. Now when the bonders who were

---

[1] Or rather, burial mounds (*haugar*); it is not known which they were.
[2] Either Vangsmjösen or Slidrefjord.

assembled saw what the king was doing, namely, plundering and burning, and saw the smoke and flame of their houses, they dispersed, and each hastened to his own home to see if he could find those he had left. As soon as there came a dispersion among the crowd, the one slipped away after the other, until the whole multitude was dissolved. Then the king rowed across the lake again, burning also on that side of the country. Now came the bonders to him begging for mercy, and offering to submit to him. He gave every man who came to him peace if he desired it, and restored to him his goods; and nobody refused to adopt Christianity. The king then had the people christened, and took hostages from the bonders. He remained a long time here in autumn, and had his ships drawn across the neck of land between the two lakes.[1] The king did not go far from the sides of the lakes into the country, for he did not much trust the bonders. He ordered churches to be built and consecrated, and placed teachers in them. When the king thought that frost might be expected, he went farther up the country, and came to Thoten. Arnor Earlscald refers to King Olaf burning in the Uplands, in the poem he composed concerning the king's brother King Harald:—

" Against the Upland people wroth,
  Our king, our lord of men, went forth:
    The houses burning,
    All people mourning;
    Who could not fly
    Hung on gallows high.
  It was, I think, in Harald's race
  The Upland people to oppress." [2]

Afterwards King Olaf went north through the Dales to Dovrefjeld, and did not halt until he reached the Drontheim district and arrived at Nidaros, where he had ordered winter provisions to be collected, and remained all winter. This was the tenth year of his reign.

CHAPTER CXXX. OF EINAR TAMBARSKELVE [1023-1024].
—The summer before, Einar Tambarskelve left the country, and went westward to England. There he met his relative Earl Hakon, and stayed some time with him. He then visited King Canute, from whom he received great presents. Einar then went south all the way to Rome, and came back the following

---

[1] i.e. between the Mjösen and the Slidre lakes.
[2] On Harald's treatment of the Uplanders, see Sagas of the Norse Kings, pp. 217–18.

summer, and returned to his house and land. King Olaf and Einar did not meet this time.

CHAPTER CXXXI. THE BIRTH OF KING MAGNUS [1024].— There was a girl whose name was Alfhild, and who was usually called the king's hand-maiden, although she was of good descent. She was a remarkably handsome girl, and lived in King Olaf's court. It was reported this spring that Alfhild was with child, and the king's confidential friends knew that he was father of the child. It happened one night that Alfhild was taken ill, and only few people were at hand; namely, some women, priests, Sigvat the scald, and a few others. Alfhild was so ill that she was nearly dead; and when she was delivered of a man-child, it was some time before they could discover whether the child was in life. But when the infant drew breath, although very weak, the priest told Sigvat to hasten to the king, and tell him of the event.

He replies, " I dare not on any account waken the king; for he has forbidden that any man should break his sleep until he awakens of himself."

The priest replies, " It is of necessity that this child be immediately baptized, for it appears to me there is but little life in it."

Sigvat said, " I would rather venture to take upon me to let thee baptize the child, than to awaken the king; and I will take the blame on myself, and will give the child a name."

They did so; and the child was baptized, and got the name of Magnus. The next morning, when the king awoke and had dressed himself, the circumstance was told him. He ordered Sigvat to be called, and said, " How camest thou to be so bold as to have my child baptized before I knew anything about it? "

Sigvat replies, " Because I would rather give two men to God than one to the devil."

The king:—" What meanest thou? "

Sigvat:—" The child was near death, and must have been the devil's if it had died as a heathen, and now it is God's. And I knew besides that if thou shouldst be so angry on this account that it affected my life, I would be God's also."

The king asked, " But why didst thou call him Magnus, which is not a name of our race? "

Sigvat:—" I called him after King Carl Magnus,[1] who, I knew, had been the best man in the world."

[1] i.e. Charlemagne.

Then said the king, " Thou art a very lucky man, Sigvat; but it is not wonderful that luck should accompany understanding. It is only wonderful how it sometimes happens that luck attends ignorant men, and that foolish counsel turns out lucky." The king was overjoyed at the circumstance. The boy grew up, and gave good promise as he advanced in age.

CHAPTER CXXXII. THE MURDER OF ASBIORN SELSBANE.— The same spring the king gave into the hands of Aasmund Grankelsson the half of the sheriffdom of the district of Halogaland, which Harek of Thiotto had formerly held, partly in fief, partly for defraying the king's entertainment in guest-quarters. Aasmund had a ship manned with nearly thirty well-armed men. When Aasmund came north he met Harek, and told him what the king had determined with regard to the district, and produced to him the tokens of the king's full powers. Harek said, " The king had the right to give the sheriffdom to whom he pleased; but the former sovereigns had not been in use to diminish our rights who are entitled by birth to hold powers from the king and to give them into the hands of peasants who never before held such offices." But although it was evident that it was against Harek's inclination, he allowed Aasmund to take the sheriffdom according to the king's order. Then Aasmund proceeded home to his father, stayed there a short time, and then went north to Halogaland to his sheriffdom; and he came north to Langö,[1] an island where there dwelt two brothers called Gunstein and Carl, both very rich and respectable men. Gunstein, the eldest of the brothers, was a good husbandman. Carl was a handsome man in appearance, and splendid in his dress; and both were, in many respects, expert in all feats. Aasmund was well received by them, remained with them a while, and collected such revenues of his sheriffdom as he could get. Carl spoke with Aasmund of his wish to go south with him and take service in the court of King Olaf, to which Aasmund encouraged him much, promising his influence with the king for obtaining for Carl such a situation as he desired; and Carl accordingly accompanied Aasmund. Aasmund heard that Asbiorn, who had killed Thore Sel, had gone to the spring fishmarket at Vaage with a large ship of burden manned with nearly twenty men, and that he was now expected from the south. Aasmund and his retinue proceeded on their way southwards along the coast with a contrary wind, but there was

[1] The most westerly island in Vesteraalen.

little of it. They saw some of the fleet for Vaage sailing towards them; and they privately inquired of them about Asbiorn, and were told he was upon the way coming from the south. Aasmund and Carl were bedfellows, and excellent friends. One day, as Aasmund and his people were rowing through a sound, a ship of burden came sailing towards them. The ship was easily known, having high bulwarks, was painted with white and red colours, and coloured cloth was woven in the sail. Carl said to Aasmund, "Thou hast often said thou wast curious to see Asbiorn who killed Thore Sel; and if I know one ship from another, that is his which is coming sailing along."

Aasmund replies, "Be so good, comrade, and tell me which is he when thou seest him."

When the ships came alongside of each other, "That is Asbiorn," said Carl; "the man sitting at the helm in a blue cloak."

Aasmund replied, "I shall make his blue cloak red;" threw a spear at Asbiorn, and hit him in the middle of the body, so that it flew through and through him, and stuck fast in the upper part of the stern-post, and Asbiorn fell down dead from the helm. Then each vessel sailed on its course, and Asbiorn's body was carried north to Thrandenæs. Then Sigrid sent a message to Biark Isle to Thore Hund, who came to her while they were, in the usual way, dressing the corpse of Asbiorn. When he returned Sigrid gave presents to all her friends, and followed Thore to his ship; but before they parted she said, " It has so fallen out, Thore, that my son Asbiorn followed thy friendly counsel, but he did not retain life to reward thee for it; but although I have not his ability, yet will I show my good will. Here is a gift I give thee, which I expect thou wilt use. Here is the spear which went through Asbiorn my son, and there is still blood upon it, to remind thee that it fits the wound thou hast seen on the corpse of thy brother's son Asbiorn. It would be a manly deed, if thou shouldst throw this spear from thy hand so that it stood in Olaf's breast; and this I can tell thee, that thou wilt be named coward in every man's mouth if thou dost not avenge Asbiorn." Thereupon she turned about and went her way.

Thore was so enraged at her words that he could not speak. He neither thought of casting the spear from him, nor took notice of the gangway; so that he would have fallen into the sea, if his men had not laid hold of him as he was going on board his ship. It was a maal-spear;[1] not large, but the socket for the spear head was gold-mounted. Now Thore rowed away with his people, and went home to Biark Isle. Aasmund and his companions also proceeded on their way until they came south to Drontheim, where they waited on King Olaf; and Aasmund related to the king all that had happened on the voyage. Carl became one of the king's court-men, and the friendship continued between him and Aasmund. They did not keep secret the words that had passed between Aasmund and Carl before Asbiorn was killed; for they even told them to the king. But then it happened, according to the proverb, that every one has a friend in the midst of his enemies. There were some present who took notice of the words, and they reached Thore Hund's ears.

CHAPTER CXXXIII. OF KING OLAF.—When spring was advanced King Olaf rigged out his ships, and sailed southwards in summer along the land. He held Things with the bonders on the way, settled the law business of the people, put to rights the faith of the country, and collected the king's taxes wherever he came. In autumn he proceeded south to the frontier of the country; and King Olaf had now made the people Christians in all the great districts, and everywhere, by laws, had introduced order into the country. He had also, as before related [pp. 228-229], brought the Orkney Islands under his power, and by messages had made many fri nds in Iceland, Greenland, and the Faroe Islands. King Olaf had sent timber for building a church to Iceland, of which a church was built upon the Thingfield where the General Thing is held, and had sent a bell for it, which is still there. This was after the Iceland people had altered their laws, and introduced Christianity, according to the word King Olaf had sent them. After that time, many considerable persons came from Iceland and entered into King Olaf's service; as Thorkel Eyolfsson, and Thorleif Bollason, Thord Kolbeinsson, Thord Baarkson, Thorgeir Haavardson, Thormod Kolbrunar the scald.[2] King Olaf had sent many friendly presents to chief people in Iceland; and they in return sent him such things as they had which they thought most acceptable. Under this show of friendship which the king gave Iceland were concealed many things which afterwards appeared.

[1] *Málaspjót*, a spear with the head inlaid with gold or silver.
[2] More correctly, " Kolbrun's scald," so named for his verses to a girl called Kolbrun. See *Fóstbræðra Saga* (trans. Lee M. Hollander).

Chapter CXXXIX. King Olaf's Message to Iceland, and the Counsels of the Icelanders [1024].—King Olaf this summer sent Thorarin Nefiolfsson to Iceland on his errands; and Thorarin went out of Drontheim fjord along with the king, and followed him south to Möre. From thence Thorarin went out to sea, and got such a favourable breeze that after four days' sail he came to land at Eyrarbakki, in Iceland. He proceeded immediately to the Al-thing, and came just as the people were upon the Law hillock,[1] to which he repaired. When the cases of the people before the Thing had been determined according to law, Thorarin Nefiolfsson took up the word as follows:—

" We parted four days ago from King Olaf Haraldsson, who sends God Almighty's and his own salutation to all the chiefs and principal men of the land; as also to all the people in general, men and women, young and old, rich and poor. He also lets you know that he will be your sovereign if ye will become his subjects, so that he and you will be friends, assisting each other in all that is good."

The people replied in a friendly way that they would gladly be the king's friends if he would be a friend of the people of their country.

Then Thorarin again took up the word:—" This follows, in addition to the king's message, that he will in friendship desire of the people of the north district that they give him the island, or out-rock, which lies at the mouth of Eyjafjord, and is called Grimsö, for which he will give you from his country whatever good the people of the district may desire. He sends this message particularly to Gudmund of Modrovald to support this matter, because he understands that Gudmund has most influence in that quarter."

Gudmund replies, " My inclination is greatly for King Olaf's friendship, and that I consider much more useful than the out-rock he desires. But the king has not heard rightly if he think I have more power in this matter than any other, for the island is a common. We, however, who have the most use of the isle will hold a meeting among ourselves about it."

Then the people went to their tent-houses; and the Northland people had a meeting among themselves, and talked over the business, and every one spoke according to his judgment. Gudmund supported the matter, and many others formed their opinions by his. Then some asked why his brother Einar did

---

[1] The mound at Thingvellir where the Law-Speaker sat.

not speak on the subject. " We think he has the clearest insight into most things."

Einar answers, " I have said so little about the matter because nobody has asked me about it; but if I may give my opinion, our countrymen might just as well make themselves at once liable to land-scatt to King Olaf, and submit to all his exactions as he has them among his people in Norway; and this heavy burden we will lay not only upon ourselves, but on our sons, and their sons, and all our race, and on all the community dwelling and living in this land, which never after will be free from this slavery. Now although this king is a good man, as I well believe him to be, yet it must be hereafter, when kings succeed each other, that some will be good and some bad. Therefore if the people of this country will preserve the freedom they have enjoyed since the land was first inhabited, it is not advisable to give the king the smallest spot to fasten himself upon the country by, and not to give him any kind of scatt or service that can have the appearance of a duty. On the other hand, I think it very proper that the people send the king such friendly presents of hawks or horses, tents or sails, or such things which are suitable gifts; and these are well applied if they are repaid with friendship. But as to Grimsö, I have to say that if nothing that serves as food were ever shipped away, a whole army could find food there. And if a foreign army were there and were sallying out in long-ships, then I should think poor peasants would find trouble at their door."

When Einar had thus explained the proper connection of the matter, the whole community were of one mind that such a thing should not be permitted; and Thorarin saw sufficiently well what the result of his errand was to be.

CHAPTER CXXXV. THE ANSWER OF THE ICELANDERS.—The day following, Thorarin went again to the Law-hill, and brought forward his errand in the following words:—" King Olaf sends his message to his friends here in the country, among whom he reckons Gudmund Eyolfsson, Snorre gode, Thorkel Eyolfsson, Skopte the lagman, and Thorstein Hallsson,[1] and desires them by me to come to him on a friendly visit; and adds, that ye must not excuse yourselves, if you regard his friendship as worth anything." In their answer they thanked the king for his message; and added, that they would afterwards give a reply to it by Thorarin when they had more closely con-

[1] All chieftains of power and influence.

sidered the matter with their friends. The chiefs now weighed
the matter among themselves, and each gave his own opinion
about the journey. Snorre and Skopte dissuaded from such a
dangerous proceeding with the people of Norway; namely,
that all the men who had the most to say in the country should
at once leave Iceland. They added, that from this message,
and from what Einar had said, they had the suspicion that the
king intended to use force and strong measures against the
Icelanders if he ruled in the country. Gudmund and Thorkel
Eyolfsson insisted much that they should follow King Olaf's
invitation, and called it a journey of honour. But when they
had considered the matter on all sides, it was at last resolved that
they should not travel themselves, but that each of them should
send in his place a man whom they thought best suited for it.
After this determination the Thing was closed, and there was
no journey that summer. Thorarin made two voyages that
summer, and about harvest was back again at King Olaf's,
and reported the result of his mission, and that some of the
chiefs, or their sons, would come from Iceland according to his
message.

CHAPTER CXXXVI. OF THE PEOPLE OF THE FARÖE ISLANDS
[1024].—The same summer there came from the Faröe Islands
to Norway, on the king's invitation, Gille the lagman, Leif
Ossursson, Thoralf of Dimon and many other bonders' sons.[1]
Thrand of Gata[2] made himself ready for the voyage; but just
as he was setting out he got a stroke of palsy, and could not
come, so he remained behind. Now when the people from the
Faröe Isles arrived at King Olaf's, he called them to him to a
conference, and explained the purpose of the journey he had
made them take; namely, that he would have scatt from the
Faröe Islands, and also that the people there should be subject
to the laws which the king should give them. In that meeting
it appeared from the king's words that he would make the
Faröe people who had come answerable, and would bind them
by oath to conclude this union. He also offered to the men
whom he thought the ablest to take them into his service, and
bestow honour and friendship on them. These Faröe men
understood the king's words so, that they must dread the turn
the matter might take if they did not submit to all that the king

---

[1] Snorri's source here is the *Færeyinga Saga* (*cf.* **p.** 301). See *The Saga
of the Faroe Islanders*, trans. M. A. C. Press, 1934.
[2] A chieftain bitterly opposed to Christianity and to the claims of Norway.

desired. Although they held several meetings about the business before it ended, the king's desire at last prevailed. Leif Gille and Thoralf went into the king's service and became his court-men; and they, with all their travelling companions, swore the oath to King Olaf, that the law and land privilege which he set them should be observed in the Faröe Islands, and also the scatt be levied that he laid upon them. Thereafter the Faröe people prepared for their return home, and at their departure the king gave those who had entered into his service presents in testimony of his friendship, and they went their way. Now the king ordered a ship to be rigged, manned it, and sent men to the Faröe Islands to receive the scatt from the inhabitants which they should pay him. It was late before they were ready; but they set off at last: and of their journey all that is to be told is that they did not come back, and no scatt either, the following summer; for nobody had come to the Faröe Isles, and no man had demanded scatt there.

CHAPTER CXXXVII. OF THE MARRIAGE OF KETEL AND OF THORD TO THE KING'S SISTERS [1025].—King Olaf proceeded about harvest time to Viken, and sent a message before him to the Uplands that they should prepare guest-quarters for him, as he intended to be there in winter. Afterwards he made ready for his journey, and went to the Uplands, and remained the winter there; going about in guest-quarters, and putting things to rights where he saw it needful, advancing also the cause of Christianity wheresoever it was requisite. It happened while King Olaf was in Hedemark that Ketel Kalf of Ringaness [1] courted Gunhild, a daughter of Sigurd Syr and of King Olaf's mother Aasta. Gunhild was a sister of King Olaf, and therefore it belonged to the king to give consent and determination to the business. He took it in a friendly way; for he knew Ketel, that he was of high birth, wealthy, and of good understanding, and a great chief; and also he had long been a great friend of King Olaf, as before related [p. 182]. All these circumstances induced the king to approve of the match, and so it was that Ketel got Gunhild. King Olaf was present at the wedding. From thence the king went north to Gudbrandsdal, where he was entertained in guest-quarters. There dwelt a man, by name Thord Guttormsson, on a farm called Steig; [2] and he was

[1] *Vide* p. 150.
[2] Steig is a farm two miles south-east of Fron church in Gudbrandsdal. Thord is Thord Istromaga, *vide* p. 239.

the most powerful man in the north end of the valley. When Thord and the king met, Thord made proposals for Isrid, the daughter of Gudbrand, and the sister of King Olaf's mother, as it belonged to the king to give consent. After the matter was considered, it was determined that the marriage should proceed, and Thord got Isrid. Afterwards Thord was the king's faithful friend, and also many of Thord's relations and friends, who followed his footsteps. From thence King Olaf returned south through Thoten and Hadeland, from thence to Ringerike, and so to Viken. In spring he went to Tunsberg, and stayed there while there was the market-meeting, and a great resort of people. He then had his vessels rigged out, and had many people about him.

CHAPTER CXXXVIII. OF THE ICELANDERS. — The same summer came Stein, a son of the lagman Skopte, from Iceland, in compliance with King Olaf's message; and with him Thorodd, a son of Snorre the gode,[1] and Gelle, a son of Thorkel Eyolfsson, and Egil, a son of Sida Hall, brother of Thorstein Hall.[2] Gudmund Eyolfsson had died the winter before. These Iceland men repaired to King Olaf as soon as they had opportunity; and when they met the king they were well received, and all were in his house. The same summer King Olaf heard that the ship was missing which he had sent the summer before to the Faröe Islands after the scatt, and nobody knew what had become of it. The king fitted out another ship, manned it, and sent it to the Faröe Islands for the scatt. They got under weigh, and proceeded to sea; but as little was ever heard of this vessel as of the former one, and many conjectures were made about what had become of them.

CHAPTER CXXXIX. HERE BEGINS THE STORY OF CANUTE THE GREAT. — During this time Canute the Great, called by some Canute the Old, was king of England and Denmark. Canute the Great was a son of Swend Haraldsson Forked-beard, whose forefathers, for a long course of generations, had ruled over Denmark. Harald Gormsson, Canute's grandfather, had conquered Norway after the fall of Harald Greyskin, Gunhild's son, had taken scatt from it, and had placed Earl Hakon the Great to defend the country. The Danish king, Swend Haraldsson, ruled also over Norway, and placed his son-in-law Earl Eric, the son of Earl Hakon, to defend the country. The brothers

---

[1] *Goði, i.e.* chieftain.　　　[2] This should read " Hallsson "; *cf.* p. 263.

Eric and Swend, Earl Hakon's sons, ruled the land until Earl
Eric went west to England, on the invitation of his brother-in-
law Canute the Great, when he left behind his son Earl Hakon,
sister's son of Canute the Great, to govern Norway. But when
Olaf the Thick came first to Norway, as before related, he took
prisoner Earl Hakon, the son of Eric, and deposed him from
the kingdom. Then Hakon proceeded to his mother's brother,
Canute the Great, and had been with him constantly until the
time to which here in our saga we have now come. Canute
the Great had conquered England by blows and weapons, and
had a long struggle before the people of the land were subdued.
But when he had set himself perfectly firm in the government
of the country, he remembered that he also had right to a
kingdom which he had not brought under his authority; and
that was Norway. He thought he had hereditary right to all
Norway; and his sister's son Hakon, who had held a part of it,
appeared to him to have lost it with disgrace. The reason why
Canute and Hakon had remained quiet with respect to their
claims upon Norway was, that when King Olaf Haraldsson
landed in Norway the people and commonalty ran together in
crowds, and would hear of nothing but that Olaf should be king
over all the country, although some afterwards, who thought
that the people upon account of his power had no self-govern-
ment left to them, went out of the country. Many powerful
men, or rich bonders' sons, had therefore gone to Canute the
Great, and pretended various errands; and every one who came
to Canute and desired his friendship was loaded with presents.
With Canute, too, could be seen greater splendour and pomp
than elsewhere, both with regard to the multitude of people
who were daily in attendance, and also to the other magnificent
things about the houses he owned and dwelt in himself. Canute
the Great drew scatt and revenue from the people who were the
richest of all in northern lands; and in the same proportion as
he had greater revenues than other kings, he also made greater
presents than other kings. In his whole kingdom peace was so
well established that no man dared break it. The people
of the country kept the peace towards each other, and had
their old country law: and for this he was greatly celebrated in all countries. And many of those who came from
Norway represented their hardships to Earl Hakon, and some
even to King Canute himself; and that the Norway people
were ready to turn back to the government of King Canute, or
Earl Hakon, and receive deliverance from them. This con-

versation suited well the earl's inclination, and he carried it to the king, and begged of him to try if King Olaf would not surrender the k.ngdom, or at least come to an agreement to divide it; and many supported the earl's views.

CHAPTER CXL. CANUTE'S MESSAGE TO KING OLAF.—Canute the Great sent men from the West, from England, to Norway, and equipped them magnificently for the journey. They were bearers of the English king Canute's letter and seal. They came about spring to the king of Norway, Olaf Haraldsson, in Tunsberg. Now when it was told the king that ambassadors had arrived from Canute the Great he was ill at ease, and said that Canute had not sent messengers hither with any messages that could be of advantage to him or his people; and it was some days before the ambassadors could come before the king. But when they got permission to speak to him they appeared before the king, and made known King Canute's letter, and their errand which accompanied it; namely, "that King Canute considers all Norway as his property, and insists that his fore-fathers before him have possessed that kingdom; but as King Canute offers peace to all countries, he will also offer peace to all here, if it can be so settled, and will not invade Norway with his army if it can be avoided. Now if King Olaf Haraldsson wishes to remain king of Norway, he will come to King Canute, and receive his kingdom as a fief from him, become his vassal, and pay the scatt which the earls before him formerly paid." There-upon they presented their letters, which contained precisely the same conditions.

Then King Olaf replies, "I have heard say, by old stories, that the Danish king Gorm was considered a fine and powerful king, yet he indeed ruled over Denmark only; but the kings who succeeded him thought that was too little. It has since come so far that King Canute rules over Denmark and England, and has conquered for himself a great part of Scotland.[1] Now he claims also my paternal heritage, and will then show some moderation in his covetousness. Does he wish to rule over all the countries of the North? Will he eat up all the kail in England? He shall do so, and reduce that country to a desert, before I lay my head in his hands, or show him any other kind of vassalage. Now ye shall tell him these my words,—I will defend Norway

[1] In 1018 the Scots invaded England and were victorious; and in 1031 Canute's forces tried to subdue the whole of Scotland.

with battle-axe and sword as long as life is given me, and will pay scatt to no man for my kingdom."

After this answer King Canute's ambassadors made themselves ready for their journey home, and were by no means rejoiced at the success of their errand.

Sigvat the scald had been with King Canute, who had given him a gold ring that weighed half a mark. The scald Berse Thorfeson was also there, and to him King Canute gave two gold rings, each weighing half a mark, and also a sword inlaid with gold. Sigvat made this song about it:—

" When we came o'er the wave, you cub,[1] when we came o'er the wave,
To me one ring, to thee two rings, the mighty Canute gave:

> Half a mark to me,
> One mark to thee,—
> A sword too, fine and brave.
> Now God knows well,
> And scalds can tell,
> What justice here would crave."

Sigvat the scald was very intimate with King Canute's messengers, and asked them many questions. They answered all his inquiries about their conversation with King Olaf, and the result of their message. They said the king listened unwillingly to their proposals. " And we do not know," say they, " to what he is trusting when he refuses becoming King Canute's vassal, and going to him, which would be the best thing he could do; for King Canute is so mild that however much a chief may have done against him, he is pardoned if he only show himself obedient. It is but lately that two kings came to him from the North, from Fife in Scotland, and he gave up his wrath against them, and allowed them to retain all the lands they had possessed before, and gave them besides very valuable gifts." Then Sigvat sang:—

> " From the North land, the midst of Fife,
> Two kings came begging peace and life;
> Craving from Canute life and peace,—
> May Olaf's good luck never cease!
> For he, our gallant Norse king, never
> Was brought, like these, his head [2] to offer
> As ransom to a living man
> For the broad lands his sword has won."

King Canute's ambassadors proceeded on their way back, and

[1] Berse, the name of the more fortunate scald, signifies also a young bear; and Sigvat puns upon it.

[2] To lay one's head on a king's or chieftain's knee symbolized submission and acknowledgment that one had offended him and that he was entitled to have one put to death.

had a favourable breeze across the sea. They came to King Canute, and told him the result of their errand, and King Olaf's last words. King Canute replies, " King Olaf guesses wrong, if he thinks I shall eat up all the kail in England; for I will let him see that there is something else than kail under my ribs, and cold kail it shall be for him." The same summer Aslak and Skialg, the sons of Erling of Jœderen, came from Norway to King Canute, and were well received; for Aslak was married to Sigrid, a daughter of Earl Swend Hakonsson, and she and Earl Hakon Ericsson were brothers' children. King Canute gave these brothers great fiefs over there, and they stood in great favour.

CHAPTER CXLI. KING OLAF'S ALLIANCE WITH ONUND THE KING OF SWEDEN.—King Olaf summoned to him all the lender-men, and had a great many people about him this summer, for a report was abroad that King Canute would come from England. People had heard from merchant vessels that Canute was assembling a great army in England. When summer was advanced, some affirmed and others denied that the army would come. King Olaf was all summer in Viken, and had spies out to learn if Canute was come to Denmark. In autumn he sent messengers eastward to Sweden to his brother-in-law King Onund, and let him know King Canute's demand upon Norway; adding that, in his opinion, if Canute subdued Norway, King Onund would not long enjoy the Swedish dominions in peace. He thought it advisable, therefore, that they should unite for their defence. " And then," said he, " we will have strength enough to hold out against Canute." King Onund received King Olaf's message favourably, and replied to it, that he for his part would make common cause with King Olaf, so that each of them should stand by the one who first required help with all the strength of his kingdom. In these messages between them it was also determined that they should have a meeting and consult with each other. The following winter King Onund intended to travel across West Gotland, and King Olaf made preparations for taking his winter abode at Sarpsborg.

CHAPTER CXLII. KING CANUTE'S AMBASSADORS TO ONUND OF SWEDEN.—In autumn King Canute the Great came to Denmark, and remained there all winter with a numerous army. It was told him that ambassadors with messages had been passing between the Swedish and Norwegian kings, and that some great plans must be concerting between them. In winter King Canute sent messengers to Sweden, to King Onund, with great gifts and messages of friendship. He also told Onund that he might sit altogether quiet in this strife between him and Olaf the Thick; " for thou, Onund," says he, " and thy kingdom shall be in peace as far as I am concerned." When the ambassadors came to King Onund they presented the gifts which King Canute sent him, together with the friendly message. King Onund did not hear their speech very willingly, and the ambassadors could observe that King Onund was most inclined to a friendship with King Olaf. They returned accordingly, and told King Canute the result of their errand, and told him not to depend much upon the friendship of King Onund.

CHAPTER CXLIII. THE EXPEDITION TO BIARMELAND [1026]. —This winter King Olaf sat in Sarpsborg, and was surrounded by a very great army of people. He sent the Halogalander Carl to the north country upon his business. Carl went first to the Uplands, then across the Dovrefjeld, and came down to Nidaros, where he received as much money as he had the king's order for, together with a good ship, such as he thought suitable for the voyage which the king had ordered him upon; and that was to proceed north to Biarmeland.[1] It was settled that the king should be in partnership with Carl, and each of them have the half of the profit. Early in spring Carl directed his course to Halogaland, where his brother Gunstein prepared to accompany him, having his own merchant goods with him. There were about twenty-five men in the ship: and in spring they sailed north to Finmark. When Thore Hund heard this, he sent a man to the brothers with the verbal message that he intended in summer to go to Biarmeland, and that he would sail with them, and that they should divide what booty they made equally between them. Carl sent him back the message that Thore must have twenty-five men as they had, and they were willing to divide the booty that might be taken equally, but not the merchant goods which each had for himself. When Thore's messenger came back he had put a stout long-ship he owned into the water, and rigged it, and he had put eighty men on board of his house-servants. Thore alone had the command over this crew, and he alone had all the goods they might acquire on the cruise. When Thore was ready for sea he set out northwards along the coast, and found Carl a little north of

[1] The coasts of the White Sea.

Sandvær.[1] They then proceeded with good wind. Gunstein said to his brother, as soon as they met Thore, that in his opinion Thore was strongly manned. "I think," said he, "we had better turn back than sail so entirely in Thore's power, for I do not trust him." Carl replies, "I will not turn back, although if I had known when we were at home on Langö that Thore Hund would join us on this voyage with so large a crew as he has, I would have taken more hands with us." The brothers spoke about it to Thore, and asked what was the meaning of his taking more people with him than was agreed upon between them. He replies, "We have a large ship which requires many hands, and methinks there cannot be too many brave lads for so dangerous a cruise." They went in summer as fast in general as the vessels could go. When the wind was light the ship of the brothers sailed fastest, and they separated; but when the wind freshened Thore overtook them. They were seldom together, but always in sight of each other. When they came to Biarmeland they went straight to the merchant town,[2] and the market began. All who had money to pay with got filled up with goods. Thore also got a number of grey pelts, and of beaver and sable skins. Carl had a considerable sum of money with him, with which he purchased skins and furs. When the fair was at an end they went out of the Dvina river, and then the truce with the country people was also at an end. When they came out of the river they he'd a seaman's council, and Thore asked the crews if they would like to go on the land and get booty.

They replied, that they would like it well enough, if they saw the booty before their eyes.

Thore replies, that there was booty to be got, if the voyage proved fortunate; but that in all probability there would be danger in the attempt.

All said they would try, if there was any chance of booty. Thore explained, that it was so established in this land that when a rich man died all his movable goods were divided between the dead man and his heirs. He got the half part, or the third part, or sometimes less, and that part was carried out into the forest and buried,—sometimes under a mound, sometimes in the earth, and sometimes even a house was built over it. He tells them at the same time to get ready for this

---

[1] Fishing ground off Ringvatsö in Tromsö county.
[2] Oppe in the river Dvina, possibly that which the Russians afterwards called Cholmogorg.

expedition at the fall of day. It was resolved that one should not desert the other, and none should hold back when the commander ordered them to come on board again. They now left people behind to take care of the ships, and went on land, where they found flat fields at first, and then great forests. Thore went first, and the brothers Carl and Gunstein in rear. Thore commanded the people to observe the utmost silence. "And let us peel the bark off the trees," says he, "so that one tree-mark can be seen from the other." They came to a large cleared opening, where there was a high fence upon which there was a gate that was locked. Six men of the country people held watch every night at this fence, two at a time keeping guard, each two for a third part of the night. When Thore and his men came to the fence the guard had gone home, and those who should relieve them had not yet come upon guard. Thore went to the fence, struck his axe up in it above his head, hauled himself up by it, and so came over the fence, and inside the gate. Carl had also come over the fence, and to the inside of the gate; so that both came at once to the door, took the bar away, and opened the door; and then the people got in within the fence. Then said Thore, "Within this fence there is a mound in which gold, and silver, and earth are all mixed together: seize that. But within here stands the Biarmeland people's god Jomala:[1] let no one be so presumptuous as to rob him." Thereupon they went to the mound, and took as much of the money as they could carry away in their clothes, with which, as might be expected, much earth was mixed. Thereafter Thore said that the people now should retreat. "And ye brothers, Carl and Gunstein," says he, "do ye lead the way, and I will go last." They all went accordingly out of the gate: but Thore went back to Jomala, and took a silver bowl that stood upon his knee full of silver money. He put the silver in his kirtle, and put his arm within the handle of the bowl, and so went out of the gate. The whole troop had come without the fence; but when they perceived that Thore had stayed behind, Carl returned to trace him, and when they met upon the path Thore had the silver bowl with him. Thereupon Carl immediately ran to Jomala; and observing he had a thick gold ornament hanging around his neck, he lifted his axe, cut the string with which the ornament was tied behind his neck, and the stroke was so strong that the

[1] *Jómali*, a word of Finno-Ugrian origin, still exists in Finnish as the name of a god; the men of Bjarmeland were probably Karelians (A. Ross, *The Terfinnas and Beormas of Ohthere*, 1940).

head of Jomala rang with such a great sound that they were all astonished. Carl seized the ornament, and they all hastened away. But the moment the sound was made the watchmen came forward upon the cleared space and blew their horns. Immediately the sound of the lur [1] was heard all around from every quarter, calling the people together. They hastened to the forest, and rushed into it; and heard the shouts and cries on the other side of the Biarmeland people in pursuit. Thore Hund went the last of the whole troop; and before him went two men carrying a great sack between them, in which was something that was like ashes. Thore took this in his hand, and strewed it upon the footpath, and sometimes over the people. They came thus out of the woods, and upon the fields, but heard incessantly the Biarmeland people pursuing with shouts and dreadful yells. The army of the Biarmeland people rushed out after them upon the field, and on both sides of them; but neither the people nor their weapons came so near as to do them any harm: from which they perceived that the Biarmeland people did not see them. Now when they reached their ships Carl and his brother went on board; for they were the foremost, and Thore was far behind on the land. As soon as Carl and his men were on board they struck their tents, cast loose their land ropes, hoisted their sails, and their ship in all haste went to sea. Thore and his people, on the other hand, did not get on so quickly, as their vessel was heavier to manage; so that when they got under sail Carl and his people were far off from land. Both vessels sailed across the White Sea. The nights were clear, so that both ships sailed night and day; until one day, towards the time the day turns to shorten, Carl and his people took up the land near an island, let down the sail, cast anchor, and waited until the slack-tide set in, for there was a strong rost [2] before them. Now Thore came up, and lay at anchor there also. Thore and his people then put out a boat, went into it, and rowed to Carl's ship. Thore came on board, and the brothers saluted him. Thore told Carl to give him the ornament. "I think," said he, "that I have best earned the ornaments that have been taken, for methinks ye have to thank me for getting away without any loss of men; and also I think thou, Carl, led us into the greatest peril."

[1] The *lúðr*, "war-horn" or "trumpet," as used in Scandinavia at this period, was probably of wood, straight and hollowed out.

[2] Rost, or race, the heavy sea made by a strong current running against the wind. It was at Sviatoi Nos, "the holy point."

Carl replied, " King Olaf has the half part of all the goods I gather on this voyage, and I intend the ornament for him. Go to him, if you like, and it is possible he will give thee the ornament, although I took it from Jomala."

Then Thore insisted that they should go upon the island and divide the booty.

Gunstein says, " It is now the turn of the tide, and it is time to sail." Whereupon they began to raise their anchor.

When Thore saw that, he returned to his boat and rowed to his own ship. Carl and his men had hoisted sail, and were come a long way before Thore got under way. They now sailed so that the brothers were always in advance, and both vessels made all the haste they could. They sailed thus until they came to Geirsvær,[1] which is the first roadstead of the traders from the North. They both came there towards evening, and lay in the harbour near the landing place. Thore's ship lay inside, and the brothers' the outside vessel in the port. When Thore had set up his tents he went on shore, and many of his men with him. They went to Carl's ship, which was well provided. Thore hailed the ship, and told the commanders to come on shore; on which the brothers, and some men with them, went on the land. Now Thore began the same discourse, and told them to bring the goods they got in booty to the land to have them divided. The brothers thought that was not necessary, until they had arrived at their own neighbourhood. Thore said it was unusual not to divide booty but at their own home, and thus to be left to the honour of other people. They spoke some words about it, but could not agree. Then Thore turned away; but had not gone far before he came back, and tells his comrades to wait there. Thereupon he calls to Carl, and says he wants to speak with him alone. Carl went to meet him; and when he came near, Thore struck at him with a spear, so that it went through him. " There," said Thore, " now thou hast learnt to know a Biarkö man. I thought thou shouldst feel Asbiorn's spear." [2] Carl died instantly, and Thore with his people went immediately on board their ship. When Gunstein and his men saw Carl's fall they ran instantly to him, took his body and carried it on board their ship, struck their tents, and cast off from the pier, and left the land. When Thore and his men saw this, they took down their tents, and made preparations to follow. But as they were hoisting the sail the fastenings to

---

[1] Now Gjesvær, a fishing ground north-west of Magerö off Finmarken.
[2] *Vide* p. 260.

the mast broke in two, and the sail fell down across the ship, which caused a great delay before they could hoist the sail again. Gunstein had already got a long way ahead before Thore's ship fetched way, and now they used both sails and oars. Gunstein did the same. On both sides they made great way day and night; but so that they did not gain much on each other, because when they came to the small sounds among the islands Gunstein's vessel was lighter in turning. But Thore's ship made way upon them, so that when they came up to Lenvik,[1] Gunstein turned towards the land, and with all his men ran up into the country, and left his ship. A little after Thore came there with his ship, sprang upon the land after them, and pursued them. There was a woman who helped Gunstein to conceal himself, and it is told that she was much acquainted with witchcraft. Thore and his men returned to the vessels, and took all the goods out of Gunstein's vessel, and put on board stones in place of the cargo, and then hauled the ship out into the fjord, cut a hole in its bottom, and sank it to the bottom. Thereafter Thore, with his people, returned home to Biarkö. Gunstein and his people proceeded in small boats at first, and lay concealed by day, until they had passed Biarkö, and had got beyond Thore's district. Gunstein went home first to Langö for a short time, and then proceeded south, without any halt, until he came to King Olaf, to whom he told all that had happened on this Biarmeland expedition. The king was ill pleased with the voyage, but told Gunstein to remain with him, promising to assist him when opportunity offered. Gunstein took the invitation with thanks, and stayed with King Olaf.

CHAPTER CXLIV. MEETING OF KING OLAF AND KING ONUND [1026].—King Olaf was, as before related [p. 271], in Sarpsborg the winter that King Canute was in Denmark. The Swedish king Onund rode across West Gotland the same winter, and had 3000 men with him. Men and messages passed between them; and they agreed to meet in spring at Konghelle. The meeting had been postponed, because they wished to know before they met what King Canute intended doing. As it was now approaching towards winter, King Canute made ready to go over to England with his forces, and left his son Hardaknut to rule in Denmark, and with him Earl Ulf, a son of Thargels Sprakalegg. Ulf was married to Astrid, King Swend's daughter, and sister of Canute the Great. Their son Swend was after-

---

[1] On the peninsula to the west of Malangen.

wards king of Denmark. Earl Ulf was a very distinguished man. When the kings Olaf and Onund heard that Canute the Great had gone west to England, they hastened to hold their conference, and met at Konghelle, on the Gotha river. They had a joyful meeting, and had many friendly conversations, of which something might become known to the public; but they also spake often a great deal between themselves, with none but themselves present, of which only some things afterwards were carried into effect, and thus became known to every one. At parting the kings presented each other with gifts, and parted the best of friends. King Onund went up into Gotland, and Olaf northwards to Viken, and afterwards to Agder, and thence northwards along the coast, but lay a long time at Egersund[1] waiting a wind. Here he heard that Erling Skialgsson, and the inhabitants of Jœderen with him, had assembled a large force. One day the king's people were talking among themselves whether the wind was south or south-west, and whether with that wind they could sail past Jœderen or not. The most said it was impossible to fetch round. Then answers Haldor Bryniolfsson,[2] "I am of opinion that we would go round Jœderen with this wind fast enough, if Erling Skialgsson had prepared a feast for us at Sole." Then King Olaf ordered the tents to be struck, and the vessels to be hauled out, which was done. They sailed the same day past Jœderen with the best wind, and in the evening reached the Whiting Isles,[3] from whence the king proceeded to Hordaland, and was entertained there in guest-quarters.

CHAPTER CXLV. THORALF'S MURDER [1026].—The same summer a ship sailed from Norway to the Faröe Islands, with messengers carrying a verbal message from King Olaf, that one of his court-men, Leif Ossursson, or Lagman Gille, or Thoralf of Dimon, should come over to him from the Faröe Islands. Now when this message came to the Faröe Islands, and was delivered to those whom it concerned, they held a meeting among themselves, to consider what might lie under this message, and they were all of opinion that the king wanted to inquire into the real state of the event which some said had taken place upon the islands; namely, the failure and disappearance of the former messengers of the king, and the loss of the two ships,

---

[1] Now Ekersund, in the south-west of Jœderen.
[2] Son of Bryniulf Ulvalde of Vettaland, p. 163.
[3] Hvitingsö, off Tungenes.

of which not a man had been saved. It was resolved that Thoralf should undertake the journey. He got himself ready, and rigged out a merchant-vessel belonging to himself, manned with ten or twelve men. When it was ready, waiting a wind, it happened at Osterö, in the house of Thrand of Gata, that he went one fine day into the room where his brother's two sons, Sigurd and Thord the Low, sons of Thorlak, were lying upon the benches in the room. Gaut the Red was also there, who was one of their relations and a man of distinction. Sigurd was the oldest, and their leader in all things. Thord had a distinguishing name, and was called Thord the Low, although in reality he was uncommonly tall, and yet in proportion more strong than large. Then Thrand said, " How many things are changed in the course of a man's life. When we were young, it was rare for young people who were able to do anything to sit or lie still upon a fine day, and our forefathers would scarcely have believed that Thoralf of Dimon would be bolder and more active than ye are. I believe the vessel I have standing here in the boat-house will be so old that it will rot under its coat of tar. Here are all the houses full of wool, which is neither used nor sold. It should not be so if I were a few winters younger." Sigurd sprang up, called upon Gaut and Thord, and said he would not endure Thrand's scoffs. They went out to the house-servants, and launched the vessel upon the water, brought down a cargo, and loaded the ship. They had no want of a cargo at home, and the vessel's rigging was in good order, so that in a few days they were ready for sea. There were ten or twelve men in the vessel. Thoralf's ship and theirs had the same wind, and they were generally in sight of each other. They came to the land in Hernar[1] in the evening, and Sigurd with his vessel lay outside on the strand, but so that there was not much distance between the two ships. It happened towards evening, when it was dark, that just as Thoralf and his people were preparing to go to bed, Thoralf and another went on shore for a certain purpose. When they were ready, they prepared to return on board. The man who had accompanied Thoralf related afterwards this story,—that a cloth was thrown over his head, and that he was lifted up from the ground, and he heard a great bustle. He was taken away, and thrown head foremost down; but there was sea under him, and he sank under the water. When he got to land, he went to the place where he and Thoralf had been parted, and there he found Thoralf with

[1] The Hennöe islands off Manger, Nordhordland.

his head cloven down to his shoulders, and dead. When the ship's people heard of it they carried the body out to the ship, and kept watch beside it all night. King Olaf was at that time in guest-quarters at Lygre,[1] and thither they sent a message. Now a Thing was called by message-token, and the king came to the Thing. He had also ordered the Faröe people of both vessels to be summoned, and they appeared at the Thing. Now when the Thing was seated, the king stood up and said, " Here an event has happened which (and it is well that it is so) is very seldom heard of. Here has a good man been put to death without any cause. Is there any man upon the Thing who can say who has done it? "

Nobody could answer.

" Then," said the king, " I cannot conceal my suspicion that this deed has been done by the Faröe people themselves. It appears to me that it has been done in this way,—that Sigurd Thorlaksson has killed the man, and Thord the Low has cast his comrade into the sea. I think, too, that the motives to this must have been to hinder Thoralf from telling about the misdeed of which he had information; namely, the murder which I suspect was committed upon my messengers."

When he had ended his speech, Sigurd Thorlaksson stood up, and desired to be heard. " I have never before," said he, " spoken at a Thing, and I do not expect to be looked upon as a man of ready words. But I think there is sufficient necessity before me to reply something to this. I will venture to make a guess that the speech the king has made comes from some man's tongue who is of far less understanding and goodness than he is, and has evidently proceeded from those who are our enemies. It is speaking improbabilities to say that I could be Thoralf's murderer; for he was my foster-brother and good friend. Had the case been otherwise, and had there been anything outstanding between me and Thoralf, yet I am surely born with sufficient understanding to have done this deed in the Faröe Islands, rather than here between your hands, sire. But I am ready to clear myself, and my whole ship's crew, of this act, and to make oath according to what stands in your laws. Or, if ye find it more satisfactory, I offer to clear myself by the ordeal of hot iron; and I wish, sire, that you may be present yourself at the proof." [2]

When Sigurd had ceased to speak there were many who

---

[1] A farm on the mainland, east of Manger.
[2] Means, of course, proof of innocence at the ordeal.

supported his case, and begged the king that Sigurd might be allowed to clear himself of this accusation. They thought that Sigurd had spoken well, and that the accusation against him might be untrue.

The king replies, " There can be two very different views about this man. If he is belied in this affair he may well be a good man, but on the other hand he may be the most bold-faced fellow ever seen—and the latter is still my guess. But I expect that he himself will provide evidence on the point."

At the desire of the people, the king took Sigurd's obligation to take the iron ordeal: he should come the following day to Lygre, where the bishop should preside at the ordeal; and so the Thing closed. The king went back to Lygre, and Sigurd and his comrades to their ship.

As soon as it began to be dark at night, Sigurd said to his ship's people, " To say the truth, we have come into a great misfortune; for a great lie is got up against us, and this king is a deceitful crafty man. Our fate is easy to be foreseen where he rules; for first he made Thoralf be slain, and then made us the misdoers, outlaws whose death can entail no fine. For him it is an easy matter to falsify the iron ordeal, so that I doubt he will come ill off who tries it against him. Now there is coming a brisk mountain breeze, blowing right out of the sound and off the land; and it is my advice that we hoist our sail and set out to sea. Let Thrand himself come with his wool to market another summer; but if I get away, it is my opinion I shall never think of coming to Norway again."

His comrades thought the advice good, hoisted their sail, and in the night time took to the open sea with all speed. They did not stop until they came to Faröe, and home to Gata. Thrand was ill pleased with their voyage, and they did not answer him in a very friendly way; but they remained at home, however, with Thrand. The morning after, King Olaf heard of Sigurd's departure, and heavy reports went round about this case; and there were many who believed that the accusation against Sigurd was true, although they had denied and opposed it before the king. King Olaf spoke but little about the matter, but seemed to know of a certainty that the suspicion he had taken up was founded in truth. The king afterwards proceeded in his progress, taking up his abode where it was provided for him.

CHAPTER CXLVI. Of the Icelanders [1027].—King Olaf

called before him the men who had come from Iceland, Thorodd Snorresson, Gelle Thorkelsson, Stein Skoptason, and Egil Hallsson, and spoke to them thus:—" Ye have spoken to me much in summer about making yourselves ready to return to Iceland, and I have never given you a distinct answer. Now I will tell you what my intention is. ` Thee, Gelle, I propose to allow to return, if thou wilt carry my message there; but none of the other Icelanders who are now here may go to Iceland before I have heard how the message which thou, Gelle, shalt bring thither has been received."

When the king had made this resolution known, it appeared to those who had a great desire to return, and were thus forbidden, that they were unreasonably and hardly dealt with, and that they were placed in the condition of unfree men. In the meantime Gelle got ready for his journey, and sailed in summer to Iceland, taking with him the message he was to bring before the Thing the following summer. The king's message was, that he required the Icelanders to adopt the laws which he had set in Norway, also to pay him thane-tax[1] and nose-tax;[2] namely, a penny for every nose, and the penny at the rate of ten pennies to the yard of wadmal.[3] At the same time he promised them his friendship if they accepted, and threatened them with all his vengeance if they refused his proposals.

The people sat long in deliberation on this business; but at last they were unanimous in refusing all the taxes and burdens which were demanded of them. That summer Gelle returned back from Iceland to Norway to King Olaf, and found him in autumn in the east in Viken, just as he had come from Gotland; of which I shall speak hereafter in this story of King Olaf [p. 316]. Towards the end of autumn King Olaf repaired north to Drontheim, and went with his people to Nidaros, where he ordered a winter residence to be prepared for him. The winter that he passed here in the merchant town of Nidaros was the thirteenth year of his reign.

---

[1] *Þegnigildi*, compensation to be paid to the king if any liegeman (*þegn*) of his were killed; this implies a claim to feudal overlordship in Iceland.

[2] The nose-tax was payable to the king. This tax was frequently imposed by the Norsemen on countries overrun by them. Thus King Thorgils, who conquered Ireland (830–45), is said to have levied such a tax on each hearth, the penalty for refusal being the loss of a nose.

[3] *Vaðmál*, homespun cloth, was in early Iceland a staple of exchange and a measure cf value; " yard " should be " ell " (half a yard).

It is doubtful whether pennies of so low a value were in use at this date.

CHAPTER CXLVII. OF THE JEMTELAND PEOPLE.— There was once a man called Ketel Jemte, a son of Earl Onund of Sparbu, in the Drontheim district. He fled over the ridge of mountains from Eystein Ildraade, cleared the forest, and settled the country now called the province of Jemteland. A great many people joined him from the Drontheim land, on account of the disturbances there; for this King Eystein had laid taxes on the Drontheim people, and set his dog, called Saur, to be king over them. Thore Helsing was Ketel's grandson, and he colonised the province called Helsingeland, which is named after him. When Harald Haarfager subdued the kingdom by force, many people fled out of the country from him, both Drontheim people and Naumedal people, and thus new settlements were added to Jemteland; and some settlers went even eastwards to Helsingeland and down to the Baltic coast, and all became subjects of the Swedish king. While Hakon Athelstan's foster-son was over Norway there was peace, and merchant traffic from Drontheim to Jemteland; and, as he was an excellent king, the Jemtelanders came from the east to him, paid him scatt, and he gave them laws and administered justice. They would rather submit to his government than to the Swedish king's, because they were of Norwegian race; and all the Helsingeland people, who had their descent from the north side of the mountain ridge, did the same. This continued long after those times, until Olaf the Thick and the Swedish king Olaf quarrelled about the boundaries. Then the Jemteland and Helsingeland people went back to the Swedish king; and then the forest of Eida was the eastern boundary of the land, and the mountain ridge, or keel of the country, the northern: and the Swedish king took scatt of Helsingeland, and also of Jemteland. Now, thought the king of Norway, Olaf, in consequence of the agreement between him and the Swedish king, the scatt of Jemteland should be paid differently than before; although it had long been established that the Jemteland people paid their scatt to the Swedish king, and that he appointed officers over the country. The Swedes would listen to nothing but that all the land to the east of the keel of the country belonged to the Swedish king. Now this went so, as it often happens, that although the kings were brothers-in-law and friendly, each would hold fast the dominions which he thought he had a right to. King Olaf had sent a message round in Jemteland, declaring it to be his will that the Jemteland people should be subject to him, threatening them with violence if they refused;

but the Je. iteland people preferred being subjects of the Swedish king.

CHAPTER CXLVIII. STEIN'S STORY [1027].—The Icelanders, Thorodd Snorresson and Stein Skoptason, were ill pleased at not being allowed to do as they liked. Stein was a remarkably handsome man, dexterous at all feats, a great poet, splendid in his apparel, and very ambitious of distinction. His father, Skopte, had composed a poem on King Olaf, which he had taught Stein, in the intention that he should bring it to King Olaf. Stein could not now restrain himself from making the king reproaches in word and speech, both in verse and prose. Both he and Thorodd were imprudent in their conversation, and said the king would be looked upon as a worse man than those who, under faith and law, had sent their sons to him, as he now treated them as men without liberty. The king was angry at this. One day Stein stood before the king, and asked if he would listen to the poem which his father Skopte had composed about him. The king replies, "Thou must first repeat that, Stein, which thou hast composed about me." Stein replies, that it was not the case that he had composed any. " I am no scald, sire," said he; "and if I even could compose anything, it, and all that concerns me, would appear to thee of little value." Stein then went out, but thought he perceived what the king alluded to. Thorgeir, one of the king's land-bailiffs, who managed one of his farms in Orkedal, happened to be present, and heard the conversation of the king and Stein, and soon afterwards Thorgeir returned home. One night Stein left the city, and his footboy with him. They went up Gulaasen and into Orkedal. One evening they came to one of the king's farms which Thorgeir had the management of, and Thorgeir invited Stein to pass the night there, and asked where he was travelling to. Stein begged the loan of a horse and sledge,[1] for he saw they were just driving home corn.

Thorgeir replies, " I do not exactly see how it stands with thy journey, and if thou art travelling with the king's leave. The other day, methinks, the words were not very sweet that passed between the king and thee."

Stein said, " If it be so that I am not my own master for the king, yet I will not submit to such treatment from his slaves; " and, drawing his sword, he killed the land-bailiff. Then he

[1] Sledges were often used on steep slopes and over rough ground in the summer.

took the horse, put the boy upon him, and sat himself in the sledge, and so drove the whole night. They travelled until they came to Surendal [1] in Möre. There they had themselves ferried across the fjord, and proceeded onwards as fast as they could. They told nobody about the murder; but wherever they came called themselves king's men, and met good entertainment everywhere. One day at last they came towards evening to Giskö, [2] to Thorberg Arneson's house. He was not at home himself, but his wife Ragnhild, a daughter of Erling Skialgsson, was. There Stein was well received, because formerly there had been great friendship between them. It had once happened, namely, that Stein, on his voyage from Iceland with his own vessel, had come to Giskö from sea, and had anchored at the island. At that time Ragnhild was in the pains of childbirth, and very ill, and there was no priest on the island, or in the neighbourhood of it. There came a message to the merchant-vessel to inquire if, by chance, there was a priest on board. There happened to be a priest in the vessel, who was called Baard; but he was a young man from West-fjord, who had little learning. The messengers begged the priest to go with them, but he thought it was a difficult matter; for he knew his own ignorance, and would not go. Stein added his word to persuade the priest. The priest replies, " I will go if thou wilt go with me; for then I will have confidence, if I should require advice." Stein said he was willing; and they went forthwith to the house, and to where Ragnhild was in labour. Soon after she brought forth a female child, which appeared to be rather weak. Then the priest baptized the infant, and Stein held it at the baptism, at which it got the name of Thora; and Stein gave it a gold ring. Ragnhild promised Stein her perfect friendship, and bade him come to her whenever he thought he required her help. Stein replied that he would hold no other female child at baptism, and then they parted. Now it was come to the time when Stein required this kind promise of Ragnhild to be fulfilled, and he told her what had happened, and that the king's wrath had fallen upon him. She answered, that all the aid she could give should stand at his service; but bade him wait for Thorberg's arrival. She then showed him to a seat beside her son Eystein Orre, who was then twelve years old. Stein presented gifts to Ragnhild and

<hr />

[1] In Nordmöre, to the west of Orkedal, the road went from Meldal via Rindal to Surendal.

[2] An island in Sondmöre, north-west of Aalesund.

Eystein. Thorberg had already heard how Stein had conducted himself before he got home, and was rather vexed at it. Ragnhild went to him, and told him how matters stood with Stein, and begged Thorberg to receive him, and take care of him.

Thorberg replied, "I have heard that the king, after sending out a message-token, held a Thing concerning the murder of Thorgeir, and has condemned Stein to outlawry, and likewise that the king is highly incensed; and I have too much sense to take the cause of a foreigner in hand, and draw upon myself the king's wrath. Let Stein, therefore, withdraw from hence as quickly as he can."

Ragnhild replied, that they should either both go or both stay.

Thorberg told her to go where she pleased. "For I expect," said he, "that wherever thou goest thou wilt soon come back, for here is thy importance greatest."

Her son Eystein Orre then stood forward, and said he would not stay behind if Ragnhild goes.

Thorberg said that they showed themselves very stiff and obstinate in this matter. "And it appears that ye must have your way in it, since ye take it so near to heart; but thou art reckoning too much, Ragnhild, upon thy descent, in paying so little regard to King Olaf's word."

Ragnhild replied, "If thou art so much afraid to keep Stein with thee here, go with him to my father Erling, or give him attendants, so that he may get there in safety."

Thorberg said he would not send Stein there; "for there are enough of things besides to enrage the king against Erling." Stein thus remained there all winter.

After Yule a king's messenger came to Thorberg, with the order that Thorberg should come to him before mid-lent (5th March); and the order was serious and severe. Thorberg laid it before his friends, and asked their advice if he should venture to go to the king after what had taken place. The greater number dissuaded him, and thought it more advisable to let Stein slip out of his hands than to venture within the king's power; but Thorberg himself had rather more inclination not to decline the journey. Soon after Thorberg went to his brother Finn,[1] told him the circumstances, and asked him to accompany him. Finn replied that he thought it foolish to be so completely under woman's influence that he dared not, on account of his wife, keep fealty to his liege lord.

"Thou art free," replied Thorberg, "to go with me or not;

[1] Finn lived at Ostraat on Orlandet.

but I believe it is more fear of the king than love to him that keeps thee back." And so they parted in anger.

Then Thorberg went to his brother Arne Arneson, and asked him to go with him to the king. Arne says, "It appears to me wonderful that such a sensible, prudent man should fall into such a misfortune, without necessity, as to incur the king's indignation. It might be excused if it were thy relation or foster-brother whom thou hadst thus sheltered; but not at all that thou shouldst take up an Iceland man, and harbour the king's outlaw, to the injury of thyself and all thy relations."

Thorberg replies, "It stands good, according to the proverb,—a rotten branch will be found in every tree. My father's greatest misfortune evidently was that he had such ill luck in producing sons that at last he produced one incapable of acting, and without any resemblance to our race, and whom in truth I never would have called brother, if it were not that it would have been to my mother's shame to have refused."

Thorberg turned away in a gloomy temper, and went home. Thereafter he sent a message to his brother Kalf in the Drontheim district, and begged him to meet him at Agdaness; and when the messengers found Kalf he promised, without more ado, to make the journey. Ragnhild sent men east to Jœderen to her father Erling, and begged him to send people. Erling's sons, Sigurd and Thord, came out, each with a ship of twenty benches of rowers and ninety men. When they came north Thorberg received them joyfully, entertained them well, and prepared for the voyage with them. Thorberg had also a vessel with twenty benches, and they steered their course northwards. When they came to the mouth of the Drontheim fjord Thorberg's two brothers, Finn and Arne, were there already, with two ships each of twenty benches. Thorberg met his brothers with joy, and observed that his whetstone had taken effect; and Finn replied he seldom needed sharpening for such work. Then they proceeded north with all their forces to Drontheim, and Stein was along with them. When they came to Agdaness, Kalf Arneson was there before them; and he also had a well-manned ship of twenty benches. With this war-force they sailed up to Nidaros, where they lay all night. The morning after they had a consultation with each other. Kalf and Erling's sons were for attacking the town with all their forces, and leaving the event to fate; but Thorberg wished that they should first proceed with moderation, and make an offer; in which opinion Finn and Arne also concurred. It was accordingly resolved that Finn and Arne, with a few men, should first wait upon the king. The king had previously heard that they had come so strong in men, and was therefore very sharp in his speech. Finn offered to pay mulct for Thorberg, and also for Stein, and bade the king to fix what the penalties should be, however large; stipulating only for Thorberg the right to stay in Norway and keep his fiefs, and for Stein life and limb.

The king replies, " It appears to me that ye come from home so equipped that ye can determine half as much as I can myself, or more; but this I expected least of all from you brothers, that ye should come against me with an army: and this counsel, I can observe, has its origin from the people of Jœderen; but ye have no occasion to offer me money in mulct."

Finn replies, " We brothers have collected men, not to offer hostility to you, sire, but to offer rather our services; but if you will bear down Thorberg altogether, we must all go to King Canute the Great with such forces as we have."

Then the king looked at him, and said, " If ye brothers will give your oaths that ye will follow me in the country and out of the country, and not part from me without my leave and permission, and shall not conceal from me any treasonable design that may come to your knowledge against me, then will I agree to a peace with you brothers."

Then Finn returned to his forces, and told the conditions which the king had proposed to them. Now they held a council upon it, and Thorberg, for his part, said he would accept the terms offered. " I have no wish," says he, " to fly from my property, and seek foreign masters; but, on the contrary, will always consider it an honour to follow King Olaf and be where he is." Then says Kalf, " I will make no oath to King Olaf, but will be with him always, so long as I retain my fiefs and dignities, and so long as the king will be my friend; and my opinion is that we should all do the same." Finn says, " My advice now is to let King Olaf himself determine in this matter." Arne Arneson says, " I was resolved to follow thee, brother Thorberg, even if thou hadst given battle to King Olaf, and I shall certainly not leave thee for listening to better counsel; so I intend to follow thee and Finn, and accept the conditions ye have taken."

Thereupon the brothers Thorberg, Finn, and Arne went on board a vessel, rowed into the fjord, and waited upon the king. The agreement went accordingly into fulfilment, so that the brothers gave their oaths to the king. Then Thorberg endeavoured to make peace for Stein with the king; but the king replied that Stein might for him depart in safety, and go where he pleased, but " in my house he can never be again." Then Thorberg and his brothers went back to their men. Kalf went to Egge, and Finn to the king; and Thorberg, with the other men, went south to their homes. Stein went with Erling's sons; but early in the spring he went west to England into the service of Canute the Great, and was long with him, and was treated with great distinction.

CHAPTER CXLIX. FINN ARNESON'S EXPEDITION TO HALOGA-LAND.—Now when Finn Arneson had been a short time with King Olaf, the king called him to a conference, along with some other persons he usually held consultation with; and in this conference the king spoke to this effect:—" The decision remains fixed in my mind that in spring I should raise the whole country to a levy both of men and ships, and then proceed, with all the force I can muster, against King Canute the Great; for I know for certain that he does not intend to treat as a jest the claim he has awakened upon my kingdom. Now I let thee know my will, Finn Arneson, that thou proceed on my errand to Haloga-land, and raise the people there to an expedition, men and ships, and summon that force to meet me at Agdaness." Then the king named other men whom he sent to Drontheim, and some southwards in the country, and he commanded that this order should be circulated through the whole land. Of Finn's voyage we have to relate that he had with him a ship with about thirty men, and when he was ready for sea he prosecuted his journey until he came to Halogaland. There he summoned the bonders to a Thing, laid before them his errand, and craved a levy. The bonders in that district had large vessels, suited to a levy expedition, and they obeyed the king's message, and rigged their ships. Now when Finn came farther north in Halogaland he held a Thing again, and sent some of his men from him to crave a levy where he thought it necessary. He sent also men to Biarkö to Thore Hund, and there, as elsewhere, craved the quota to the levy. When the message came to Thore he made himself ready, and manned with his house-servants the same vessel he had sailed with on his cruise to Biarmeland, and which he equipped at his own expense. Finn summoned all the people of Haloga-land who were to the north to meet at Vaage. There came a great fleet together in spring, and they waited there until Finn returned from the North. Thore Hund had also come there.

When Finn arrived he ordered the signal to sound for all the people of the levy to attend a House-Thing; and at it all the men produced their weapons, and also the fighting men from each ship-district were mustered. When that was all finished Finn said, " I have also to bring thee a salutation, Thore Hund, from King Olaf, and to ask thee what thou wilt offer him for the murder of his court-man Carl, or for the robbery in taking the king's goods north in Lenvik [p. 276]. I have the king's orders to settle that business, and I wait thy answer to it."

Thore looked about him, and saw standing on both sides many fully armed men, among whom were Gunstein and others of Carl's kindred. Then said Thore, " My proposal is soon made. I will refer altogether to the king's pleasure the matter he thinks he has against me."

Finn replies, " Thou must put up with a less honour; for thou must refer the matter altogether to my decision, if any agreement is to take place."

Thore replies, " And even then I think it will stand well with my case, and therefore I will not decline referring it to thee."

Thereupon Thore came forward, and confirmed what he said by giving his hand upon it; and Finn repeated first all the words he should say.

Finn now pronounced his decision upon the agreement,— that Thore should pay to the king ten marks of gold,[1] and to Gunstein and the other kindred ten marks, and for the robbery and loss of goods ten marks more; and all which should be paid immediately.

Thore says, " This is a heavy money mulct."

" Without it," replies Finn, " there will be no agreement."

Thore says, there must time be allowed to gather so much in loan from his followers; but Finn told him to pay immediately on the spot; and besides, Thore should lay down the great ornament which he took from Carl when he was dead. Thore asserted that he had not got the ornament. Then Gunstein pressed forward, and said that Carl had the ornament around his neck when they parted, but it was gone when they took up his corpse. Thore said he had not observed any ornament; but if there was any such thing, it must be lying at home in Biarkö. Then Finn put the point of his spear to Thore's breast, and said that he must instantly produce the ornament; on which Thore took the ornament from his neck and gave it to Finn. There-

---

[1] A mark of gold was equal to 8 marks silver; the whole sum was therefore equal to 240 marks silver (one mark = 8 oz.).

after Thore turned away, and went on board his ship. Finn, with many other men, followed him, went through the whole vessel, and took up the hatches. At the mast they saw two very large casks; and Finn asked, " What are these puncheons? "

Thore replies, " It is my liquor."

Finn says, " Why don't you give us something to drink then, comrade, since you have so much liquor? "

Thore ordered his men to run off a bowlful from the puncheons, from which Finn and his people got liquor of the best quality. Now Finn ordered Thore to pay the mulcts. Thore went backwards and forwards through the ship, speaking now to the one, now to the other, and Finn calling out to produce the pence. Thore begged him to go to the shore, and said he would bring the money there, and Finn with his men went on shore. Then Thore came and paid silver; of which, from one purse, there were weighed ten marks. Thereafter Thore brought many knotted kerchiefs; and in some was one mark, in others half a mark, and in others some small money. " This is money, my friends, which good people have lent me," said he; " for I think all my travelling money is gone." Then Thore went back again to his ship, and returned, and paid the silver by little and little; and this lasted so long that the day was drawing towards evening. When the Thing had closed the people had gone to their vessels and made ready to depart; and as fast as they were ready they hoisted sail and set out, so that most of them were under sail. When Finn saw that they were most of them under sail, he ordered his men to get ready too; but as yet little more than a third part of the mulct had been paid. Then Finn said, " This goes on very slowly, Thore, with the payment. I see it costs thee a great deal to pay money. I shall now let it stand for the present, and what remains thou shalt pay to the king himself." Finn then got up and went away.

Thore replies, " I am well enough pleased, Finn, to part now; but the good will is not wanting to pay this debt, so that both thou and the king shall say it is not unpaid."

Then Finn went on board his ship, and followed the rest of his fleet. Thore was late before he was ready to come out of the harbour. When the sails were hoisted he steered out over Westfjord,[1] and went to sea, keeping south along the land so far off that the hill-tops were half sunk, and soon the land altogether was sunk from view by the sea. Thore held this course until

[1] The broad bay between the Lofodens and the mainland.

he got into the English sea, and landed in England. He betook himself to King Canute forthwith, and was well received by him. It then came out that Thore had with him a great deal of property; and, with other things, all the money he and Carl had taken in Biarmeland. In the great liquor-casks there were sides within the outer sides, and the liquor was between them. The rest of the casks were filled with greyskins,[1] and beaver and sable skins. Thore was then with King Canute. Finn came with his forces to King Olaf, and related to him how all had gone upon his voyage, and told at the same time his suspicion that Thore had left the country and gone west to England to King Canute. " And there I doubt he will be of little service to us."

The king replies, " I believe that Thore must be our enemy, and it appears to me always better to have him at a distance than near."

CHAPTER CL. DISPUTE BETWEEN HAREK AND AASMUND GRANKELSSON.—Aasmund Grankelsson had been this winter in Halogaland in his sheriffdom, and was at home with his father Grankel. There lies a rock out in the sea, on which there is both seal and bird catching, and a fishing ground, and egg-gathering; and from old times it had been an appendage to the farm which Grankel owned, but now Harek of Thiotto laid claim to it. It had gone so far that some years he had taken by force all the gain of this rock; but Aasmund and his father thought that they might expect the king's help in all cases in which the right was upon their side. Both father and son went therefore in spring to Harek, and brought him a message and tokens from King Olaf that he should drop his claim. Harek answered Aasmund crossly, because he had gone to the king with such insinuations—" for the just right is upon my side. Thou shouldst learn moderation, Aasmund, although thou hast so much confidence in the king's favour. It has succeeded with thee to kill some chiefs, and leave their slaughter unpaid for by any mulct; and also to plunder us, although we thought ourselves at least equal to all of equal birth, and thou art far from being my equal in family."

Aasmund replies, " Many have experienced from thee, Harek, that thou art of great connections, and too great power; and many in consequence have suffered loss in their property through thee. But it is likely that now thou must turn thyself elsewhere,

[1] Squirrel skins.

and not against us with thy violence, and not go altogether against law, as thou art now doing." Then they separated.

Harek sent ten or twelve of his house-servants with a large rowing boat, with which they rowed to the rock, took all that was to be got upon it, and loaded their boat. But when they were ready to return home, Aasmund Grankelsson came with thirty men and ordered them to give up all they had taken. Harek's house-servants were not quick in complying, so that Aasmund attacked them. Some of Harek's men were cudgelled, some wounded, some thrown into the sea, and all they had caught was taken from on board of their boat, and Aasmund and his people took it along with them. Then Harek's servants came home, and told him the event. Harek replies, " That is called news indeed that seldom happens: never before has it happened that my people have been beaten."

The matter dropped. Harek never spoke about it, but was very cheerful. In spring, however, Harek rigged out a cutter of twenty seats of rowers, and manned it with his house-servants, and the ship was remarkably well fitted out both with people and all necessary equipment; and Harek went to the levy: but when he came to King Olaf, Aasmund was there before him. The king summoned Harek and Aasmund to him, and reconciled them so that they left the matter entirely to him. Aasmund then produced witnesses to prove that Grankel had owned the rock, and the king gave judgment accordingly. The case had a one-sided result. No mulct was paid for Harek's house-servants, and the rock was declared to be Grankel's. Harek observed it was no disgrace to obey the king's decision, whatever way the case itself was decided.

CHAPTER CLI. THORODD'S STORY [1026].—Thorodd Snorresson had remained in Norway according to King Olaf's commands, when Gelle Thorkelsson got leave to go to Iceland, as before related [p. 281]. He remained there with King Olaf, but was ill pleased that he was not free to travel where he pleased. Early in winter, King Olaf, when he was in Nidaros, made it known that he would send people to Jemteland to collect the scatt; but nobody had any great desire to go on this business, after the fate of those whom King Olaf had sent before,—namely, Thrand White and others, twelve in number, who lost their lives, as related [p. 166]; and the Jemtelanders had ever since been subject to the Swedish king. Thorodd Snorresson now offered to undertake this journey, for he cared little what became of him if he

could but become his own master again. The king consented,
and Thorodd set out with eleven men in company. They came
east to Jemteland, and went to a man called Thore, who was
lagman, and a person in high estimation. They met with a
hospitable reception; and when they had been there a while,
they explained their business to Thore. He replied, that other
men and chiefs of the country had in all respects as much power
and right to give an answer as he had, and for that purpose he
would call together a Thing. It was so done; the message-
token was sent out, and a numerous Thing assembled. Thore
went to the Thing, but the messengers in the meantime remained
at home. At the Thing, Thore laid the business before the people,
but all were unanimous that no scatt should be paid to the king of
Norway; and some were for hanging the messengers, others for
sacrificing them to the gods. At last it was resolved to hold
them fast until the king of Sweden's sheriffs arrived, and they
could treat them as they pleased with consent of the people; and
that, in the meantime, this decision should be concealed, and
the messengers treated well, and detained under pretext that
they must wait until the scatt is collected; and that they should
be separated, and placed two and two, as if for the convenience
of boarding them. Thorodd and another remained in Thore's
house. There was a great Yule feast and ale-drinking, to which
each brought his own liquor; for there were many peasants in
the village, who all drank in company together at Yule. There
was another village not far distant, where Thore's brother-in-law
dwelt, who was a rich and powerful man, and had a grown-up
son. The brothers-in-law intended to pass the Yule in drinking
feasts, half of it at the house of the one and half with the other;
and the feast began at Thore's house. The brothers-in-law
drank together, and Thorodd and the son of that bonder also
together; and it was a drinking match. In the evening words
arose, and comparisons between the men of Sweden and of
Norway, and then between their kings both of former times and
at the present, and of the manslaughters and robberies that had
taken place between the countries. Then said that bonder's
son, " If our king has lost most people, his sheriffs will make it
even with the lives of twelve men when they come from the south
after Yule; and ye little know, ye silly fools, why ye are kept
here." Thorodd took notice of these words, and many made
jest about it, and scoffed at them and their king. When the ale
began to talk out of the hearts of the Jemtelanders, what Thorodd
had before long suspected became evident. The day after

Thorodd and his comrade took all their clothes and weapons, and laid them ready; and at night, when the people were all asleep, they fled to the forest. The next morning, when the Jemtelanders were aware of their flight, men set out after them with dogs to trace them, and found them in a wood in which they had concealed themselves. They brought them home to a room in which there was a deep cellar, into which they were thrown, and the door locked upon them. They had little meat, and only the clothes they had on them. In the middle of Yule,[1] Thore, with all his freeborn men, went to his brother-in-law's where he was to be a guest until the last of Yule. Thore's slaves were to keep guard upon the cellar, and they were provided with plenty of liquor; but as they observed no moderation in drinking, they became towards evening confused in the head with the ale. As they were quite drunk, those who had to bring meat to the prisoners in the cellar said among themselves that they should want for nothing. Thorodd amused the slaves by singing to them. They said he was a clever man, and gave him a large candle that was lighted; and the slaves who were in went to call the others to come in: but they were all so confused with the ale, that in going out they neither locked the cellar nor the room after them. Now Thorodd and his comrade tore up their skin clothes in strips, knotted them together, made a noose at one end, and threw up the rope on the floor of the room. It fastened itself around a chest, by which they tried to haul themselves up. Thorodd lifted up his comrade until he stood on his shoulders, and from thence scrambled up through the hatch-hole. There was no want of ropes in the chamber, and he threw a rope down to Thorodd; but when he tried to draw him up, he could not move him from the spot. Then Thorodd told him to cast the rope over a cross-beam that was in the house, make a loop in it, and place as much wood and stones in the loop as would outweigh him; and the heavy weight went down into the cellar, and Thorodd was drawn up by it. Now they took as much clothes as they required in the room; and among other things they took some reindeer hides, out of which they cut sandals, and bound them under their feet, with the hoofs of the reindeer feet trailing behind. But before they set off they set fire to a large corn barn which was close by, and then ran out into the pitch-dark night. The barn blazed, and set fire to many other houses in the village. Thorodd and his comrade travelled the

[1] Yule was reckoned as equal to half a month, from 25th December to 7th January, so that the middle of Yule was New Year's day.

whole night until they came to a lonely wood, where they concealed themselves when it was daylight. In the morning they were missed. There was chase made with dogs to trace the footsteps all round the house; but the hounds always came back to the house, for they had the smell of the reindeer hoofs, and followed the scent back on the road that the hoofs had left, and therefore could not find the right direction. Thorodd and his comrade wandered long about in the desert forest, and came one evening to a small house, and went in. A man and a woman were sitting by the fire. The man called himself Thore, and said it was his wife who was sitting there, and the hut belonged to them. The peasant asked them to stop there, at which they were well pleased. He told them that he had come to this place because he had fled from the inhabited district on account of a murder. Thorodd and his comrade were well received, and they all got their supper at the fireside; and then the benches were cleared for them, and they lay down to sleep, but the fire was still burning with a clear light. Thorodd saw a man come in from another house, and never had he seen so big a man. He was dressed in a scarlet cloak beset with gold clasps, and was of very handsome appearance. Thorodd heard him scold them for taking guests, when they had scarcely food for themselves. The housewife said, " Be not angry, brother; seldom such a thing happens; and rather do them some good too, for thou hast better opportunity to do so than we." Thorodd heard also the stout man named by the name of Arnliot Gelline,[1] and observed that the woman of the house was his sister. Thorodd had heard speak of Arnliot as the greatest of robbers and malefactors. Thorodd and his companion slept the first part of the night, for they were wearied with walking; but when a third of the night was still to come, Arnliot woke them, told them to get up, and make ready to depart. They arose immediately, put on their clothes, and some breakfast was given them; and Arnliot gave each of them also a pair of skis. Arnliot made himself ready to accompany them, and got upon his skis, which were both broad and long; but scarcely had he swung his ski staff before he was a long way past them. He waited for them, and said they would make no progress in this way, and told them to stand upon the surface of his skis beside him. They did so. Thorodd stood

---

[1] Arnliot's part in the battle of Stiklestad (*vide* p. 365) is also mentioned in the *Legendary Saga*, but no other account gives the circumstances of his meeting with Thorodd; these Snorri probably took directly from some current oral tale. There are obvious marks of folk-tale in this episode.

nearest to him, and held by Arnliot's belt, and his comrade held by him. Arnliot strode on as quickly with them both as if he was alone and without any weight. The following day they came, towards night, to a hospice, struck fire, and prepared some food; but Arnliot told them to throw away nothing of their food, neither bones nor crumbs. Arnliot took a silver plate out of the pocket of his cloak, and ate from it. When they were done eating, Arnliot gathered up the remains of their meal and they prepared to go to sleep. In the other end of the house there was a loft upon cross-beams, and Arnliot and the others went up, and laid themselves down to sleep. Arnliot had a large halberd, of which the upper part was mounted with gold, and the shaft was so long that with his arm stretched out he could scarcely touch the top of it; and he was girt with a sword. They had both their weapons and their clothes up in the loft beside them. Arnliot, who lay outermost in the loft, told them to be perfectly quiet. Soon after twelve men came to the house, who were merchants going with their wares to Jemteland; and when they came into the house they made a great disturbance, were merry, and made a great fire before them; and when they took their supper they cast away all the bones around them. They then prepared to go to sleep, and laid themselves down upon the benches around the fire. When they had been asleep a short time, a huge witch came into the house; and when she came in, she carefully swept together all the bones and whatever was of food kind into a heap, and threw it into her mouth. Then she gripped the man who was nearest to her, riving and tearing him asunder, and threw him upon the fire. The others awoke in dreadful fright and sprang up; but she took them, and sent them one by one to hell, so that one only remained in life. He ran under the loft calling for help, if there was any one in the loft to help him. Arnliot reached down his hand, seized him by the shoulder, and drew him up into the loft. The witch-wife had turned towards the fire, and began to eat the men who were roasting. Now Arnliot stood up, took his halberd, and struck her between the shoulders, so that the point came out at her breast. She writhed with it, gave a dreadful shriek, and sprang up. The halberd slipped from Arnliot's hands, and she ran out with it. Arnliot then went in; cleared away the dead corpses out of the house; set the door and the door-posts up, for she had torn them down in going out; and they slept the rest of the night. When the day broke they got up; and first they took their breakfast. When they had got food, Arnliot said, " Now we must part here.

Ye can proceed upon the new-traced path the merchants have made in coming here yesterday. In the meantime I will seek after my halberd, and in reward for my labour I will take so much of the goods these men had with them as I find useful to me. Thou, Thorodd, must take my salutation to King Olaf; and say to him that he is the man I am most desirous to see, although my salutation may appear to him of little worth." Then he took his silver plate, wiped it dry with a cloth, and said, " Give King Olaf this plate; salute him, and say it is from me." Then they made themselves ready for their journey, and parted. Thorodd went on with his comrade and the man of the merchants' company who had escaped. He proceeded until he came to King Olaf in the town (Nidaros), told the king all that had happened, and presented to him the silver plate. The king said it was wrong that Arnliot himself had not come to him; " for it is a pity so brave a hero, and so distinguished a man, should have given himself up to misdeeds."

Thorodd remained the rest of the winter with the king, and in summer got leave to return to Iceland; and he and King Olaf parted the best of friends.

CHAPTER CLII. KING OLAF'S LEVY OF MEN [1027].—King Olaf made ready in spring to leave Nidaros, and many people were assembled about him, both from Drontheim and the Northern country; and when he was ready he proceeded first with his men to Möre, where he gathered the men of the levy, and did the same at Raumsdal. He went from thence to South Möre. He lay a long time at the Herö Isles[1] waiting for his forces; and he often held House-things, as many reports came to his ears about which he thought it necessary to hold councils. In one of these Things he made a speech, in which he spoke of the loss he suffered from the Faröe islanders. " The scatt which they promised me," he said, " is not forthcoming; and I now intend to send men thither after it." Then he proposed to different men to undertake this expedition; but the answer was, that all declined the adventure.

Then there stood up a stout and very remarkable-looking man in the Thing. He was clad in a red kirtle, had a helmet on his head, a sword in his belt, and a large halberd in his hands. He took up the word and said, " In truth there is great contrast here. Ye have a good king; but he has bad servants. Ye say no to this expedition he offers you, although ye have received

[1] West of Hareidland.

many gifts of friendship and tokens of honour from him. I have hitherto been no friend of the king, and he has been my enemy, and says, besides, that he has good grounds for being so. Now I offer, sire, to go upon this expedition, if no better will undertake it."

The king answers, " Who is this brave man who replies to my offer? Thou showest thyself different from the other men here present, in offering thyself for this expedition from which they excuse themselves, although I expected they would willingly have undertaken it; but I do not know thee in the least, and do not know thy name."

He replies, " My name, sire, is not difficult to know, and I think thou hast heard my name before. I am Karl Mærske."

The king—" So this is Karl! I have indeed heard thy name before; and, to say the truth, there was a time when our meeting must have been such, if I had had my will, that thou shouldst not have lived to tell it. But I will not show myself worse than thou, but will join my thanks and my favour to the side of the help thou hast offered me. Now thou shalt come to me, Karl, and be my guest to-day; and then we shall consult together about this business." Karl said it should be so.

CHAPTER CLIII. KARL MÆRSKE'S STORY.—Karl Mærske had been a viking, and a celebrated robber. Often had the king sent out men against him, and wished to make an end of him; but Karl, who was a man of high connection, was quick in all his doings, and besides a man of great dexterity, and expert in all feats. Now when Karl had undertaken this business the king was reconciled to him, gave him his friendship, and let him be fitted out in the best manner for this expedition. There were about twenty men in the ship; and the king sent messages to his friends in the Faröe Islands, and recommended him also to Leif Ossursson and Lagman Gille, for aid and defence; and for this purpose furnished Karl with tokens of the full powers given him. Karl set out as soon as he was ready; and as he got a favourable breeze soon came to the Faröe Islands, and landed at Thorshaven, in the island Stromö.[1] A Thing was called, to which there came a great number of people. Thrand of Gata came with a great retinue, and Leif and Gille came there also, with many in their following. After they had set up their tents, and put themselves in order, they went to Karl Mærske, and saluted

[1] The largest and the central island of the Faeroes with the present capital Thorshavn.

each other on both sides in a friendly way. Then Karl produced
King Olaf's words, tokens, and friendly message to Leif and Gille,
who received them in a friendly manner, invited Karl to come to
them, and promised him to support his errand, and give him all
the aid in their power, for which he thanked them. Soon after
came Thrand of Gata, who also received Karl in the most friendly
manner, and said he was glad to see so able a man coming to their
country on the king's business, which they were all bound to
promote. " I will insist, Karl," says he, " on thy taking up thy
winter abode with me, together with all those of thy people who
may appear to thee necessary for thy dignity."

Karl replies, that he had already settled to lodge with Leif;
" otherwise I would with great pleasure have accepted thy
invitation."

" Then fate has given great honour to Leif," says Thrand;
" but is there any other way in which I can be of service? "

Karl replies that he would do him a great service by collecting
the scatt of the Auströ, and of all the northern islands.

Thrand said it was both his duty and interest to assist in the
king's business, and thereupon Thrand returned to his tent: and
at that Thing nothing else worth speaking of occurred. Karl
took up his abode with Leif Ossursson, and was there all winter.
Leif collected the scatt of Stromö, and all the islands south of it.
The spring after Thrand of Gata fell ill, and had sore eyes and
other complaints; but he prepared to attend the Thing, as was
his custom. When he came to the Thing he had his tent put up,
and within it another black tent, that the light might not pene-
trate. After some days of the Thing had passed, Leif and Karl
came to Thrand's tent, with a great many people, and found some
persons standing outside. They asked if Thrand was in the tent,
and were told he was. Leif told them to bid Thrand come out,
as he and Karl had some business with him. They came back,
and said that Thrand had sore eyes, and could not come out;
" but he begs thee, Leif, to come to him within." Leif told his
comrades to come carefully into the tent, and not to press
forward, and that he who came last in should go out first. Leif
went in first, followed by Karl, and then his comrades; and all
fully armed as if they were going into battle. Leif went into the
black tent, and asked if Thrand was there. Thrand answered,
and saluted Leif. Leif returned his salutation, and asked if he
had brought the scatt from the northern islands, and if he would
pay the scatt that had been collected. Thrand replies that he
had not forgotten what had been spoken of between him and

Karl, and that he would now pay over the scatt. "Here is a purse, Leif, full of silver, which thou canst receive." Leif looked around, and saw but few people in the tent, of whom some were lying upon the benches, and a few were sitting up. Then Leif went to Thrand, and took the purse, and carried it into the outer tent, where it was light, turned out the money on his shield, groped about in it with his hand, and told Karl to look at the silver. When they had looked at it a while, Karl asked Leif what he thought of the silver. He replied, "I am thinking that each bad coin there is in the north isles has turned up here." Thrand heard this, and said, "Do you not think, Leif, the silver is good?" "No," says he. Thrand replies, "Our relations, then, are rascals not to be trusted. I sent them in spring to collect the scatt in the north isles, as I could not myself go anywhere, and they have allowed themselves to be bribed by the bonders to take false money, which nobody looks upon as current and good; it is better, therefore, Leif, to look at this silver which has been paid me as land-rent." Leif thereupon carried back this silver, and received another bag, which he carried to Karl, and they looked over the money together. Karl asked Leif what he thought of this money. He answered, that it appeared to him so bad that it would not be taken in payment, however little hope there might be of getting a debt paid in any other way; "therefore I will not take this money upon the king's account." A man who had been lying on the bench now cast the skin coverlet off which he had drawn over his head, and said, "True is the old word,—he grows worse who grows older: so it is with thee, Thrand, who allowest Karl Mærske to handle thy money all the day." This was Gaut the Red. Thrand sprang up at Gaut's words, and reprimanded his relation with many angry words. At last he said that Leif should leave this silver, and take a bag which his own peasants had brought him in spring. "And although I am weak-sighted, yet my own hand is the truest test." Another man who was lying on the bench raised himself now upon his elbow; and this was Thore the Low. He said, "These are no ordinary reproaches we suffer from Karl Mærske, and therefore he well deserves a reward for them." Leif in the meantime took the bag, and carried it to Karl; and when they cast their eyes on the money, Leif said, "We need not look long at this silver, for here the one piece of money is better than the other; and this is the money we will have. Let a man come to be present at the counting it out." Thrand says that he thought Leif was the fittest man to do it upon his account.

Leif and Karl thereupon went a short way from the tent, sat
down, and counted and weighed the silver. Karl took the
helmet off his head, and received in it the weighed silver. They
saw a man coming to them who had a stick with an axe-head on
it in his hand, a hat low upon his head, and a short green cloak.
He was bare-legged, and had linen breeches on tied at the knee.
He laid his stick down in the field, and went to Karl, and said,
" Take care, Karl Mærske, that thou dost not hurt thyself against
my axe-stick." Immediately, a man came running, and calls
with great haste to Leif Ossursson, telling him to come as quick
as possible to Lagman Gille's tent; " for," says he, " Sigurd
Thorlakson ran in just now into the mouth of the tent, and gave
one of Gille's men a desperate wound." Leif rose up instantly,
and went off to Gille's tent along with his men. Karl remained
sitting, and the Norway people stood round him in a circle.
Gaut immediately sprang up, and struck with a hand-axe over
the heads of the people, and the stroke came on Karl's head;
but the wound was slight. Thord the Low seized the stick-axe,
which lay in the field at his side, and struck the axe-blade right
into Karl's skull. Many people now streamed out of Thrand's
tent. Karl was carried away dead. Thrand was much grieved
at this event, and offered money-mulcts for his relations; but
Leif and Gille, who had to prosecute the business, would accept
no mulct. Sigurd was banished the country for having wounded
Gille's tent comrade, and Gaut and Thord for the murder of
Karl. The Norway people rigged out the vessel which Karl had
with him, and sailed eastward to Olaf, and gave him these
tidings. He was in no pleasant humour at it, and threatened a
speedy vengeance; but it was not allotted by fate to King Olaf
to revenge himself on Thrand and his relations, because of the
hostilities which had begun in Norway, and which are now to be
related. And there is nothing more to be told of what happened
after King Olaf sent men to the Faröe Islands to take scatt of
them. But great strife arose after Karl's death in the Faröe
Islands between the family of Thrand of Gata and Leif Ossursson, and of which there are great sagas.

CHAPTER CLIV. KING OLAF'S EXPEDITION WITH HIS LEVY
[1027].—Now we must proceed with the relation we began before
[p. 297],—that King Olaf set out with his men, and raised a levy
over the whole country. All lendermen in the North followed
him excepting Einar Tambarskelve, who sat quietly at home
upon his farm since his return to the country, and did not serve

the king. Einar had great estates and wealth, although he held
no fiefs from the king, and he lived splendidly. King Olaf
sailed with his fleet south around Stad, and many people from
the districts around joined him. King Olaf himself had a ship
which he had got built the winter before, and which was called
the Bison.[1] It was a very large ship, with a bison's head gilded
all over upon the bow. Sigvat the scald speaks thus of it:—

> " Trygvesson's Long Serpent bore,
> Grim gaping o'er the waves before,
> A dragon's head with open throat,
> When last the hero was afloat:
>   His cruise was closed,
>   As God disposed.
> Olaf has raised a bison's head,
> Which proudly seems the waves to tread,
> While o'er its golden forehead dashing
> The waves its glittering horns are washing:
>   May God dispose
>   A luckier close."

The king went on to Hordaland: there he heard the news
that Erling Skialgsson had left the country with a great force,
and four or five ships. He himself had a large war-ship, and
his sons had three of twenty rowing banks each; and they had
sailed westward to England to Canute the Great. Then King
Olaf sailed eastward along the land with a mighty war-force, and
he inquired everywhere if anything was known of Canute's
proceedings; and all agreed in saying he was in England,[2] but
added that he was fitting out a levy, and intended coming to
Norway. As Olaf had a large fleet, and could not discover with
certainty where he should go to meet King Canute, and as his
people were dissatisfied with lying quiet in one place with so
large an armament, he resolved to sail with his fleet south to
Denmark, and took with him all the men who were best
appointed and most warlike; and he gave leave to the others to
return home. And it is told in the song:—

> " The Bison's oars, in sunshine glancing,
>   Wake the slumb'ring deep,
>   As they southwards sweep
> While northward Onund's fleet's advancing."

Now the people whom he thought of little use having gone
home, King Olaf had many excellent and stout men-at-arms
besides those who, as before related, had fled the country or sat

---

[1] *Visundr*, the wild European bison ox or aurochs. The ship's stern-
post was shaped to represent the beast's tail, and this too was gilded (*Sagas
of the Norse Kings*, p. 142).
[2] It is recorded that Canute was in Rome on 26th March, so that he must
have returned to England.

quietly at home; and most of the chief men and lendermen of
Norway were along with him.

CHAPTER CLV. OF KING OLAF AND KING ONUND.—When
King Olaf sailed to Denmark, he set his course for Sealand; and
when he came there he made incursions on the land, and began to
plunder. The country people were severely treated; some were
killed, some bound and dragged to the ships. All who could
do so took to flight, and made no opposition. King Olaf committed there the greatest ravages. While Olaf was in Sealand,
the news came that King Onund Olafsson of Sweden had raised
a levy and fallen upon Scania, and was ravaging there; and
then it became known what the resolution had been that the two
kings had taken at the Gotha river, where they had concluded a
union and friendship, and had bound themselves to oppose King
Canute. King Onund continued his march until he met his
brother-in-law King Olaf. When they met they made proclamation, both to their own people and to the people of the
country, that they intended to conquer Denmark; and asked the
support of the people of the country for this purpose. And it
happened, as we find examples of everywhere, that if hostilities
are brought upon the people of a country not strong enough to
withstand, the greatest number will submit to the conditions by
which peace can be purchased at any rate. So it happened here
that many men went into the service of the kings, and agreed to
submit to them. Wheresoever they went they laid the country
all round in subjection to them, and otherwise laid waste all
with fire and sword. Of this foray Sigvat the scald speaks in a
ballad he composed concerning King Canute the Great:—

> " Canute is on the sea!
>   The news is told,
>   That Olaf now grows bold
>   And forth to war goes he.
> This boasting word is in his mouth:
>   ' On a lucky day
>   We came away
> From Drontheim to the south.'
> Across the cold East sea,
>   The Swedish king
>   His host did bring,
> To gain great victory.
> King Onund came to fight,
>   In Sealand's plains,
>   Against the Danes,
> With his steel-clad men so bright.
> Canute is on the land;
>   Side to side
>   His long-ships ride

> Along the yellow strand.
> Where waves wash the green banks,
>> Mast to mast,
>> All bound fast,
> His great fleet lies in ranks."

CHAPTER CLVI. OF KING CANUTE THE GREAT.—King Canute had heard in England that King Olaf of Norway had called out a levy, and had gone with his forces to Denmark, and was making great ravages in his dominions there. Canute began to gather people, and he had speedily collected a great army and a numerous fleet. Earl Hakon was second in command over the whole.

Sigvat the scald came this summer from the West, from Rouen in Valland, and with him was a man called Berg. They had made a merchant voyage there the summer before. Sigvat had made a little poem about this journey, called " The Western Traveller's Song," which begins thus:—

> " Berg! many a merry morn was pass'd,
> When our vessel was made fast
> And we lay on the glittering tide
> Of Rouen river's western side."

When Sigvat came to England he went directly to King Canute, and asked his leave to proceed to Norway; for King Canute had forbidden all merchant vessels to sail until he himself was ready with his fleet. When Sigvat arrived he went to the house in which the king lodged; but the doors were locked, and he had to stand a long time outside, but when he got admittance he obtained the permission he desired. He then sang:—

> " The way to Jutland's king I sought;
> A little patience I was taught.
> The doors were shut—all full within;
> The udaller could not get in.
> But Gorm's great son did condescend
> To his own chamber me to send,
> And grant my prayer—although I'm one
> Whose arms the armour's weight have known-"

When Sigvat became aware that King Canute was equipping an armament against King Olaf, and knew what a mighty force King Canute had, he made these lines:—

> " The mighty Knut, and Earl Hakon,
> Have leagued themselves, and counsel taken
> Against King Olaf's life,
> And are ready for the strife.
> In spite of king and earl, I say,
> ' I love him well—may he get away:'
> On the Fjelds, wild and dreary,
> With him I'd live, and ne'er be weary."

Sigvat made many other songs concerning this expedition of
Canute and Hakon.   He made this among others:—

> " It was the earl's intention then
> 'Twixt Olaf and the udalmen
> Peace to establish, yea, whenever
> Both sides should meet and speak together.
> Noble are those of Eric's blood!
> Yet Hakon could not heal this feud,
> For bonders in their furious strife
> Had robbed too many men of life."

CHAPTER CLVII. OF KING CANUTE'S SHIP THE DRAGON.—
Canute the Great was at last ready with his fleet, and left the
land; and a vast number of men he had, and ships frightfully
large.   He himself had a dragon-ship so large that it had sixty
benches of rowers, and the head was gilt all over.   Earl Hakon
had another dragon of forty benches, and it also had a gilt figure-
head.   The sails of both were in stripes of blue, red, and green,
and the vessels were painted all above the water-line; and all
that belonged to their equipment was most splendid.   They had
also many other huge ships remarkably well fitted out and grand.
Sigvat the scald talks of this in his song on Knut:—

> " Canute is out beneath the sky—
> Canute of the clear blue eye!
> The king is out on the ocean's breast,
> Leading his grand fleet from the West.
> On to the East the ship-masts glide,
> Glancing and bright each long-ship's side.
> The conqueror of great Ethelred,
> Canute, is there, his foeman's dread:
> His dragon with her sails of blue,
> All bright and brilliant to the view,
> High hoisted on the yard-arms wide,
> Carries great Canute o'er the tide.
> Brave is the royal progress—fast
> The proud ship's keel obeys the mast,
> Dashes through foam, and gains the land,
> Raising a surge on Lymfjord's strand."

It is related that King Canute sailed with this vast force from
England, and came with all his force safely to Denmark, where
he went into Lymfjord, and there he found gathered besides a
large army of the men of the country.

CHAPTER CLVIII. HARDAKNUT TAKEN TO BE KING IN DEN-
MARK.—Earl Ulf Sprakalegsson had been set as protector over
Denmark when King Canute went to England, and the king
had entrusted his son Hardaknut in the earl's hands.   This

took place the summer before, as we related. But the earl immediately gave it out that King Canute had, at parting, made known to him his will and desire that the Danes should take his son Hardaknut as king over the Danish dominions. " On that account," says the earl, " he gave the matter into our hands; as I, and many other chiefs and leading men here in the country, have often complained to King Canute of the evil consequences to the country of being without a king, and that former kings thought it honour and power enough to rule over the Danish kingdom alone; and in the times that are past many kings have ruled over this kingdom. But now there are greater difficulties than have ever been before; for we have been so fortunate hitherto as to live without disturbance from foreign kings, but now we hear the king of Norway is going to attack us, to which is added the fear of the people that the Swedish king will join him; and now King Canute is in England." The earl then produced King Canute's letter and seal, confirming all that the earl asserted. Many other chiefs supported this business; and in consequence of all these persuasions the people resolved to take Hardaknut as king, which was done at the same Thing. The Queen Emma had been principal promoter of this determination; for she had got the letter to be written, and provided with the seal, having cunningly got hold of the king's signet: but from him it was all concealed. Now when Hardaknut and Earl Ulf heard for certain that King Olaf was come from Norway with a large army, they went to Jutland, where the greatest strength of the Danish kingdom lies, sent out message-tokens, and summoned to them a great force; but when they heard the Swedish king was also come with his army, they thought they would not have strength enough to give battle to both, and therefore kept their army together in Jutland, and resolved to defend that country against the kings. The whole of their ships they assembled in Lymfjord, and waited thus for King Canute. Now when they heard that King Canute had come from the West to Lymfjord, they sent men to him, and to Queen Emma, and begged her to find out if the king was angry at them or not, and to let them know. The queen talked over the matter with him, and said, " Your son Hardaknut will pay the full mulct the king may demand, if he has done anything which is thought to be against the king." He replies that Hardaknut has not done this of his own judgment. " And therefore," says he, " it has turned out as might have been expected, that when he, a child, and without understanding, wanted to be called king, the country, when any evil came and an enemy appeared, must be conquered by foreign princes, if our might had not come to his aid. If he will have any reconciliation with me, let him come to me and lay down the mock title of king he has given himself." The queen sent these very words to Hardaknut, and at the same time she begged him not to decline coming; for, as she truly observed, he had no force to stand against his father. When this message came to Hardaknut, he asked advice of the earl and other chief people who were with him; but it was soon found that when the people heard King Canute the Old was arrived they all streamed to him, and seemed to have no confidence but in him alone. Then Earl Ulf and his fellows saw they had but two roads to take; either to go to the king and leave all to his mercy, or to fly the country. All pressed Hardaknut to go to his father, which advice he followed. When they met he fell at his father's feet, and laid his seal, which accompanied the kingly title, on his knee. King Canute took Hardaknut by the hand, and placed him in as high a seat as he used to sit in before. Earl Ulf sent his son Swend, who was a sister's son of King Canute, and the same age as Hardaknut, to the king. He prayed for grace and reconciliation for his father, and offered himself as hostage for the earl. King Canute ordered him to tell the earl to assemble his men and ships, and come to him, and then they would talk of reconciliation. The earl did so.

CHAPTER CLIX. FORAY IN SCANIA.—When King Olaf and King Onund heard that King Canute was come from the West, and also that he had a vast force, they sailed east to Scania, and allowed themselves to ravage and burn in the districts there, and then proceeded eastward along the land to the frontier of Sweden. As soon as the country people heard that King Canute was come from the West, no one thought of going into the service of the two kings. Sigvat speaks of these matters:—

> " Canute is bold!
>   Kings could not hold
>   The Danish land
>   With warrior band;
>   But then the foe
>   Of Danes did go
>   And ravage round
>   All Scania's bound."

Now the kings sailed eastward along the coast, and brought up in a river called Helge-aa,[1] and remained there some time.

[1] In the east of Skaane.

When they heard that King Canute was coming eastward with his forces against them, they held a council; and the result was, that King Olaf with his people went up the country to the forest, and to the lake out of which the river Helge flows. There at the river-head they made a dam of timber and turf, and dammed in the lake. They also dug a deep ditch, through which they led several waters, so that the lake waxed very high. In the river-bed they laid large logs of timber. They were many days about this work, and King Olaf had the management of this piece of artifice; but King Onund had only to command the fleet and army. When King Canute heard of the proceedings of the two kings, and of the damage they had done to his dominions, he sailed right against them to where they lay in Helge river. He had a war-force which was one half greater than that of both the kings together. Sigvat speaks of these things:—

> " Canute is brave!
> This prince did save
> From scaith or harm
> By foeman's arm,
> Men of his realm
> Whom war would whelm.
> He'll not allow
> Wild plundering now."

CHAPTER CLX. BATTLE IN HELGE RIVER.—One day, towards evening, King Onund's spies saw King Canute coming sailing along, and he was not far off. Then King Onund ordered the war-horns to sound; on which his people struck their tents, put on their weapons, rowed out of the harbour and east round the land, bound their ships together, and prepared for battle. King Onund made his spies run up the country to look for King Olaf, and tell him the news. Then King Olaf broke up the dam and let the river take its course. King Olaf travelled down in the night to his ships. When King Canute came outside the harbour he saw the forces of the kings ready for battle. He thought that it would be too late in the day to begin the fight by the time his forces could be ready; for his fleet required a great deal of room at sea, and there was a long distance between the foremost of his ships and the hindmost, and between those outside and those nearest the land. Now, as Canute saw that the Swedes and Norwegians had quitted the harbour, he went into it with as many ships as it could hold; but the main strength of the fleet lay without the harbour. In the morning, when it was light, a great part of the men went on shore; some for amusement, some

to converse with the people of other ships. They observed
nothing until the water came rushing over them like a waterfall,
carrying huge trees, which drove in among their ships, damaging
all they struck; and the water covered all the fields. The men
on shore perished, and many who were in the ships. All who
could do it cut their cables; so that the ships were loose, and
drove before the stream, and were scattered here and there.
The great dragon, which King Canute himself was in, drove
before the stream; and as it could not so easily be turned with
oars, drove out among Olaf's and Onund's ships. As they knew
the ship, they laid her on board on all quarters. But the ship
was so high in the hull, as if it were a castle, and had besides such
a numerous and chosen crew on board, well armed and exercised,
that it was not easy to attack her. After a short time also Earl
Ulf came up with his fleet; and then the battle began, and King
Canute's fleet gathered together from all quarters. But the kings
Olaf and Onund, seeing they had for this time got all the victory
that fate permitted them to gain, let their ships retreat, cast
themselves loose from King Canute's ship, and the fleets
separated. But as the attack had not been made as King
Canute had determined, he made no farther attempt; and the
kings on each side arranged their fleets and put their ships in
order. When the fleets were parted, and each sailing its course,
Olaf and Onund looked over their forces, and found they had
suffered no loss of men. In the meantime they saw that if they
waited until King Canute got his large fleet in order to attack
them, the difference of force was so great that for them there was
little chance of victory. It was also evident that if the battle
was renewed, they must suffer a great loss of men. They took
the resolution, therefore, to row with the whole fleet eastward
along the coast.[1] Observing that King Canute did not pursue
them, they raised up their masts and set sail. Ottar Black tells
thus of it in the poem he composed upon King Canute the Great :—

> " The king, in battle fray,
>   Drove the Swedish host away;
>   The wolf did not miss prey,
>   Nor the raven on that day.
>   Great Canute could withstand
>   Two kings to keep his land
>   For at Helge river's side
>   They would not his sword abide."

[1] According to the *Anglo-Saxon Chronicle*, this battle was in 1025 and
was between Canute and " Ulf and Eilaf " (? Earl Ulf and a brother of his).
Saxo says that Earl Ulf, Olaf, and Onund made concerted attacks on
Canute, who routed the latter two but was outwitted by Ulf at Helge river.

Thord Siareksson the poet made a death-song on King Olaf (called the Rood Song) where this encounter is spoken of thus:—

> " King Olaf, Agder's lord,
> Ne'er shunned the Jutland king,
> But with his blue-edged sword
> Broke many a mailcoat-ring.
> King Canute was not slow:
> His strong arm filled the plain
> With dead, killed by his bow:
> The wolf howled o'er the slain."

CHAPTER CLXI. KING OLAF AND KING ONUND'S PLANS.—
King Olaf and King Onund sailed eastward to the Swedish king's dominions; and one day, towards evening, landed at a place called Barvik,[1] where they lay all night. But then it was observed of the Swedes that they were home-sick; for the greater part of their forces sailed eastward along the land in the night, and did not stop their course until they came home to their houses. Now when King Onund observed this, he ordered, as soon as the day dawned, to sound the signal for a House-thing; and the whole people went on shore, and the Thing sat down. Then King Onund took up the word, and spake thus: " So it is, King Olaf, that, as you know, we have been assembled in summer and have forayed wide around in Denmark, and have gained much booty, but no land. I had 350 vessels, and now have not above 100 remaining with me. Now it appears to me we can make no greater progress than we have made, although you have still the 60 vessels which have followed you the whole summer. It therefore appears to me best that we come back to my kingdom; for it is always good to drive home with the waggon safe. In this expedition we have won something and lost nothing. Now I will offer you, King Olaf, to come with me, and we shall remain assembled during the winter. Take as much of my kingdom as you will, so that you and the men who follow you may support yourselves well; and when spring comes let us take such measures as we find serviceable. If you, however, will prefer to travel across our country, and go overland to Norway, it shall be free for you to do so."

King Olaf thanked King Onund for his friendly offer. " But if I may advise," says he, " then we should take another resolution, and keep together the forces we have still remaining. I had in the first of summer, before I left Norway, 350 ships; but when I left the country I chose from among the whole war-levy

---

[1] Possibly this is Baraakra in Blekinge.

those I thought to be the best, and with them I manned 60 ships; and these I still have. Now it appears to me that the part of your war-force which has now run away is the most worthless and of least assistance; but now I see here all your chiefs and leaders, and I know well that the people who belong to the court-troops [1] are by far the best suited to carry arms. We have here chosen men and superb ships, and we can very well lie all winter in our ships, as vikings' custom is. But Canute cannot lie long in Helge river; for the harbour will not hold so many vessels as he has. If he steers eastward after us, we can escape from him, and then people will soon gather to us; but if he return to the harbours where his fleet can lie, I know for certain that the desire to return home will not be less in his army than in ours. I think, also, we have ravaged so widely in summer, that the small-holders, both in Sealand and Scania, know well whose favour they have to seek. Canute's army will thus be dispersed so widely, that it is uncertain to whom fate may at last give the victory; but let us first find out what resolution he takes."

Thus King Olaf ended his speech, and it found much applause, and his advice was followed. Spies were sent into King Canute's army, and both the kings Olaf and Onund remained lying where they were.

CHAPTER CLXII. OF KING CANUTE AND EARL ULF.—When King Canute saw that the kings of Norway and Sweden steered eastward with their forces along the coast, he sent men to ride night and day on the land to follow their movements. Some spies went forward, others returned; so that King Canute had news every day of their progress. He had also spies always in their army. Now when he heard that a great part of the fleet had sailed away from the kings, he turned back with his forces to Sealand, and lay with his whole fleet in the Sound; so that part lay on the Scania [2] side, and a part on the Sealand side. King Canute himself, the day before Michaelmas (28th September), rode with a great retinue to Roskilde. There his brother-in-law, Earl Ulf, had prepared a great feast for him. The earl was the most agreeable host; but the king was silent and sullen. The earl talked to him in every way to make him cheerful, and brought forward everything which he thought would amuse him; but the king remained stern, and speaking little. At last the earl proposed to him a game at chess, which he agreed to; and a

---

[1] The *hirðmenn*, picked men who formed the king's bodyguard.
[2] Scania, on the northern or Swedish side of the Sound.

chess-board was produced, and they played together. Earl Ulf
was hasty in temper, stiff, and in nothing yielding; but everything he managed went on well in his hands: and he was a great
warrior, about whom there are many stories. He was the most
powerful man in Denmark next to the king. Earl Ulf's sister
Gyda was married to Earl Gudin (Goodwin) Ulfnadsson; and
their sons were Harald king of England, and Earl Toste, Earl
Walthiof,[1] Earl Mauro-kaare,[1] and Earl Swend. Gyda was the
name of their daughter, who was married to the English king
Edward the Good.

CHAPTER CLXIII. OF THE EARL'S MURDER.—When they had
played a while the king made a false move, at which the earl took
a knight from the king; but the king set the piece again upon
the board, and told the earl to make another move; but the earl
grew angry, threw over the chess-board, stood up, and went
away. The king said, " Run away, Ulf the Fearful." The earl
turned round at the door and said, " Thou wouldst have run
farther at Helge river, if thou hadst come to battle there. Thou
didst not call me Ulf the Fearful when I hastened to thy help
while the Swedes were beating thee like a dog." The earl then
went out, and went to bed. The following morning while the
king was putting on his clothes he said to his footboy, " Go thou
to Earl Ulf and kill him."

The lad went, was away awhile, and then came back.

The king said, " Hast thou killed the earl? "

" I did not kill him, for he was gone to Saint Lucius' church."

There was a man called Ivar White, a Norwegian by birth,
who was the king's court-man and chamberlain.[2] The king said
to him, " Go thou and kill the earl."

Ivar went to the church, and in at the choir, and thrust his
sword through the earl, who died on the spot. Then Ivar went
to the king, with the bloody sword in his hand.

The king said, " Hast thou killed the earl? "

" I have killed him," says he.

" Thou didst well."

After the earl was killed the monks closed the church and
locked the doors. When that was told the king he sent a
message to the monks, ordering them to open the church and sing

---

[1] Earl Walthiof and Mauro-Kaare (*i.e.* Earl Morcar) were not Godwin's
sons, but sons of Siward of Northumberland and Aelfgar of Mercia respectively. See *Sagas of the Norse Kings*, pp. 219 ff., 235.
[2] More accurately, " member of his household " (*herbergismaðr*).

high mass. They did as the king ordered; and when the king came to the church he bestowed on it great property, so that it had a large domain, by which that place was raised very high; and these lands have since always belonged to it. King Canute rode down to his ships, and lay there till late in harvest with a very large army.

CHAPTER CLXIV. OF KING OLAF AND THE SWEDES.—When King Olaf and King Onund heard that King Canute had sailed to Ore Sound, and lay there with a great force, the kings held a House-thing, and spoke much about what resolution they should adopt. King Olaf wished they should remain there with all the fleet, and see what King Canute would at last resolve to do. But the Swedes held it to be unadvisable to remain until the frost set in, and so it was determined; and King Onund went home with all his army, and King Olaf remained lying after them.

CHAPTER CLXV. OF EGIL AND TOVE.—While King Olaf lay there, he had frequently conferences and consultations with his people. One night Egil Hallsson and Tove Valgautsson had the watch upon the king's ship. Tove came from West Gotland, and was a man of high birth. While they sat on watch they heard much lamentation and crying among the people who had been taken in the war, and who lay bound on the shore at night. Tove said it made him ill to hear such distress, and asked Egil to go with him and let loose these people. This work they set about, cut the cords, and let the people escape, and that act of theirs was extremely unpopular; and indeed the king was so enraged at it that they themselves were in the greatest danger. When Egil afterwards fell sick the king for a long time would not visit him, until many people entreated it of him. It vexed Egil much to have done anything the king was angry at, and he begged his forgiveness. The king now dismissed his wrath against Egil, laid his hands upon the side on which Egil's pain was, and sang a prayer; upon which the pain ceased instantly, and Egil grew better. Tove came, after entreaty, into reconciliation with the king, on condition that he should exhort his father Valgaut to come to the king. He was a heathen; but after conversation with the king he went over to Christianity, and died instantly when he was baptized.

CHAPTER CLXVI. TREACHERY TOWARDS KING OLAF.—King Olaf had now frequent conferences with his people, and asked advice from them, and from his chiefs, as to what he should determine upon. But there was no unanimity among them— some considering that unadvisable which others considered highly serviceable; and there was much indecision in their councils. King Canute had always spies in King Olaf's army, who entered into conversation with many of his men, offering them presents and favour on account of King Canute. Many allowed themselves to be seduced, and gave promises of fidelity, and to be King Canute's men, and bring the country into his hands if he came to Norway. This was apparent, afterwards, of many who at first kept it concealed. Some took at once money bribes, and others were promised money afterwards; and a great many there were who had got great presents of money from him before: for it may be said with truth of King Canute, that every man who came to him, and who he thought had the spirit of a man and would like his favour, got his hands full of gifts and money. On this account he was very popular, although his generosity was principally shown to foreigners, and was greatest the greater distance they came from.

CHAPTER CLXVII. KING OLAF'S CONSULTATIONS. — King Olaf had often conferences and meetings with his people, and asked their counsel; but as he observed they gave different opinions, he had a suspicion that there must be some who spoke differently from what they really thought advisable for him, and he was thus uncertain if all gave him due fidelity in council. Some pressed that with the first fair wind they should sail to Ore Sound, and so to Norway. They said the Danes would not dare to attack them, although they lay with so great a force right in the way. But the king was a man of too much understanding not to see that this was impracticable. He knew also that Olaf Trygvesson had found it quite otherwise, as to the Danes not daring to fight, when he with a few people went into battle against a great body of them. The king also knew that in King Canute's army there were a great many Norwegians; therefore he entertained the suspicion that those who gave this advice were more favourable to King Canute than to him. King Olaf came at last to the determination, from all these considerations, that the people who would follow him should make themselves ready to proceed by land across Gotland, and so to Norway. "But our ships," said he, "and all things that we cannot take with us, I will send eastward to the Swedish king's dominions, and let them be taken care of for us there."

CHAPTER CLXVIII. HAREK OF THIOTTO'S VOYAGE.—Harek of Thiotto replied thus to the king's speech: " It is evident that I cannot travel on foot to Norway. I am old and heavy, and little accustomed to walking. Besides, I am unwilling to part with my ship; for on that ship and its apparel I have bestowed so much labour that it would go much against my inclination to put her into the hands of my enemies."

The king said, " Come along with us, Harek, and we shall carry thee when thou art tired of walking."

Then Harek sang these lines:—

> " I'll mount my ocean steed,
> And o'er the sea I'll speed;
> Forests and hills are not for me,—
> I love the moving sea.
> Though Canute block the Sound,
> Rather than walk the ground,
> And leave my ship, I'll see
> What my ship will do for me."

Then King Olaf let everything be put in order for the journey. The people had their walking clothing and weapons, but their other clothes and effects they packed upon such horses as they could get. Then he sent off people to take his ships east to Calmar. There he had the vessels laid up, and the ships' apparel and other goods taken care of. Harek did as he had said, and waited for a wind, and then sailed west to Scania, until, about the decline of the day, he came with a fresh and fair wind to the eastward of Holene.[1] There he let the sail and the vane, and flag and mast be taken down, and let the upper works of the ship be covered over with some grey tilt-canvas, and let a few men sit at the oars in the fore part and aft, but the most were sitting low down in the vessel.

When Canute's watchmen saw the ship, they talked with each other about what ship it might be, and made the guess that it must be one loaded with herrings or salt, as they only saw a few men at the oars; and the ship, besides, appeared to them grey, and wanting tar, as if burnt up by the sun, and they saw also that it was deeply loaded. Now when Harek came farther through the Sound, and past the fleet, he raised the mast, hoisted sail, and set up his gilded vane. The sail was white as snow, and in it were red and blue stripes of cloth interwoven. When the king's men saw the ship sailing in this state, they told the king that probably King Olaf had sailed through them. But King Canute replies, that King Olaf was too prudent a man to

[1] The bay inside Skanör.

sail with a single ship through King Canute's fleet, and thought it more likely to be Harek of Thiotto, or the like of him. Many believed the truth to be that King Canute knew of this expedition of Harek, and that it would not have succeeded so if they had not concluded a friendship beforehand with each other; which seemed likely, after King Canute's and Harek's friendly understanding became generally known.

Harek made this song as he sailed northward round the isle of Vederey [1]:—

> " Let the ladies of Denmark and Lund never sneer,
>   Saying I dare not sail now that autumn is here;
>   Fair maidens, no smiles!
>   For out past the isles
>   My dragon, my sea-horse, my good ship I steer."

Harek went on his way, and never stopped till he came north to Halogaland, to his own house in Thiotto Isle.

CHAPTER CLXIX. KING OLAF'S COURSE FROM SWEDEN.— When King Olaf began his journey, he came first into Smaaland, and then into West Gotland. He marched quietly and peaceably, and the country people gave him all assistance on his journey. Thus he proceeded until he came into Viken, and north through Viken to Sarpsborg, where he remained, and ordered a winter abode to be prepared. Then he gave most of the chiefs leave to return home, but kept the lendermen by him whom he thought the most serviceable. There were with him also all the sons of Arne Armodsson, and they stood in great favour with the king. Gelle Thorkelsson, who the summer before had come from Iceland, also came there to the king, as before related [p. 281].

CHAPTER CLXX. OF SIGVAT THE SCALD.—Sigvat the scald had long been in King Olaf's household, as related [p. 148], and the king made him his marshal. Sigvat had no talent for speaking in prose; but in scaldcraft he was so practised that the verses came as readily from his tongue as if he were speaking in usual language. He had made a mercantile journey to Normandy, and in the course of it had come to England, where he met King Canute, and obtained permission from him to sail to Norway, as before related [p. 304]. When he came to Norway, he proceeded straight to King Olaf, and found him at Sarpsborg. He presented himself before the king just as he was sitting down to

---

[1] Now Hallands Væderö off the north-west point of Skaane.

table. Sigvat saluted him. The king looked at Sigvat and was
silent. Then Sigvat sang:—

> " Great king! thy marshal is come home,
> No more by land or sea to roam,
>   But by thy side
>   Still to abide.
> Great king! what seat here shall he take
> Among thy men, for honour's sake?
>   Yet all seats here
>   To me are dear."

Then was verified the old saying, that " many are the ears of a
king; " for King Olaf had heard all about Sigvat's journey, and
that he had spoken with Canute. He says to Sigvat, " I do not
know if thou art my marshal, or hast become one of Canute's
men." Sigvat said:—

> " Canute, whose golden gifts display
> A generous heart, would have me stay,
> Service in his great court to take,
> And my own Norway king forsake.
> Two masters at a time, I said,
> Were one too many for men bred
> Where truth and virtue, shown to all,
> Make all men true in Olaf's hall."

Then King Olaf told Sigvat to take his seat where he before
used to sit; and in a short time Sigvat was in as high favour with
the king as ever.

CHAPTER CLXXI. OF ERLING SKIALGSSON AND HIS SONS.—
Erling Skialgsson and all his sons had been all summer in King
Canute's army, in the retinue of Earl Hakon. Thore Hund was
also there, and was in high esteem. Now when King Canute
heard that King Olaf had gone overland to Norway, he discharged his army, and gave all men leave to go to their winter
abodes. There was then in Denmark a great army of foreigners,
both English, Norwegians, and men of other countries, who had
joined the expedition in summer. In autumn Erling Skialgsson
went to Norway with his men, and received great presents from
King Canute at parting; but Thore Hund remained behind in
King Canute's court. With Erling went messengers from King
Canute well provided with money; and in winter they travelled
through all the country, paying the money which King Canute
had promised to many in autumn for their assistance. They
gave presents in money, besides, to many whose friendship could
be purchased for King Canute. They received much assistance
in their travels from Erling. In this way it came to pass that

many turned their support to King Canute, promised him their services, and agreed to oppose King Olaf. Some did this openly, but many more concealed it from the public. King Olaf heard this news, for many had something to tell him about it; and the conversation in the court often turned upon it. Sigvat the scald made a song upon it:—

> " The base traitors ply
>   With purses of gold,
>   Wanting to buy
>   What is not to be sold,—
>   The king's life and throne
>   Wanting to buy:
>   But our souls are our own,
>   And to hell we'll not hie.
>   No pleasure in heaven,
>   As we know full well,
>   To the traitor is given,—
>   His soul is his hell."

Often also the conversation turned upon how ill it beseemed Earl Hakon to raise his hand in arms against King Olaf, who had given him his life when he fell into the king's power; but Sigvat was a particular friend of Earl Hakon, and when he heard the earl spoken against he sang:—

> " Our own court people we may blame,
>   If they take gold to their own shame,
>   Their king and country to betray.
>   With those who give it's not the same,
>   From them we have no faith to claim:
>   'Tis we are wrong, if we give way."

CHAPTER CLXXII. OF KING OLAF'S PRESENTS AT YULE [1028].—King Olaf gave a great feast at Yule, and many great people had come to him. It was the seventh day of Yule (31st December) that the king, with a few persons, among whom was Sigvat, who attended him day and night, went to a house in which the king's most precious valuables were kept. He had, according to his custom, collected there with great care the valuable presents he was to make on New Year's eve. There was in the house no small number of gold-mounted swords; and Sigvat sang:—

> " The swords stand there,
>   All bright and fair,—
>   Those oars that dip in blood:
>   If I in favour stood,
>   I too might have a share.
>   A sword the scald would gladly take,
>   And use it for his master's sake:
>   In favour once he stood,
>   And a sword has stained in blood."

The king took a sword of which the handle was twisted round with gold, and the guard was gold-mounted, and gave it to him. It was a valuable article; but the gift was not seen without envy, as will appear hereafter.

Immediately after Yule the king began his journey to the Uplands; for he had a great many people about him, but had received no income that autumn from the North country, for there had been an armament in summer, and the king had laid out all the revenues he could command; and also he had no vessels with which he and his people could go to the North. At the same time he had news from the North from which he could see that there would be no safety for him in that quarter, unless he went with a great force. For these reasons he determined to proceed through the Uplands, although it was not so long a time since he had been there in guest-quarters as the law prescribes,[1] and as the kings usually had the custom of observing in their visits. When he came to the Uplands the lendermen and the richest bonders invited him to be their guest, and thus lightened his expenses.

CHAPTER CLXXIII. OF BIORN THE BAILIFF.—There was a man called Biorn who was of Gotland family, and a friend and acquaintance of Queen Astrid, and in some way related to her. She had given him farm-management and other offices in the upper part of Hedemark. He had also the management of Osterdal district. Biorn was not in esteem with the king, nor liked by the bonders. It happened in a hamlet which Biorn ruled over that many swine and cattle were missing; therefore Biorn ordered a Thing to be called to examine the matter. Such pillage he attributed chiefly to the people settled in forest-farms far from other men; by which he referred particularly to those who dwelt in Osterdal, for that district was very thinly inhabited, and full of lakes and forest clearings, and but in few places did the people live close together.

CHAPTER CLXXIV. OF RAUD'S SONS.—There was a man called Raud who dwelt in Osterdal. His wife was called Ragnhild; and his sons, Dag and Sigurd, were men of great talent. They were present at the Thing, made a reply in defence of the Osterdal people, and removed the accusation from them. Biorn thought they were too pert in their answer, and too fine in

---

[1] Olaf had visited the Uplands in 1025 (*vide* p. 265), so that three years had now elapsed and it was full time for this visit. (*cf.* p. 179).

their clothes and weapons; and therefore turned his speech against these brothers, and said it was not unlikely they may have committed these thefts. They denied it, and the Thing closed. Soon after King Olaf, with his retinue, came to guest-quarters in the house of bailiff Biorn. The matter which had been before the Thing was then complained of to the king; and Biorn said that Raud's sons appeared to him to have committed these thefts. A messenger was sent for Raud's sons; and when they appeared before the king he said they had not at all the appearance of thieves, and acquitted them. Thereupon they invited the king, with all his retinue, to a three days' entertainment at their father's; and although Biorn dissuaded him from it, the king went. At Raud's there was a very excellent feast. The king asked Raud what people he and his wife were. Raud answered that he was originally a Swedish man, rich, and of high birth; " but I ran away with the wife I have ever since had, and she is a sister of King Ring Dagsson." The king then remembered both their families. He found that father and sons were men of understanding, and asked them what they could do. Sigurd said he could interpret dreams and determine the time of the day although no heavenly bodies could be seen. The king made trial of his art, and found it was as Sigurd had said. Dag stated, as his accomplishment, that he could see the misdeeds and vices of every man who came under his eye, when he chose to observe him closely. The king told him to declare what faults of disposition he saw in the king himself. Dag mentioned a fault which the king was sensible he really had. Then the king asked what fault the bailiff Biorn had. Dag said Biorn was a thief; and told also where Biorn had concealed on his farm the bones, horns, and hides of the cattle he had stolen in autumn; " for he committed," said Dag, " all the thefts in autumn which he accuses other people of." Dag also told the king the places where the king should go after leaving them. When the king departed from Raud's house he was accompanied on the way, and presented with friendly gifts; and Raud's sons remained with the king. The king went first to Biorn's, and found there that all Dag had told him was true. Upon which he drove Biorn out of the country, and he had to thank the queen that he got off safe with life and limbs.

CHAPTER CLXXV. THORE'S DEATH.—Thore, a son of Olve of Egge, a stepson of Kalf Arneson, and a sister's son of Thore Hund, was a remarkably handsome man, stout and strong.

He was at this time eighteen years old; had made a good marriage in Hedemark, by which he got great wealth; and was besides one of the most popular of men, and formed to be a chief. He invited the king and his retinue home to him to a feast. The king accepted the invitation, went to Thore's, and was well received. The entertainment was very splendid; they were excellently treated, and all that was set before the guests was of the best that could be got. The king and his people talked among themselves of the excellence of everything, and knew not what they should admire the most,—whether Thore's house outside, or the inside furniture, the table service or the liquors, or the host who gave them such a feast. But Dag said little about it. The king used often to speak to Dag, and ask him about various things; and he had proved the truth of all that Dag had said, both of things that had happened or were to happen, and therefore the king had much confidence in what he said. The king called Dag to him to have a private conversation together, and spoke to him about many things. Afterwards the king turned the conversation on Thore,—what an excellent man Thore was, and what a superb feast he had made for them. Dag answered but little to this, but agreed it was true what the king said. The king then asked Dag what disposition or faith he found in Thore. Dag replied that he must certainly consider Thore of a good disposition, if he be really what most people believe him to be. The king told him to answer direct what he was asked, and said that it was his duty to do so. Dag replies, "Then thou must allow me to determine the punishment if I disclose his faith." The king replied that he would not submit his decision to another man, but again ordered Dag to reply to what he asked.

Dag replies, "The sovereign's order goes before all. I find this disposition in Thore, as in so many others, that he is too greedy of money."

The king:—"Is he then a thief, or a robber?"

"He is neither."

"What is he then?"

"To win money he is a traitor to his sovereign. He has taken money from King Canute the Great for thy head."

The king asks, "What proof hast thou of the truth of this?"

Dag:—"He has upon his right arm, above the elbow, a thick gold ring, which King Canute gave him, and which he lets no man see."

This ended their conference, and the king was very wroth.

Now as the king sat at table, and the guests had drunk a while with great mirth, and Thore went round to see the guests well served, the king ordered Thore to be called to him. He went up before the table, and laid his hands upon it.

The king asked, " How old a man art thou, Thore? "

He answered, " I am eighteen years old."

" A stout man thou art for those years, and thou hast been fortunate also."

Then the king took his right hand, and felt it towards the elbow.

Thore said, " Take care, for I have a boil upon my arm."

The king held his hand there, and felt there was something hard under it. " Hast thou not heard," said he, " that I am a physician? Let me see the boil."

As Thore saw it was of no use to conceal it longer, he took off the ring and laid it on the table.

The king asked if that was the gift of King Canute.

Thore replied that he could not deny it was.

The king ordered him to be seized and laid in irons. Kalf came up and entreated for mercy, and offered money for him, which also was seconded by many; but the king was so wroth that nobody could get in a word. He said Thore should suffer the doom he had prepared for himself. Thereupon he ordered Thore to be killed. This deed was much detested in the Uplands, and not less in the Drontheim country, where many of Thore's connections were. Kalf took the death of this man much to heart, for he had been his foster-son in childhood.

CHAPTER CLXXVI. THE FALL OF GRIOTGARD.—Griotgard Olvesson, Thore's brother, and the eldest of the brothers, was a very wealthy man, and had a great troop of people about him. He lived also at this time in Hedemark. When he heard that Thore had been killed, he made an attack upon the places where the king's goods and men were; but, between whiles, he kept himself in the forest and other secret places. When the king heard of this disturbance, he had inquiry made about Griotgard's haunts, and found out that he had taken up night-quarters not far from where the king was. King Olaf set out in the night-time, came there about day-dawn, and placed a circle of men round the house in which Griotgard was sleeping. Griotgard and his men, roused by the stir of people and clash of arms, ran to their weapons, and Griotgard himself sprang to the front room. He asked who commanded the troop; and it was answered him,

" King Olaf was come there." Griotgard asked if the king
would hear his words. The king, who stood at the door, said
that Griotgard might speak what he pleased, and he would hear
his words. Griotgard said, " I do not beg for mercy; " and at
the same moment he rushed out, having his shield over his head
and his drawn sword in his hand. It was not so much light that
he could see clearly. He struck his sword at the king; but
Arnbiorn Arneson ran in, and the thrust pierced him under his
armour into his stomach, and Arnbiorn got his death-wound.
Griotgard was killed immediately, and most of his people with
him. After this event the king turned back to the south to
Viken.

CHAPTER CLXXVII. KING OLAF SENDS FOR HIS SHIPS AND
GOODS.—Now when the king came to Tunsberg he sent men out
to all the districts, and ordered the people out upon a levy. He
had but a small provision of shipping, and there were only
bonders' vessels to be got. From the districts in the near neighbourhood many people came to him, but few from any distance;
and it was soon found that the people had turned away from the
king. King Olaf sent people to Gotland for his ships, and other
goods and wares which had been left there in autumn; but the
progress of these men was very slow, for it was no better now
than in autumn to sail through the Sound, as King Canute had
in spring fitted out an army throughout the whole of the Danish
dominions and had no fewer than 1200 (*i.e.* 1440) vessels.

CHAPTER CLXXVIII. KING OLAF'S COUNSELS.—The news
came to Norway that King Canute had assembled an immense
armament through all Denmark, with which he intended to
conquer Norway. When this became known the people were
less willing to join King Olaf, and he got but little aid from the
bonders. The king's men often spoke about this among themselves. Sigvat tells of it thus:—

> " Our men are few, our ships are small,
>   While England's king is strong in all;
>   But yet our king is not afraid—
>   O! never be such king betrayed!
>   'Tis evil counsel to deprive
>   Our king of countrymen to strive
>   To save their country, sword in hand:
>   'Tis money that betrays our land."

The king held meetings with the men of the court, and sometimes House-things with all his people, and consulted with them

what they should, in their opinion, undertake. "We must not conceal from ourselves," said he, "that Canute will come here this summer; and that he has, as ye all know, a large force, and we have at present but few men to oppose to him; and, as matters now stand, we cannot depend much on the fidelity of the country people." The king's men replied to his speech in various ways; but it is said that Sigvat the scald replied thus, advising flight, as treachery, not cowardice, was the cause of it:—

> "We ought to flee, then pay our foe
> For what we wrought of harm and woe.
> I may be blamed, accused of fear;
> But treachery, not faith, rules here.
> Men may retire who long have shown
> Their faith and love, and now alone
> Retire because they cannot save—
> This is no treachery in the brave."

CHAPTER CLXXIX. HAREK OF THIOTTO BURNS GRANKEL AND HIS MEN.—The same spring it happened in Halogaland that Harek of Thiotto remembered how Asmund Grankelson had plundered and beaten his house-servants. A ten-oared cutter which belonged to Harek was afloat in front of the house, with tent and deck, and he spread the report that he intended to go south to Drontheim. One evening Harek went on board with his house-servants, about eighty men, who rowed the whole night; and he came towards morning to Grankel's house, and surrounded it with his men. They then made an attack on the house and set fire to it; and Grankel with his people were burnt, and some were killed outside; and in all about thirty men lost their lives. After this deed Harek returned home and sat quietly in his farm. Asmund was with King Olaf when he heard of it; therefore there was nobody in Halogaland to sue Harek for mulct for this deed, and also he offered none.

CHAPTER CLXXX. KING CANUTE'S EXPEDITION TO NORWAY.—Canute the Great collected his forces, and went to Lymfjord. When he was ready with his equipment he sailed from thence with his whole fleet to Norway; made all possible speed, and did not land to the eastward of the Fjord, but crossed Folden,[1] and landed in Agder, where he summoned a Thing. The bonders came down from the upper country to hold a Thing with Canute, who was everywhere in that country accepted as king. Then he placed men over the districts, and took hostages from

[1] The mouth of Oslo fjord.

the bonders, and no man opposed him. King Olaf was in Tunsberg when Canute's fleet sailed across the mouth of the fjord. Canute sailed northwards along the coast, and people came to him from all the districts, and promised him fealty. He lay a while in Ekersund, where Erling Skialgsson came to him with many people, and King Canute and Erling renewed their league of friendship. Among other things, Canute promised Erling the whole country between Stad and Rygiarbit [1] to rule over. Then King Canute proceeded; and, to be short in our tale, did not stop until he came to Drontheim, and landed at Nidaros. In Drontheim he called together a Thing for the eight districts, at which King Canute was chosen king of all Norway. Thore Hund, who had come with King Canute from Denmark, was there, and also Harek of Thiotto; and both were made sheriffs of the king, and took the oath of fealty to him. King Canute gave them great fiefs, and also sole right to the Lapland trade, and presented them besides with great gifts. He enriched all men who were inclined to enter into friendly accord with him both with fiefs and money, and gave them greater power than they had before.

CHAPTER CLXXXI. OF KING CANUTE.—When King Canute had laid the whole of Norway under his authority, he called together a numerous Thing, both of his own people and of the people of the country; and at it he made proclamation, that he made his relation Earl Hakon the governor-in-chief of all the land in Norway that he had conquered in this expedition. In like manner he led his son Hardaknut to the high seat at his side, gave him the title of king, and therewith the whole Danish dominion. King Canute took as hostages from all lendermen and great bonders in Norway either their sons, brothers, or other near connections, or the men who were dearest to them and appeared to him most suitable; by which he, as before observed, secured their fidelity to him. As soon as Earl Hakon had attained this power in Norway his brother-in-law, Einar Tambarskelve, made an agreement with him, and received back all the fiefs he formerly had possessed while the earls ruled the country. King Canute gave Einar great gifts, and bound him by great kindness to his interests; and promised that Einar should be the greatest and most important man in Norway, among those who did not hold the highest dignity, as long as he had power over the country. He added to this, that Einar appeared to him the most suitable man to hold the highest title

[1] Now Jernestangen, between the counties of Nedenes and Bratsberg.

of honour in Norway if no earls remained, and his son Eindride also, on account of his high birth. Einar placed a great value on these promises, and, in return, promised the greatest fidelity. Einar's chiefship began anew with this.

CHAPTER CLXXXII. OF THORARIN LOFTUNGE.—There was a man by name Thorarin Loftunge, an Icelander by birth, and a great scald, who had been much with the kings and other great chiefs. He was now with King Canute the Great, and had composed a flokk, or short poem without refrain, in his praise. When the king heard of this he was very angry, and ordered him to bring the next day a drapa, or long poem, by the time he went to table; and if he failed to do so, said the king, " he shall be hanged for his impudence in composing such a small poem about King Canute." Thorarin then composed a stave as a refrain, which he inserted in the poem, and also augmented it with several other strophes or verses. This was the refrain:—

> " Canute protects his realm, as Jove,[1]
> Guardian of Greece, his realm above."

King Canute rewarded him for the poem with fifty marks of silver. The poem was called the " Head-ransom." Thorarin composed another poem about King Canute, which was called the " Campaign Poem; "[2] and therein he tells of King Canute's expedition when he sailed from Denmark to Norway; and the following are strophes from one of the parts of his poem:—

> " Canute with all his men is out,
> Under the heavens in war-ships stout,—
> Out on the sea, from Lymfiord's green,
> My good, my brave friend's fleet is seen.
> The men of Agder on the coast
> Tremble to see this mighty host:
> Though once the raven's beak they filled
> With flesh of men whom they had killed.

> " The sight surpasses far the tale,
> As glancing in the sun they sail;
> The king's ship glittering all with gold,
> And splendour there not to be told.
> Round Lyster many a coal-black mast
> Of Canute's fleet is gliding past.
> And now through Eyka sound they ride,
> Upon the gently heaving tide.

[1] A mistaken paraphrase; the " Guardian of Greece " is Christ, as Snorri says in his *Edda*.

[2] *Tøgdrápa :* the precise meaning of this title is not known, but it may be connected with the name of the metre (*Tøglag*), of which this poem is the oldest known example; it has four syllables to the line, and much internal rhyme and assonance.

" And all the sound is covered o'er
With ships and sails, from shore to shore,
A mighty king, a mighty host,
Hiding the sea on Eyka coast.[1]
And peaceful men in haste now hie
Up Hiorngla-hill [2] the fleet to spy,
As round the ness where Stade lies
Each high-stemmed ship in splendour flies.

" Nor seemed the voyage long, I trow,
To warrior on the high-built bow,
As o'er the ocean-mountains riding
The land and hills seem past him gliding.
With whistling breeze and flashing spray
Past Stim [3] the gav ships dashed away;
In open sea, the southern gale
Filled every wide out-bellying sail.

" Still on they fly, still northwards go,
Till he who conquers every foe,
The mighty Canute, came to land,
Far in the north on Drontheim's strand.
There this great king of Jutland race,
Whose deeds and gifts surpass in grace
All other kings', bestowed the throne
Of Norway on his sister's son.

" To his own son he gave the crown
(This I must add o his renown)
Of Denmark—Canute's shield is red
And wet with blood in battle shed."

Here it is told that King Canute's expedition was grander
than saga can tell; but Thorarin sang thus, because he would
pride himself upon being one of King Canute's retinue when
he came to Norway.

CHAPTER CLXXXIII. OF THE MESSENGERS SENT BY KING
OLAF FOR HIS SHIPS.—The men whom King Olaf had sent eastwards to Gotland after his ships took with them the vessels they
thought the best, and burnt the rest. The ship-apparel and
other goods belonging to the king and his men they also took with
them; and when they heard that King Canute had gone to
Norway they sailed west (north) through Ore Sound, and then
north to Viken to King Olaf, to whom they delivered his ships.
He was then at Tunsberg. When King Olaf learnt that King
Canute was sailing north along the coast, King Olaf steered
with his fleet into Oslo fjord, and into a branch of it called

[1] Ekersund, south of Stavanger.
[2] Tjœrnaglen in Söndhordland.
[3] Now Stenmet, a mountain on the boundary between Romsdal and
Nordmöre.

Drafn, where he lay quiet until King Canute's fleet had sailed southwards again. On this expedition which King Canute made from the North along the coast, he held a Thing in each district, and in every Thing the country was bound by oath in fealty to him, and hostages were given him. He went eastward across the mouths of the fjords to Sarpsborg, and held a Thing there, and, as elsewhere, the country was surrendered to him under oath of fidelity. King Canute then returned south to Denmark, after having conquered Norway without stroke of sword, and he ruled now over three kingdoms. So says Halvard Hareksblese when he sang of King Canute:—

> " The warrior-king, whose blood-stain'd shield
> Has shone on many a hard-fought field,
> England and Denmark now has won,
> And o'er three kingdoms rules alone.
> Peace now he gives us fast and sure,
> Since Norway too is made secure
> By him who oft, in days of yore,
> Glutted the hawk and wolf with gore."

CHAPTER CLXXXIV. OF KING OLAF AND HIS PROCEEDINGS. —King Olaf sailed with his ships out to Tunsberg, as soon as he heard that King Canute had turned back, and was gone south to Denmark. He then made himself ready with the men who liked to follow him, and had then thirteen ships. Afterwards he sailed out along Viken; but got little money, and few men, as those only followed him who dwelt in islands, or on outlying points of land. The king landed in such places, but got only the money and men that fell in his way; and he soon perceived that the country had abandoned him. He proceeded on according to the winds. This was in the beginning of winter. The wind turned very late in the season in their favour, so that they lay long in the Sel Islands,[1] where they heard the news from the North, through merchants, who told the king that Erling Skialgsson had collected a great force in Jœderen, and that his ship lay fully rigged outside of the land, together with many other vessels belonging to the bonders; namely, skiffs, fisher-yachts, and great row-boats. Then the king sailed with his fleet from the East, and lay a while in Ekersund. Both parties heard of each other now, and Erling assembled all the men he could.

CHAPTER CLXXXV. OF KING OLAF'S VOYAGE [1028].—On

[1] The manuscripts read " Sól Isles," which are unknown; the Sel Isles are a little north-west of the Naze.

Thomasmas (21st December), before Yule, the king left the harbour as soon as day appeared. With a good but rather strong gale he sailed northwards past Jœderen. The weather was rainy, with dark flying clouds in the sky. The spies went immediately in through the Jœderen country when the king sailed past it; and soon as Erling heard that the king was sailing past from the East, he let the war-horn call all the people on board, and the whole force hastened to the ships, and prepared for battle. The king's ship passed by Jœderen at a great rate; but thereafter turned in towards the land, intending to run up the fjords to gather men and money. Erling Skialgsson perceived this, and sailed after him with a great force and many ships. Swiftly their vessels flew, for they had nothing on board but men and arms; but Erling's ship went much faster than the others; therefore he took in a reef in the sails, and waited for the other vessels. Then the king saw that Erling with his fleet gained upon him fast; for the king's ships were heavily laden, and were besides water-soaked, having been in the sea the whole summer, autumn, and winter, up to this time. He saw also that the odds would be much against him, if he should go against the whole of Erling's fleet when it was assembled. He hailed from ship to ship the orders to let the sails gently sink, and to unship the booms and out-riggers, which was done. When Erling saw this he calls out to his people, and orders them to get on more sail. " Ye see," says he, " that their sails are diminishing, and they are getting fast away from our sight." He took the reef out of the sails of his ship, and outsailed all the others immediately; for Erling was very eager in his pursuit of King Olaf.

CHAPTER CLXXXVI. OF ERLING SKIALGSSON'S FALL.—
King Olaf then steered in towards Böken,[1] by which the ships came out of sight of each other. Thereafter the king ordered his men to strike the sails, and row forwards through a narrow sound that was there, and all the ships lay collected within a rocky point. Then all the king's men put on their weapons. Erling sailed in through the sound, and observed nothing until the whole fleet was before him, and he saw the king's men rowing towards him with all their ships at once. Erling and his crew let fall the sails, and seized their weapons; but the king's fleet surrounded his ship on all sides. Then the fight began, and it was of the sharpest; but soon the greatest loss

[1] Store Bokn.

was among Erling's men. Erling stood on the quarter-deck
of his ship. He had a helmet on his head, a shield before him,
and a sword in his hand. Sigvat the scald had remained behind
in Viken, and heard the tidings. He was a great friend of Erling,
had received presents from him, and had been at his house.
Sigvat composed a poem upon Erling's fall, in which there is the
following verse:—

> " Erling has set his ship on sea—
> Against the king away is he:
> He who oft lets the eagle stain
> Her yellow feet in blood of slain.
> His little war-ship side by side
> With the king's fleet, the fray will bide.
> Now sword to sword the fight is raging,
> Which Erling with the king is waging."

Then Erling's men began to fall, and at the same moment his
ship was carried by boarding, and every man of his died in his
place. The king himself was among the foremost in the fray.
So says Sigvat:—

> " The bold king hewed with hasty sword,—
> The king urged on the ship to board,—
> All o'er the decks the wounded lay:
> Right fierce and bloody was that fray.
> In Tunger sound,[1] on Jœderen shore,
> The decks were slippery with red gore;
> Warm blood was dropping in the sound,
> Where the king's sword was gleaming round."

So entirely had Erling's men fallen, that not a man remained
standing in his ship but himself alone; for there was none who
asked for quarter, or none who got it if he did ask. There was
no opening for flight, for there lay ships all round Erling's ship
on every side, and it is told for certain that no man attempted
to fly; and Sigvat says:—

> " All Erling's men fell in the fray,
> Off Böken Isle, this hard-fought day.
> The brave king boarded, onward cheered,
> And north of Tung the deck was cleared.
> Erling alone, the brave, the stout,
> Cut off from all, yet still held out;
> High on the stern—a sight to see—
> In his lone ship alone stood he."

Then Erling was attacked both from the forecastle and from
the other ships. There was a large space upon the poop which
stood high above the other ships, and which nobody could reach
but by arrow-shot, or partly with the thrust of spear, but which

[1] Tunger, the islands north of Tungenes.

he always struck from him by parrying. Erling defended himself so manfully, that no example is known of one man having sustained the attack of so many men so long. Yet he never tried to get away, nor asked for quarter. So says Sigvat:—

> " Skialg's brave son no mercy craves,—
> The battle's fury still he braves;
> The spear-storm, through the air sharp singing,
> Against his shield was ever ringing.
> So Erling stood; but fate had willed
> His life off Böken should be spilled.
> No braver man has, since his day,
> Past Böken Island ta'en his way."

When Olaf went back a little upon the fore-deck he saw Erling's behaviour; and the king accosted him thus:—" Thou hast turned to face me to-day, Erling."

He replies, " Eagles stand face to face to claw each other." Sigvat the scald tells thus of these words of Erling:—

> " Erling, our best defence of old,—
> Erling the brave, the brisk, the bold,—
> Cried boldly in that fearsome place:
> ' Let eagles claw now, face to face! '
> It was the truth that there he spoke
> To Olaf, when the battle broke
> At Utstein,[1]—battle once he sought,
> And valiantly the hero fought."

Then said the king, " Wilt thou enter into my service, Erling? "

" That I will," said he; took the helmet off his head, laid down his sword and shield, and went forward to the forecastle deck.

The king stuck him in the chin with the sharp point of his battle-axe, and said, " I shall mark thee as a traitor to thy sovereign."

Then Aslak Fitiaskalle rose up, and struck Erling in the head with an axe, so that it stood fast in his brain, and was instantly his death-wound. Thus Erling lost his life.

The king said to Aslak, " May all ill luck attend thee for that stroke; for thou hast struck Norway out of my hands."

Aslak replied, " It is bad enough if that stroke displease thee, for I thought it was striking Norway into thy hands; and if I have given thee offence, sire, by this stroke, and have thy ill-will for it, it will go badly with me, for I will get so many men's ill-will and enmity for this deed that I would need all your protection and favour."

[1] One of the isles to the north of Tungenes.

The king replied that he should have it.

Thereafter the king ordered every man to return to his ship, and make ready for battle as fast as he could; and scarcely was this done before the other vessels ran in from the south into the sound. It went with the bonder army as is often seen, that the men, although many in numbers, know not what to do when they have experienced a check, have lost their chief, and are without leaders. None of Erling's sons were there, and the bonders therefore made no attack, and the king sailed on his way northwards. But the bonders took Erling's corpse, adorned it, and carried it with them home to Sole, and also the bodies of all who had fallen. There was great lamentation over Erling; and it has been a common observation among people, that Erling Skialgsson was the greatest and worthiest man in Norway of those who had no high title. Sigvat made these verses upon the occasion:—

> " Thus Erling fell—and such a gain
> To buy with such a loss was vain;
> For better man than he ne'er died,
> And the king's gain was small beside.
> In truth no man I ever knew
> Was, in all ways, so firm and true;
> Honoured by all; yet soon indeed
> He lost his life—so fate decreed."

Sigvat also says that Aslak had very unthinkingly committed this murder of his own kinsman:—

> " Horland's brave defender's dead!
> Aslak has heaped on his own head
> The guilt of murdering his own kin:
> May few be guilty of such sin!
> His kinsman's murder on him lies—
> Our forefathers, in sayings wise,
> Have said, what is unknown to few,
> ' Kinsmen to kinsmen should be true.' "

CHAPTER CLXXXVII. OF THE INSURRECTION OF AGDER DISTRICT.—Of Erling's sons some at that time were north in Drontheim, some in Hordaland, and some in the Fjords district, for the purpose of collecting men. When Erling's death was reported, the news came also that there was a levy raising in Agder, Hordaland, and Rogaland. Forces were raised and a great army assembled, under Erling's sons, to pursue King Olaf.

When King Olaf sailed away after the battle with Erling, he went northward through the sounds, and it was late in the day. It is related that the king then made the following verses:—

" This night, with battle sounds wild ringing,
Small joy to pale Erling is bringing
Who lies in Jœderen:
Ravens eat
The vanquished corpses for their meat.
His plundering brought him little good!
I leaped aboard in warlike mood,
And there, for my dear country's sake,
I mowed men down for death to take."

Afterwards the king sailed with his fleet along the land north-ward, and got certain tidings of the bonders assembling an army. There were many chiefs and lendermen at this time with King Olaf, and all the sons of Arne. Of this Biorn Guldbraascald speaks in the poem he composed about Kalf Arneson:—

" Kalf! thou hast fought at Böken well;
Of thy brave doings all men tell:
When Harald's son his men urged on
To the hard strife, thy courage shone.
Thou soon hadst made a good Yule feast
For troll-wife's wolf there in the East:
Where stone and spear were flying round,
There thou wast still the foremost found.
The people suffered in the strife
When noble Erling lost his life,
And north of Utstein many a speck
Of blood lay black upon the deck.
The king, 'tis clear, has been deceived,
By treason of his land bereaved;
And Agder now, whose force is great,
Will rule o'er all parts of the state."

King Olaf continued his voyage until he came north of Stad, and brought up at the Herö Isles. Here he heard the news that Earl Hakon had a great war-force in Drontheim, and thereupon the king held a council with his people. Kalf Arneson urged much to advance to Drontheim, and fight Earl Hakon, notwith-standing the difference of numbers. Many others supported this advice, but others dissuaded from it, and the matter was left to the king's judgment.

CHAPTER CLXXXVIII. DEATH OF ASLAK FITIASKALLE.— Afterwards the king went into Steinavaag,[1] and remained there all night; but Aslak Fitiaskalle ran into Borgund,[2] where he remained the night, and where Vigleik Arneson was before him. In the morning, when Aslak was about returning on board, Vigleik assaulted him, and sought to avenge Erling's murder. Aslak fell there. Some of the king's court-men, who had been home all summer, joined the king here. They came from

[1] Between Hessöen and Aspöen, now the westmost part of Aalesund.
[2] A farmstead in Sondmöre.

Frekösund,[1] and brought the king tidings that Earl Hakon, and
many lendermen with him, had come in the morning to Frekösund with a large force; "and they will end thy days, sire, if
they have strength enough." Now the king sent his men up to
a hill that was near; and when they came to the top,[2] and looked
northwards to Björn Island, they perceived that a great armament of many ships was coming from the north, and they hastened back to the king with this intelligence. The king, who
was lying there with only twelve ships, ordered the war-horn
to sound, the tents to be taken down on his ships, and they took
to their oars. When they were quite ready, and were leaving
the harbour, the bonder army sailed north around Thiotande[3]
with twenty-five ships. The king then steered inside of Nörve
Island, and inside of the Hund skerries. Now when King Olaf
came right abreast of Borgund, the ship which Aslak had
steered came out to meet him and, when they found the king,
told him the tidings,—that Vigleik Arneson had killed Aslak
Fitiaskalle, because he had killed Erling Skialgsson. The king
took this news very angrily, but could not delay his voyage on
account of the enemy, and he sailed in by Vegsund[4] and Skottet.
There some of his people left him; among others, Kalf Arneson,
with many other lendermen and ship commanders, who all went
to meet Earl Hakon. King Olaf, however, proceeded on his
way without stopping until he came to Tcdur fjord, where he
brought up at Valdal, and landed from his ship. He had then
five ships with him, which he drew up upon the shore, and took
care of their sails and materials. Then he set up his land tent
upon a point of land called Sult,[5] where there are pretty flat
fields, and set up a cross near to the point of land. A bonder,
by name Bruse, who dwelt there in Möre,[6] and was chief over
the valley, came down to King Olaf, together with many other
bonders, and received him well, and according to his dignity;
and he was friendly, and pleased with their reception of him.
Then the king asked if there was a passable road up in the
country from the valley to Lesje; and Bruse replied, that there
was a slope in the valley called Sessur[7] not passable for man or
beast. King Olaf answers, "That we must try, bonder, and it

---

[1] The sound between Frökö and the mainland in the north-west of
Romsdalen.
[2] Sukkertoppen on Hessöen.   [3] Now Kverven.
[4] Between Sulö and Oxenö.
[5] Now Sylte on the Tafjord.
[6] Now Muri on the west bank of the river.
[7] Now Skjœrsuren on the north of the river near Gröning.

will go as God pleases. Come here in the morning with your yoke, and come yourself with it, and let us then see, when we come to the sloping precipice, what chance there may be, and if we cannot devise some means of coming over it with horses and people."

CHAPTER CLXXXIX. CLEARING OF THE ROAD [1029].—Now when day broke the bonders drove down with their yokes, as the king had told them. The clothes and weapons were packed upon horses, but the king and all the people went on foot. He went thus until he came to a place called Kros-Brekke;[1] and when he came up upon the hill he rested himself, sat down there a while, looked down over the fjord, and said, "A difficult expedition ye have thrown upon my hands, ye lendermen, who have now changed your fealty, although but a little while ago ye were my friends and faithful to me." There are now two crosses erected upon the bank on which the king sat.[2] Then the king mounted a horse, and rode without stopping up the valley, until he came to the precipice. Then the king asked Bruse if there was no summer hut of cattle-herds[3] in the neighbourhood, where they could remain. He said there was.[4] The king ordered his land-tent to be set up, and remained there all night. In the morning the king ordered them to drive to the steep slope, and try if they could get across it with the waggons. They drove there, and the king remained in the meantime in his tent. Towards evening the king's court-men and the bonders came back, and told how they had had a very fatiguing labour, without making any progress, and that there never could be a road made that they could get across; so they continued there the second night, during which, for the whole night, the king was occupied in prayer. As soon as he observed day dawning he ordered his men to drive again to the steep, and try once more if they could get across it with the waggons; but they went very unwillingly, saying nothing could be gained by it. When they were gone the man who had charge of the king's kitchen came, and said there were only two carcasses of young cattle remaining of provision: "although you, sire, have 300 men, and there are 100 bonders besides." Then the king ordered that he should set

[1] Now Langbrekke.
[2] A timber cross was still standing in 1760. An iron cross stands on the spot with a modern inscription.
[3] *Sel—sæter* in Norwegian—is a shieling, *i.e.* a hut for herdsmen keeping cattle on the mountain summer pastures.
[4] Now Alstadsœteren or Uren on the south side of Skjœrsuren.

all the kettles on the fire and put a little bit of meat in each kettle, which was done. Then the king went there, and made the sign of the cross over each kettle, and told them to make ready the meat. The king then went to the steep slope called Sessur, where a road should be cleared. When the king came all his people were sitting down, quite worn out with the hard labour. Bruse said, " I told you, sire, but you would not believe me, that we could make nothing of this steep." The king laid aside his cloak, and told them to go to work once more at the steep slope. They did so, and now twenty men could handle stones which before 100 men could not move from the place; and thus before mid-day the road was cleared so well, that it was as passable for men, and for horses with packs, as a road in the plain fields. The king, after this, went down again to where the meat was, which place is still called Olaf's Slabs.[1] Near the Slabs there is a spring, at which Olaf washed himself; and therefore at the present day, when the cattle in the valley are sick, their illness is made better by their drinking at this well. Thereafter the king sat down to table with all the others; and when he was satisfied he asked if there was any other shieling on the other side of the steep, and near the mountains, where they could pass the night. Bruse said there was such a shieling, called Grönningen; [2] but that nobody could pass the night there on account of witchcraft, and evil beings who were in the shieling. Then the king said they must get ready for their journey, as he wanted to be at the shieling for the night. Then came the kitchen-master to the king, and tells that there was come an extraordinary supply of provisions, and he did not know where it had come from, or how. The king thanked God for this blessing, and gave the bonders who drove down again to their valley some rations of food, but remained himself all night in the shieling. In the middle of the night, while the people were asleep, there was heard in the cattle-fold a dreadful cry, and these words: " Now Olaf's prayers are burning me," says the spirit, " so that I can no longer be in my habitation; now must I fly, and never more come to this fold." When the king's people awoke in the morning the king proceeded to the mountains, and said to Bruse, " Here shall now a farm be settled, and the bonder who dwells here shall never want what is needful for the support of life; and never shall his crop be destroyed by frost, although the crops be frozen on the farms both above it and

[1] The place is still called Hellaren or Olafshelleren (The Olaf Slab).
[2] Now the farm of Gröning.

below it." Then the king proceeded over the mountains, and
came to a farm called Einbö,[1] where he remained for the night.
King Olaf had then been fifteen years king of Norway, including
the year both he and Swend were in the country, and this year
we have now been telling about. It was, namely, a little past
Yule when the king left his ships and took to the land, as before
related. Of this portion of his reign the priest Are Thorgilson
the Wise was the first who wrote; and he was both faithful in his
story, of a good memory, and so old a man that he could remember
the men, and had heard their accounts, who were so old that
through their age they could remember these circumstances as he
himself wrote them in his books, and he named the men from
whom he received his information. Otherwise it is generally said
that King Olaf had been fifteen years king of Norway when he
fell; but they who say so reckon to Earl Swend's government
the last year he was in the country, for King Olaf lived fifteen
years afterwards as king.

CHAPTER CXC. OLAF'S PROPHECIES.—When the king had
been one night in Lesje he proceeded on his journey with his
men, day by day; first into Gudbrandsdal, and from thence
out to Hedemark. Now it was seen who had been his friends,
for they followed him; but those who had served him with
less fidelity separated from him, and some showed him even
indifference, or even full hostility, which afterwards was apparent; and also it could be seen clearly in many Upland people
that they took very ill his putting Thore to death, as before related
[p. 322]. King Olaf gave leave to return home to many of his
men who had farms and children to take care of; for it seemed
to them uncertain what safety there might be for the families
and property of those who left the country with him. Then the
king explained to his friends his intention of leaving the country, and going first east into Sweden, and there taking his determination as to where he should go: but he let his friends know
his intention to return to the country, and regain his kingdom,
if God should grant him longer life; and he did not conceal his
expectation that the people of Norway would again return to
their fealty to him. "I think," says he, "that Earl Hakon will
have Norway but a short time under his power, which many will
not think an extraordinary expectation, as Earl Hakon has had
but little luck against me: but probably few people will trust
to my prophecy, that Canute the Great will in the course of a

[1] High up in Lesjeskogen under the fjeld.

few years die, and his kingdoms vanish; and there will be no risings in favour of his race." When the king had ended his speech, his men prepared themselves for their departure. The king, with the troop that followed him, turned east to Eida forest. And there were along with him the Queen Astrid; their daughter Ulfhild; Magnus, King Olaf's son; Ragnvald Brusesson; the three sons of Arne, Thorberg, Finn, and Arne, with many lendermen; and the king's attendants consisted of many chosen men. Biorn the marshal got leave to go home, and he went to his farm, and many others of the king's friends returned home with his permission to their farms. The king begged them to let him know the events which might happen in the country, and which it might be important for him to know: and now the king proceeded on his way.

CHAPTER CXCI. KING OLAF PROCEEDS TO RUSSIA.—It is to be related of King Olaf's journey, that he went first from Norway eastward through Eida forest to Vermeland, then to Vatsbu,[1] and through the forests in which there are roads, until he came out in Nerike district. There dwelt a rich and powerful man in that [2] part called Sigtryg, who had a son, Ivar, who afterwards became a distinguished person. Olaf stayed with Sigtryg all spring; and when summer came he made ready for a journey, procured a ship for himself, and without stopping went on to Russia to King Jarisleif and his queen Ingigerd; but his own queen Astrid, and their daughter Ulfhild, remained behind in Sweden, and the king took his son Magnus eastward with him. King Jarisleif received King Olaf in the kindest manner, and made him the offer to remain with him, and to have so much land as was necessary for defraying the expense of the entertainment of his followers. King Olaf accepted this offer thankfully, and remained there. It is related that King Olaf was distinguished all his life for pious habits, and zeal in his prayers to God. But afterwards, when he saw his own power diminished, and that of his adversaries augmented, he turned all his mind to God's service; for he was not distracted by other thoughts, or by the labour he formerly had upon his hands, for during all the time he sat upon the throne he was endeavouring to promote what was most useful: and first to free and protect the country from foreign chiefs' oppressions, then to convert the people

---

[1] The most northerly district in West Gotland, south of Tiveden.
[2] The king had to pass over a part of Venern to Vatsbu and thence via Tiveden to Nerike.

to the right faith; and also to establish law and the rights of the country, which he did by letting justice have its way, and punishing evil-doers.

CHAPTER CXCII. CAUSES OF THE REVOLT AGAINST KING OLAF.—It had been an old custom in Norway that the sons of lendermen, or other great men, went out in war-ships to gather property, and they marauded both in the country and out of the country. But after King Olaf came to the sovereignty he protected the country, so that he abolished all plundering there; and even if they were the sons of powerful men who committed any depredation, or did what the king considered against law, he did not spare them at all, but they must suffer in life or limbs; and no man's entreaties, and no offer of money-penalties, could help them. So says Sigvat:—

> " They who on viking cruises drove
> With gifts of red gold often strove
> To buy their safety—but our chief
> Had no compassion for the thief.
> He made the bravest lose his head
> Who robbed at sea, and pirates led;
> And his just sword gave peace to all,
> Sparing no robber, great or small."

And he also says:—

> " Great king! whose sword on many a field
> Food to the wandering wolf did yield,
> And then the thief and pirate band
> Swept wholly off by sea and land—
> Good king! who for the people's sake
> Set hands and feet upon a stake,
> When plunderers of great name and bold
> Harried the country as of old.

> " The country's guardian showed his might
> When oft he made his just sword bite
> Through many a viking's neck and hair,
> And never would the guilty spare.
> King Magnus' father, I must say,
> Did many a good deed in his day.
> Olaf the Thick was stern and stout,
> Much good his victories brought out."

He punished great and small with equal severity, which appeared to the chief people of the country too severe; and animosity rose to the highest when they lost relatives by the king's just sentence, although they were in reality guilty. This was the origin of the hostility of the great men of the country to King Olaf, that they could not bear his just judgments. He again would rather renounce his dignity than omit righteous judgment. The accusation against him, of being stingy with his money, was not just, for he was a most generous man towards his friends; but that alone was the cause of the discontent raised against him, that he appeared hard and severe in his retributions. Besides, King Canute offered great sums of money, and the great chiefs were corrupted by this, and by his offering them greater dignities than they had possessed before. The inclinations of the people, also, were all in favour of Earl Hakon, who was much beloved by the country folks when he ruled the country before.

CHAPTER CXCIII. OF JOKUL BARDSON.—Earl Hakon had sailed with his fleet from Drontheim, and gone south to Möre against King Olaf, as before related [p. 334]. Now when the king bore away, and ran into the fjord, the earl followed him thither; and then Kalf Arneson came to meet him, with many of the men who had deserted King Olaf. Kalf was well received. The earl steered in through Todarfjord to Valdal, where the king had laid up his ships on the strand. He took the ships which belonged to the king, had them put upon the water and rigged, and cast lots, and put commanders in charge of them according to the lots. There was a man called Jokul, who was an Icelander, a son of Bard Jokulson of Vatsdal: [1] the lot fell upon Jokul to command the Bison, which King Olaf himself had commanded. Jokul made these verses upon it:—

> " Mine is the lot to take the helm
> Which Olaf owned, who owned the realm;
> No girl shall hear that I feel fear—
> I'm used to storms and ocean-deer.
> O lady of the golden rings!
> The ship I sail was once the king's,
> But victory was snatched away
> From Olaf's grasp one summer day."

We may here shortly tell what happened a long time after,— that this Jokul fell in with King Olaf's men in the island of Gotland, and the king ordered him to be taken out to be beheaded. A willow twig accordingly was plaited in with his hair, and a man held him fast by it. Jokul sat down upon a bank, and a man swung the axe to execute him; but Jokul hearing the sound, raised his head, and the blow struck him in the head, and made a dreadful wound. As the king saw it would be his death-

[1] For an account of this family see *Vatzdæla Saga* (trans. Gwyn Jones, *The Vatnsdalers' Saga*, 1944).

wound, he ordered them to let him lie with it. Jokul raised himself up, and he sang:—

> " My hard fate I mourn,—
> Alas! my wounds burn,
> My red wounds are gaping,
> My life-blood escaping.
> My wounds burn sore;
> But I suffer still more
> From the king's angry word,
> Than his sharp-biting sword."

CHAPTER CXCIV. OF KALF ARNESON.—Kalf Arneson went with Earl Hakon north to Drontheim, and the earl invited him to enter into his service. Kalf said he would first go home to his farm of Egge, and afterwards make his determination; and Kalf did so. When he came home he found his wife Sigrid much irritated; and she reckoned up all the sorrow inflicted on her, as she insisted, by King Olaf. First, he had ordered her first husband Olve to be killed. " And now since," says she, " my two sons; and thou thyself, Kalf, wert present when they were cut off, and which I little expected from thee." Kalf says, it was much against his will that Thore was killed. " I offered money-penalty for him," says he; " and when Griot-gard was killed, I lost my brother Arnbiorn at the same time." She replies, " It is well thou hast suffered this from the king; for thou mayst perhaps avenge him, although thou wilt not avenge my injuries. Thou sawest how thy foster-son Thore was killed, with all the regard of the king for thee." She frequently brought out such vexatious speeches to Kalf, to which he often answered angrily; but yet he allowed himself to be persuaded by her to enter into the earl's service, on condition of renewing his fiefs to him. Sigrid sent word to the earl how far she had brought the matter with Kalf. As soon as the earl heard of it, he sent a message to Kalf that he should come to the town to him. Kalf did not decline the invitation, but came directly to Nidaros, and waited on the earl who received him kindly. In their conversation it was fully agreed upon that Kalf should go into the earl's service, and should receive great fiefs. After this Kalf returned home, and had the greater part of the interior of the Drontheim country under him. As soon as it was spring Kalf rigged out a ship that belonged to him, and when she was ready he put to sea, and sailed west to England; for he had heard that in spring King Canute was to sail from Denmark to England, and that King

Canute had given **Harald,** a son of Thorkel the Tall, an earldom in Denmark. Kalf Arneson went to King Canute as soon as he arrived in England. Biorn Guldbraascald tells of this:—

> " King Olaf eastward o'er the sea
> To Russia's monarch had to flee;
> Our Harald's brother ploughed the main,
> And furrowed white its dark-blue plain.
> Whilst thou—the truth I still will say,
> Nor fear nor favour can me sway—
> Thou to King Canute hastened fast,
> As soon as Olaf's luck was past."

Now when Kalf came to King Canute the king received him particularly well, and had many conversations with him. Among other things, King Canute, in a conference, asked Kalf to bind himself to raise a warfare against King Olaf, if ever he should return to the country. " And for which," says the king, " I will give thee the earldom, and place thee to rule over Norway; and my relation Hakon shall come to me, which will suit him better, for he is so honourable and trustworthy that I believe he would not even throw a spear against the person of King Olaf if he came back to the country." Kalf lent his ear to what the king proposed, for he had a great desire to attain this high dignity; and this conclusion was settled upon between King Canute and Kalf. Kalf then prepared to return home, and on his departure he received splendid presents from King Canute. Biorn the scald tells of these circumstances:—

> " Sprung from old earls!—to England's lord
> Thou owest many a thankful word
> For many a gift: if all be true,
> Thy interest has been kept in view;
> For when thy course was bent for home,
> (To no small things thy life may come)
> ' That Norway should be thine,' 'tis said,
> The London king a promise made."

Kalf thereafter returned to Norway, and came to his farm.

CHAPTER CXCV. OF THE DEATH OF EARL HAKON. — Earl Hakon left the country this summer, and went to England, and when he came there was well received by the king. The earl had a bride in England, and he travelled to conclude this marriage; and as he intended holding his wedding in Norway, he came to procure those things for it in England which it was difficult to get in Norway. In autumn he made ready for his return, but it was somewhat late before he was clear for sea; but at last he set out. Of his voyage all that can be told is, that the vessel was lost, and not a man escaped. Some relate that the vessel was seen north of Caithness in the evening in a heavy storm, and the wind blowing out of Pentland Firth. They who believe this report say the vessel drove out among the breakers of the ocean; [1] but with certainty people knew only that Earl Hakon was missing in the ocean, and nothing belonging to the ship ever came to land. The same autumn some merchants came to Norway, who told the tidings that were going through the country of Earl Hakon being missing; and all men knew that he neither came to Norway nor to England that autumn, so that Norway that winter was without a head. [2]

CHAPTER CXCVI. OF BIORN THE MARSHAL. — Biorn the marshal sat at home on his farm after his parting from King Olaf. Biorn was a celebrated man; therefore it was soon reported far and wide that he had set himself down in quietness. Earl Hakon and the other chiefs of the country heard this also, and sent persons with a verbal message to Biorn. When the messengers arrived Biorn received them well; and afterwards Biorn called them to him to a conference, and asked their business. He who was their foreman presented to Biorn the salutations of King Canute, Earl Hakon, and of several chiefs. "K: g Canute," says he, "has heard much of thee, and that thou iast been long a follower of King Olaf the Thick, and hast been a great enemy of King Canute; and this he thinks not right, for he will be thy friend, and the friend of all worthy men, if thou wilt turn from thy friendship to King Olaf and become his enemy. And the only thing now thou canst do is to seek friendship and protection there where it is most readily to be found, and which all men in this northern world think it most honourable to be favoured with. Ye who have followed Olaf the Thick should consider how he is now separated from you; and that now ye have no aid against King Canute and his men, whose lands ye plundered last summer, and whose friends ye murdered. Therefore ye ought to accept, with thanks, the friendship which the king offers you; and it would become you better if you offered money even in mulct to obtain it."

When he had ended his speech Biorn replies, "I wish now to sit quietly at home, and not to enter into the service of any chief."

[1] Literally, "into the *svelgr*"—the whirlpool near Swona in the Pentland Firth. It is still called *Swelchie*.
[2] The earl was to be married to Canute's niece, Gunhild.

The messenger answers, " Such men as thou art are just the right men to serve the king; and now I can tell thee there are just two things for thee to choose,—either to depart as outlaw from thy property, and wander about as thy comrade Olaf is doing; or, which is evidently better, to accept King Canute's and Earl Hakon's friendship, become their man, and take the oaths of fealty to them. Receive now thy reward." And he displayed to him a large bag full of English money.

Biorn was a man fond of money, and self-interested; and when he saw the silver he was silent, and reflected with himself what resolution he should take. It seemed to him much to abandon his property, as he did not think it probable that King Olaf would ever have a rising in his favour in Norway. Now when the messenger saw that Biorn's inclinations were turned towards the money, he threw down two thick gold rings, and said, " Take the money at once, Biorn, and swear the oaths to King Canute; for I can promise thee that this money is but a trifle compared to what thou wilt receive if thou followest King Canute."

By the heap of money, the fine promises, and the great presents he was led by covetousness, took the money, went into King Canute's service, and gave the oaths of fealty to King Canute and Earl Hakon, and then the messengers departed.

CHAPTER CXCVII. OF BIORN THE MARSHAL'S JOURNEY.— When Biorn heard the tidings that Earl Hakon was missing he soon altered his mind, and was much vexed with himself for having been a traitor in his fidelity to King Olaf. He thought, now, that he was freed from the oath by which he had bound himself to Earl Hakon. It seemed to Biorn that now there was some hope that King Olaf might again come to the throne of Norway if he came back, as the country was without a head. Biorn therefore immediately made himself ready to travel, and took some men with him. He then set out on his journey, travelling night and day, on horseback when he could, and by ship when he found occasion; and never halted until he came east to Russia to King Olaf, who was very glad to see Biorn. Then the king inquired much about the news from Norway. Biorn tells him that Earl Hakon was missing, and the kingdom left without a head. At this news the men who had followed King Olaf were very glad,—all who had left property, connections, and friends in Norway; and the longing for home was awakened in them. Biorn told King Olaf much news from

Norway, and very anxious the king was to know, and asked much how his friends had kept their fidelity towards him. Biorn answered, it had gone differently with different people.

Then Biorn stood up, fell at the king's feet, held his foot, and said, " All is in your power, sire, and in God's! I have taken money from King Canute's men, and sworn them the oaths of fealty; but now will I follow thee, and not part from thee so long as we both live."

The king replies, " Stand up, Biorn: thou shalt be reconciled with me; but reconcile thy perjury with God. I can see that but few men in Norway have held fast by their fealty, when such men as thou art could be false to me. But true it is also that people sit in great danger when I am distant, and they are exposed to the wrath of my enemies."

Biorn then reckoned up those who had principally bound themselves to rise in hostility against the king and his men; and named, among others, Erling's son in Jœderen and their connections, Einar Tambarskelve, Kalf Arneson, Thore Hund, and Harek of Thiotto.

CHAPTER CXCVIII. OF KING OLAF.—After King Olaf came to Russia he was very thoughtful, and weighed what counsel he now should follow. King Jarisleif and Queen Ingigerd offered him to remain with them, and receive a kingdom called Vulgaria,[1] which is a part of Russia, and in which land the people were still heathen. King Olaf thought over this offer; but when he proposed it to his men they dissuaded him from settling himself there, and urged the king to betake himself to Norway to his own kingdom: but the king himself had resolved almost in his own mind to lay down his royal dignity, to go out into the world to Jerusalem, or other holy places, and to enter into some order of monks. But yet the thought lay deep in his soul to recover again, if there should be any opportunity for him, his kingdom in Norway. When he thought over this, it recurred to his mind how all things had gone prosperously with him during the first ten years of his reign, and how afterwards everything he undertook became heavy, difficult, and hard; and that he had been unlucky on all occasions in which he had tried his luck. On this account he doubted if it would be prudent to depend so much upon his luck, as to go with so little strength into the hands of his enemies, seeing that all the people of the

---

[1] Vulgaria was not the present Bulgaria; but the present Russian province Casan, on the east of the Volga, with its capital Bolghar.

country had taken part with them to oppose King Olaf. Such cares he had often on his mind, and he left his cause to God, praying that he would do what to him seemed best. These thoughts he turned over in his mind, and knew not what to resolve upon; for he saw how evidently dangerous that was which his inclination was most bent upon.

CHAPTER CXCIX. OF KING OLAF'S DREAM.—One night the king lay awake in his bed, thinking with great anxiety about his determination, and at last, being tired of thinking, sleep came over him towards morning; but his sleep was so light that he thought he was awake, and could see all that was doing in the house. Then he saw a great and superb man, in splendid clothes, standing by his bed; and it came into the king's mind that this was King Olaf Trygvesson who had come to him. This man said to him, " Thou art very sick of thinking about thy future resolutions; and it appears to me wonderful that these thoughts should be so tumultuous in thy soul that thou shouldst even think of laying down the kingly dignity which God hath given thee, and of remaining here, and accepting of a kingdom from foreign and unknown kings. Go back rather to that kingdom which thou hast received in heritage, and rule over it with the strength which God hath given thee, and let not thy inferiors take it from thee. It is the glory of a king to be victorious over his enemies, and it is a glorious death to die in battle. Or art thou doubtful if thou hast right on thy side in the strife with thine enemies? Thou must have no doubts, and must not conceal the truth from thyself. Thou must go back to thy country, and God will give open testimony that the kingdom is thine by property." When the king awoke he thought he saw the man's shoulders going out. From this time the king's courage rose, and he fixed firmly his resolution to return to Norway; to which his inclination also tended most, and which he also found was the desire of all his men. He bethought himself also that the country being without a chief could be easily attacked, from what he had heard, and that after he came himself many would turn back towards him. When the king told his determination to his people they all gave it their approbation joyfully.

CHAPTER CC. OF KING OLAF'S HEALING POWERS.—It is related that once upon a time, while King Olaf was in Russia, it happened that the son of an honest widow had a sore boil upon his neck, of which the lad lay very ill; and as he could not swallow any food, there was little hope of his life. The boy's mother went to Queen Ingigerd, with whom she was acquainted, and showed her the lad. The queen said she knew no remedy for it. " Go," said she, " to King Olaf, he is the best physician here; and beg him to lay his hands on thy lad, and bring him my words if he will not otherwise do it." She did as the queen told her; and when she found the king she says to him that her son is dangerously ill of a boil in his neck, and begs him to lay his hand on the boil. The king tells her he is not a physician, and bids her go to where there were physicians. She replies, that the queen had told her to come to him; " and told me to add the request from her, that you would use the remedy you understood, and she said that thou art the best physician here in the town." Then the king took the lad, laid his hands upon his neck, and felt the boil for a long time, until the boy made a very wry face. Then the king took a piece of bread, laid it in the figure of the cross upon the palm of his hand, and put it into the boy's mouth. He swallowed it down, and from that time all the soreness left his neck, and in a few days he was quite well, to the great joy of his mother and all his relations. Then first came Olaf into the repute of having as much healing power in his hands[1] as is ascribed to men who have been gifted by nature with healing by the touch; and afterwards, when his miracles were universally acknowledged, this also was considered one of his miracles.

CHAPTER CCI. KING OLAF BURNS THE WOOD SHAVINGS ON HIS HAND FOR HIS SABBATH BREACH.—It happened one Sunday that the king sat in his high seat at the dinner table, and had fallen into such deep thought that he did not observe how time went. In one hand he had a knife, and in the other a piece of fir-wood from which he cut splinters from time to time. The table-servant stood before him with a bowl in his hands; and seeing what the king was about, and that he was involved in thought, he said, " It is Monday, sire, to-morrow." The king looked at him when he heard this, and then it came into his mind what he was doing on the Sunday. Then the king ordered a lighted candle to be brought him, swept together all the shavings he had made, set them on fire, and let them burn upon

---

[1] The healing powers ascribed to Olaf here and on p. 313 are evidently not regarded by Snorri as miraculous in the fullest sense; a belief that " a king's hands are healing hands " was widespread.

his naked hand; showing thereby that he would hold fast by God's law and commandment, and not trespass without punishment on what he knew to be right.

CHAPTER CCII. OF KING OLAF. — When King Olaf had resolved on his return home, he made known his intention to King Jarisleif and Queen Ingigerd. They dissuaded him from this expedition, and said he should receive as much power in their dominions as he thought desirable; but begged him not to put himself within the reach of his enemies with so few men as he had. Then King Olaf told them of his dream; adding, that he believed it to be God's will and providence that it should be so. Now when they found he was determined on travelling to Norway, they offered him all the assistance to his journey that he would accept from them. The king thanked them in many fine words for their good will; and said that he accepted from them, with no ordinary pleasure, what might be necessary for his undertaking.

CHAPTER CCIII. OF KING OLAF'S JOURNEY FROM RUSSIA.— Immediately after Yule, King Olaf made himself ready; and had about 200 of his men with him. King Jarisleif gave him all the horses, and whatever else he required; and when he was ready he set off. King Jarisleif and Queen Ingigerd parted from him with all honour; and he left his son Magnus behind with the king. The first part of his journey, down to the sea-coast, King Olaf and his men made on the ice; but as spring approached, and the ice broke up, they rigged their vessels, and when they were ready and got a wind they set out to sea, and had a good voyage. When Olaf came to the island of Gotland with his ships he heard the news—which was told as truth, both in Sweden, Denmark, and over all Norway—that Earl Hakon was missing, and Norway without a head. This gave the king and his men good hope of the issue of their journey. From thence they sailed, when the wind suited, to Sweden, and went into the Mælare lake, to Westeraas,[1] and sent men to the Swedish King Onund appointing a meeting. King Onund received his brother-in-law's message in the kindest manner, and went to him according to his invitation. Astrid also came to King Olaf, with the men who had attended her; and great was the joy on all sides at this meeting. The Swedish king also received his brother-in-law King Olaf with great joy when they met.

[1] Áróss, the site of the present Upsala.

CHAPTER CCIV. OF THE BARONS IN NORWAY [1030].—Now we must relate what, in the meantime, was going on in Norway. Thore Hund, in these two winters, had made a Lapland journey, and each winter had been a long time on the Fjelds, and had gathered to himself great wealth by trading in various wares with the Laplanders. He had twelve large coats of reindeer-skin made for him, with so much Lapland witchcraft that no weapon could cut or pierce them any more than if they were armour of ring-mail, nor so much.[1] The spring thereafter Thore rigged a long-ship which belonged to him, and manned it with his house-servants. He summoned the bonders, demanded a levy from the most northern Thing district, collected in this way a great many people, and proceeded with this force southwards. Harek of Thiotto had also collected a great number of people; and in this expedition many people of consequence took a part, although these two were the most distinguished. They made it known publicly that with this war-force they were going against King Olaf, to defend the country against him, in case he should come from the eastward.

CHAPTER CCV. OF EINAR TAMBARSKELVE.—Einar Tambar-skelve had most influence in the outer part of the Drontheim country after Earl Hakon's death was no longer doubtful; for he and his son Eindride appeared to be the nearest heirs to the movable property the earl had possessed. Then Einar remembered the promises and offers of friendship which King Canute had made him at parting; and he ordered a good vessel which belonged to him to be got ready, and embarked with a great retinue, and when he was ready sailed southwards along the coast, then set out to sea westwards, and sailed without stopping until he came to England. He immediately waited on King Canute, who received him well and joyfully. Then Einar opened his business to the king, and said he was come there to see the fulfilment of the promises the king had made him; namely, that he, Einar, should have the highest title of honour in Norway if Earl Hakon were no more. King Canute replies, that now the circumstances were altered. " I have now," said he, " sent men and tokens to my son Swend in Denmark, and promised him the kingdom of Norway; but thou shalt retain my friendship, and get the dignity and title which thou art entitled by birth to hold. Thou shalt be lenderman with great

---

[1] The Lapps were reputed to be very powerful wizards, and many sagas contain stories of their magic.

fiefs, and be so much more raised above other lendermen as thou art more able than they." Einar saw sufficiently how matters stood with regard to his business, and got ready to return home; but as he now knew the king's intentions, and thought it probable if King Olaf came from the East the country would not be very peaceable, it came into his mind that it would be better to proceed slowly, and not to be hastening his voyage, in order to fight against King Olaf without his being advanced by it to any higher dignity than he had before. Einar accordingly went to sea when he was ready; but only came to Norway after the events were ended which took place there during that summer.

CHAPTER CCVI. OF THE CHIEF PEOPLE IN NORWAY.—The chiefs in Norway had their spies east in Sweden, and south in Denmark, to find out if King Olaf had come from Russia. As soon as these men could get across the country, they heard the news that King Olaf was arrived in Sweden; and as soon as full certainty of this was obtained, the war message-token went round the land. The whole people were called out to a levy, and a great army was collected. The lendermen who were from Agder, Rogaland, and Hordaland, divided themselves, so that some went towards the north and some towards the east; for they thought they required people on both sides. Erling's sons from Jœderen went eastward, with all the men who lived east of them, and over whom they were chiefs; Aslak of Finnö,[1] and Erlend of Garde,[2] with the lendermen north of them, went towards the north. All those now named had sworn an oath to King Canute to deprive Olaf of life, if opportunity should offer.

CHAPTER CCVII. OF HARALD SIGURDSSON'S PROCEEDINGS.— Now when it was reported in Norway that King Olaf was come from the East to Sweden, his friends gathered together to give him aid. The most distinguished man in this flock was Harald Sigurdsson, a brother [3] of King Olaf, who then was fifteen years of age, very stout, and manly of growth as if he were full-grown. Many other brave men were there also; and there were in all 600 men when they proceeded from the Uplands, and went eastward with their force through Eida forest to Vermeland.

[1] An island and district in Ryfylke.
[2] A farm and parish in Etne, Söndhordland.
[3] i.e. Harald Hardaradi, Olaf's half-brother, the son of Queen Astrid and Sigurd Syr. He later became king of Norway, and was killed in England in 1066 at Stamford Bridge.

From thence they went eastward through the forests to Sweden, and made inquiry about King Olaf's proceedings.

CHAPTER CCVIII. OF KING OLAF'S PROCEEDINGS IN SWEDEN. —King Olaf was in Sweden in spring, and had sent spies from thence into Norway. All accounts from that quarter agreed that there was no safety for him if he went there, and the people who came from the north dissuaded him much from penetrating into the country. But he had firmly resolved within himself, as before stated, to go into Norway; and he asked King Onund what strength King Onund would give him to conquer his kingdom. King Onund replied, that the Swedes were little inclined to make an expedition against Norway. "We know," says he, "that the Northmen are rough and warlike, and it is dangerous to carry hostility to their doors; but I will not be slow in telling thee what aid I can give. I will give thee 400 chosen men from my court-men, active, and warlike, and well equipt for battle; and moreover will give thee leave to go through my country, and gather to thyself as many men as thou canst get to follow thee." King Olaf accepted this offer, and got ready for his march. Queen Astrid, and Ulfhild the king's daughter, remained behind in Sweden.

CHAPTER CCIX. KING OLAF ADVANCES TO JÆRNBERALAND.— Just as King Olaf began his journey the men came to him whom the Swedish king had given, in all 400 men, and the king took the road the Swedes showed him. He advanced upwards in the country to the forests, and came to a district called Jærnbera-land.[1] Here the people joined him who had come out of Norway to meet him, as before related [p. 351]; and he met here his brother Harald, and many other of his relations, and it was a joyful meeting. They made out together 1200 men.

CHAPTER CCX. OF DAG RINGSSON.—There was a man called Dag, who is said to have been a son of King Ring, who fled the country from King Olaf (p. 182). This Ring, it is said further, had been a son of Dag, and grandson of Ring, Harald Haarfager's son. Thus Dag was King Olaf's relative. Both Ring the father and Dag the son had settled themselves in Sweden, and got land to rule over. In spring, when Olaf came from the East to Sweden, he sent a message to his relation Dag,

[1] " Iron-bearing Land," the modern Swedish province of Dalarna, rich in iron ore.

that he should join him in this expedition with all the force he could collect; and if they gained the country of Norway again, Dag should have no smaller part of the kingdom under him than his forefathers had enjoyed. When this message came to Dag it suited his inclination well, for he had a great desire to go to Norway and get the dominion his family had ruled over. He was not slow, therefore, to reply, and promised to come. Dag was a quick-speaking, quick-resolving man, mixing himself up in everything; eager, but of little understanding. He collected a force of almost 1200 men, with which he joined King Olaf.

CHAPTER CCXI. OF KING OLAF'S JOURNEY.—King Olaf sent a message before him to all the inhabited places he passed through, that the men who wished to get goods and money, and share of booty, and the lands besides which now were in the hands of his enemies, should come to him, and follow him. Thereafter King Olaf led his army through forests, often over desert moors, and often over large lakes; and they dragged, or carried the boats, from lake to lake. On the way a great many followers joined the king, partly forest settlers, partly vagabonds. The places at which he halted for the night are since called Olaf's Huts. He proceeded without any break upon his journey until he came to Jemteland, from which he marched north over the keel or ridge of the land. The men spread themselves over the hamlets, and proceeded, much scattered, so long as no enemy was expected; but always, when so dispersed, the Northmen accompanied the king. Dag proceeded with his men on another line of march, and the Swedes on a third with their troop.

CHAPTER CCXII. OF HIGHWAYMEN.—There were two men, the one called Gauka-Thore, the other Afrafaste, who were highwaymen and great robbers, and had a company of thirty men such as themselves. These two men were larger and stronger than other men, and they wanted neither courage nor impudence. These men heard speak of the army that was crossing the country, and said among themselves it would be a clever counsel to go to the king, follow him to his country, and go with him into a regular battle, and try themselves in this work; for they had never been in any battle in which people were regularly drawn up in line, and they were curious to see the king's order of battle. This counsel was approved of by their comrades, and accordingly they went to the road on which King Olaf was to pass. When they came there they presented themselves to the king, with their followers, fully armed. They saluted him, and he asked what people they were. They told their names, and said they were natives of the place; and told their errand, and that they wished to go with the king. The king said, it appeared to him there was good help in such folks. "And I have a great inclination," said he, "to take such; but are ye Christian men?"

Gauka-Thore replies, that he is neither Christian nor heathen. "I and my comrades have no faith but on ourselves, our strength, and the luck of victory; and with this faith we slip through sufficiently well."

The king replies, "A great pity it is that such brave slaughtering fellows did not believe in Christ their Creator."

Thore replies, "Is there any Christian man, king, in thy following, who stands so high to-day as we two brothers?"

The king told them to let themselves be baptized, and to accept the true faith. "Follow me then, and I will advance you to great dignities; but if ye will not do so, return to your former vocation."

Afrafaste said they would not take on Christianity, and he turned away.

Then said Gauka-Thore, "It is a great shame that the king drives us thus away from his army, and I never before came where I was not received into the company of other people, and I shall never return back on this account." They joined accordingly the rear with other forest-men, and followed the troops. Thereafter the king proceeded west up to the keel-ridge of the country (*i.e.* the border between Sweden and Norway).

CHAPTER CCXIII. OF KING OLAF'S VISION. — Now when King Olaf, coming from the east, went over the keel-ridge and descended on the west side of the fjelds, where it declines towards the sea, he could see from thence far over the country. Many people rode before the king and many after, and he himself rode so that there was a free space around him. He was silent, and nobody spoke to him, and thus he rode a great part of the day without looking much about him. Then the bishop rode up to him, asked him why he was so silent, and what he was thinking of; for, in general, he was very cheerful, and very talkative on a journey to his men, so that all who were near him were merry. The king replied, full of thought, "Wonderful things have come into my mind a while ago. As I just now looked over Norway, out to the west from the mountain, it came into my mind how many happy days I have had in that land. It appeared to me at first as if I saw over all the Drontheim country, and then over all Norway; and the longer this vision was before my eyes the farther, methought, I saw, until I saw over the whole wide world, both land and sea. Well I recognized places where I have been in former days; some even which I have only heard speak of, and some I saw of which I had never heard, both inhabited and uninhabited, in this wide world." The bishop replied that this was a holy vision, and very remarkable.

CHAPTER CCXIV. OF THE MIRACLE ON THE CORN LAND.— When the king had come lower down from the fjeld, there lay a farm before him called Suul,[1] on the highest part of Værdal district; and as they came nearer to the house the corn land appeared on both sides of the path. The king told his people to proceed carefully, and not destroy the corn of the bonder. The people observed this when the king was near; but the crowd behind paid no attention to it, and the people ran over the corn, so that it was trodden flat to the earth. There dwelt a bonder there called Thorgeir Flek, who had two sons nearly grown up. Thorgeir received the king and his people well, and offered all the assistance in his power. The king was pleased with his offer, and asked Thorgeir what was the news of the country, and if any forces were assembled against him. Thorgeir says that a great army was drawn together in the Drontheim country, and that there were some lendermen both from the south of the country, and from Halogaland in the north; " but I do not know," says he, " if they are intended against you, or going elsewhere." Then he complained to the king of the damage and waste done him by the people breaking and treading down all his corn-fields. The king said it was ill done to bring upon him any loss. Then the king rode to where the corn had stood, and saw it was laid flat on the earth; and he rode round the field, and said, " I expect, bonder, that God will repair thy loss, so that the field, within a week, will be better; " and it proved the best of the corn, as the king had said. The king remained all night there, and in the morning he made himself ready, and told Thorgeir the bonder to accompany him, and Thorgeir offered his two sons also for the journey; and although

[1] Suul is a farm still known by the same name at the head of Værdal.

the king said that he did not want them with him, the lads
would go. As they would not stay behind, the king's court-
men were about binding them; but the king seeing it said,
" Let them come with us: the lads will come safe back again."
And it was with the lads as the king foretold.

CHAPTER CCXV. OF THE BAPTISM OF THE FOREST HIGHWAY-
MEN.—Thereafter the army advanced to Staf,[1] and when the
king reached the Staf moor he halted. There he got the certain
information that the bonders were advancing with an army
against him, and that he might soon expect to have a battle
with them. He mustered his force here, and, after reckoning
them up, found he had more than 3000[2] men. There were in
the army 900[2] heathen men, and when he came to know it he
ordered them to allow themselves to be baptized, saying that
he would have no heathens with him in battle. " We must
not," says he, " put our confidence in numbers, but in God alone
must we trust; for through his power and favour we must be
victorious, and I will not mix heathen people with my own."
When the heathens heard this, they held a council among
themselves, and at last 400[3] men agreed to be baptized; but
500[3] men refused to adopt Christianity, and that body returned
home to their land. Then the brothers Gauka-Thore and Afrafaste presented themselves to the king, and offered again to
follow him. The king asked if they had now taken baptism.
Gauka-Thore replied that they had not. Then the king ordered
them to accept baptism and the true faith, or otherwise to go
away. They stepped aside to talk with each other on what
resolution they should take. Afrafaste said, " To give my
opinion, I will not turn back, but go into the battle, and take
a part on the one side or the other; and I don't care much in
which army I am." Gauka-Thore replies, " If I go into battle
I will give my help to the king, for he has most need of help.
And if I must believe in a God, why not in the White Christ as
well as in any other? Now it is my advice, therefore, that we
let ourselves be baptized, since the king insists so much upon
it, and then go into the battle with him." They all agreed to
this, and went to the king, and said they would receive baptism.
Then they were baptized by a priest, and afterwards confirmed by the bishop. The king then took them into the troop

[1] A farm in Værdal, no longer existing.
[2] *i.e.* 3600 and 1080 respectively.
[3] *i.e.* 480 and 600 respectively.

of his court-men, and said they should fight under his banner in the battle.[1]

CHAPTER CCXVI. KING OLAF'S SPEECH. — King Olaf got certain intelligence now that it would be but a short time until he had a battle with the bonders; and after he had mustered his men, and reckoned up the force, he had more than 3000 men,[2] which appears to be a great army in one field. Then the king made the following speech to the people: "We have a great army, and excellent troops; and now I will tell you, my men, how I will have our force drawn up. I will let my banner go forward in the middle of the army, and my court-men and pursuivants [3] shall follow it, together with the war forces that joined us from the Uplands, and also those who may come to us here in the Drontheim land. On the right hand of my banner shall be Dag Ringson, with all the men he brought to our aid; and he shall have the second banner. And on the left hand of our line shall be the men be whom the Swedish king gave us, together with all the people who came to us in Sweden; and they shall have the third banner. I will also have the people divide themselves into distinct flocks or parcels, so that relations and acquaintances should be together; for thus they defend each other best, and know each other. We will have all our men distinguished by a mark, so as to be a field-token upon their helmets and shields, by painting the holy cross thereupon with white colour. When we come into battle we shall all have one countersign and field-cry, — 'Forward, forward, Christ-men! cross men! king's men!' We must draw up our men in thinner ranks, because we have fewer people, and I do not wish to let them surround us with their men. Now let the men divide themselves into separate flocks, and then each flock into ranks; then let each man observe well his proper place, and take notice what banner he is drawn up under. And now we shall remain drawn up in array; and our men shall be fully armed, night and day, until we know where the meeting shall be between us and the bonders." When the king had finished speaking, the army arrayed and arranged itself according to the king's orders.

CHAPTER CCXVII. KING OLAF'S COUNSEL.—Thereafter the

[1] It is unlikely that Olaf did dismiss all heathens from his army; the verse of Sigvat given on p. 392 is evidence to the contrary.

[2] *i.e.* 3600 men.

[3] Literally, "the men of the *hirð* and the *gestir*"; see notes, pp. 158 and 311.

king had a meeting with the chiefs of the different divisions,
and then the men had returned whom the king had sent out into
the neighbouring districts to demand men from the bonders.
They brought the tidings from the inhabited places they had
gone through, that all around the country was stripped of all
men able to carry arms, as all the people had joined the bonders'
army; and where they did find any they got but few to follow
them, for the most of them answered that they stayed at home
because they would not follow either party: they would not
go out against the king, nor yet against their own relations.
Thus they had got but few people. Now the king asked his
men their counsel, and what they now should do. Finn Arneson
answered thus to the king's question: "I will say what
should be done, if I may advise. We should go with armed
hand over all the inhabited places, plunder all the goods, and
burn all the habitations, and leave not a hut standing, and thus
punish the bonders for their treason against their sovereign.
I think many a man will then cast himself loose from the bonders'
army, when he sees smoke and flame at home on his farm, and
does not know how it is going with children, wives, or old men,
fathers, mothers, and other connections. I expect also," he
added, " that if we succeed in breaking the assembled host,
their ranks will soon be thinned; for so it is with the bonders,
that the counsel which is the newest is always the dearest to
them all, and most followed." When Finn had ended his speech
it met with general applause; for many thought well of such a
good occasion to make booty, and all thought the bonders well
deserved to suffer damage; and they also thought it probable,
what Finn said, that many would in this way be brought to
forsake the assembled army of the bonders. Thormod Kolbrunar
scald made these verses then:—

> " Fire house and hut throughout the land!
> Burn all around, our mountain-band!
> And with our good swords stout and bold
> The king's own we'll win back, and hold.
> The Drontheimers should nothing find
> But ashes whirling in the wind,
> Where houses stood—what melts the ice
> Should burn the hut, by my advice."

Now when the king heard the warm expressions of his people
he told them to listen to him, and said, " The bonders have well
deserved that it should be done to them as ye desire. They also
know that I have formerly done so, burning their habitations,
and punishing them severely in many ways; but then I pro-

ceeded against them with fire and sword because they rejected the true faith, betook themselves to sacrifices, and would not obey my commands. We had then God's honour to defend. But this treason against their sovereign is a much less grievous crime, although it does not become men who have any manhood in them to break the faith and vows they have sworn to me. Now, however, it is more in my power to spare those who have dealt ill with me, than those whom God hated. I will, therefore, that my people proceed gently, and commit no ravage. First, I will proceed to meet the bonders: if we can then come to a reconciliation, it is well; but if they will fight with us, then there are two things before us: either we fail in the battle, and then it will be well advised not to have to retire encumbered with spoil and cattle; or we gain the victory, and then ye will be the heirs of all who fight now against us: for some will fall, and others will fly, but both will have forfeited their goods and properties, and then it will be good to enter into full houses and well-stocked farms; but what is burnt is of use to no man, and with pillage and force more is wasted than what turns to use. Now we will spread out far through the inhabited places, and take with us all the men we can find able to carry arms. The men will also capture cattle for slaughter, or whatever else of provision that can serve for food; but not do any other ravage. But I will see willingly that ye kill any spies of the bonder army ye may fall in with. Dag and his people shall go by the north side down along the valley, and I will go on along the country road, and so we shall meet in the evening, and all have one night quarter."

CHAPTER CCXVIII. OF KING OLAF'S SCALDS.—It is related that when King Olaf drew up his men in battle order, he made a shield rampart with his troop that should defend him in battle, for which he selected the strongest and boldest. Thereafter he called his scalds, and ordered them to go in within the shield defence. " Ye shall," says the king, " remain here, and see the circumstances which may take place, and then ye will not have to follow the reports of others in what ye afterwards tell or sing concerning it." There were Thormod Kolbrunarscald, Gissur Gulbraascald, foster-father of Hofgarde Refr,[1] and Thorfin Mudr. Then said Thormod to Gissur, " Let us not stand so close together, comrade, that Sigvat the scald should not find room when he comes. He must stand before the king, and the

[1] *i.e.* Ref Gestsön from Hovgardar, a farm on Snefjeldsnes, *vide* p. 374.

king will not have it otherwise." The king heard this, and said, " Ye need not sneer at Sigvat, because he is not here. Often has he followed me well, and now he is praying for us, and that we greatly need." Thormod replies, " It may be, sire, that ye now require prayers most; but it would be thin around the banner-staff if all thy court-men were now on the way to Rome. True it was what we spoke about, that no man who would speak with you could find room for Sigvat."

Thereafter the scalds talked among themselves that it would be well to compose a few songs of remembrance about the events which would soon be taking place. Then Gissur sang:—

> " From me shall bonder girl ne'er hear
> A thought of sorrow, care, or fear:
> I wish my girl knew how gay
> We arm us for our viking fray.
> Many and brave they are, we know,
> Who come against us there below;
> But, life or death, we, one and all,
> By Norway's king will stand or fall."

And Thorfin Mudr made another song, viz:—

> Dark is the cloud of men and shields,
> Slow moving up through Værdal's fields:
> These Værdal folks presume to bring
> Their armed force against their king.
> On! let us feed the carrion crow,—
> Give her a feast in every blow;
> And, above all, let Drontheim's hordes
> Feel the sharp edge of true men's swords."

And Thormod sang:—

> " The whistling arrows pipe to battle,
> Sword and shield their war-call rattle.
> Up! brave men, up! the faint heart here
> Finds courage when the danger's near.
> Up! brave men, up! with Olaf on!
> With heart and hand a field is won.
> One viking cheer!—then, stead of words,
> We'll speak with our death-dealing swords."

These songs were immediately got by heart by the army.

CHAPTER CCXIX. OF KING OLAF'S GIFTS FOR THE SOULS OF THOSE WHO SHOULD BE SLAIN.—Thereafter the king made himself ready, and marched down through the valley. His whole forces took up their night quarter in one place, and lay down all night under their shields; but as soon as day broke the king again put his army in order, and that being done they proceeded down through the valley. Many bonders then came to the king, of whom the most joined his army; and all, as one man, told the same tale,—that the lendermen had collected an enormous army, with which they intended to give battle to the king.

The king took many marks of silver, and delivered them into the hands of a bonder, and said, "This money thou shalt conceal, and afterwards lay out,—some to churches, some to priests, some to alms-men,—as gifts for the life and souls of those who fight against us, and may fall in battle."

The bonder replies, "Should you not rather give this money for the soul-mulct of your own men?"

The king says, "This money shall be given for the souls of those who stand against us in the ranks of the bonders' army, and fall by the weapons of our own men. The men who follow us to battle, and fall therein, will all be saved together with ourself."

CHAPTER CCXX. OF THORMOD KOLBRUNARSCALD. — This night the king lay with his army around him on the field, as before related, and lay long awake in prayer to God, and slept but little. Towards morning a slumber fell on him, and when he awoke daylight was shooting up. The king thought it too early to awaken the army, and asked where Thormod the scald was. Thormod was at hand, and asked what was the king's pleasure. "Sing us a song," said the king. Thormod raised himself up, and sang so loud that the whole army could hear him. He began to sing the old Biarkamal,[1] of which these are the first verses:—

> "The day is breaking,—
> The cock is shaking
> His rustling wings,
> His crowing rings!
> The hour is come
> When thralls at home
> Begin their toilsome task—
> Ye friends of Adils,[2] wake at last!
> Wake up! wake up!
> Nor wassail cup,

[1] *Bjarkamál*, a tenth-century poem on the last battle of Boðvar Bjarki and the other legendary champions of the Danish king Hrolf Kraki. Three more stanzas are preserved in Snorri's *Edda*, and the whole was paraphrased in Latin verse by Saxo Grammaticus. Axel Olrik (*The Heroic Legends of Denmark*, 1916) conjecturally restored the original text; a translation of this appears in L. M. Hollander, *Old Norse Poems*, 1936.

[2] Ironical; the Swedish King Adils is now their foe.

Nor woman's cheer,
Awaits you here.
Rolf of the bow!
Har of the blow!
Brave men, the battle ne'er forsaking!
'Tis Hildur's game [1] that bides your waking."

Then the troops awoke, and when the song was ended the people thanked him for it; and it pleased many, as it was suitable to the time and occasion, and they called it the House-carles' Whet.[2] The king thanked him for the pleasure, and took a gold ring that weighed half a mark and gave it him. Thormod thanked the king for the gift, and said, " We have a good king; but it is not easy to say how long the king's life may be. It is my prayer, sire, that thou shouldst never part from me either in life or death."

The king replies, " We shall all go together so long as I rule, and as ye will follow me."

Thormod says, " I hope, sire, that whether in safety or danger I may stand near you as long as I can stand, whatever we may hear of Sigvat travelling with his gold-hilted sword." Then Thormod made these lines:—

" To thee, my king, I'll still be true,
Until another scald I view,
Here in the field with golden sword,
When thinkest thou he will come, great lord?
Thy scald shall never be a craven,
Whether he feasts the greedy raven,
Or lies upon the battle-plain
(Master of ships!) among the slain."

CHAPTER CCXXI. KING OLAF COMES TO STIKLESTAD.—King Olaf led his army farther down through the valley, and Dag and his men went another way, and the king did not halt until he came to Stiklestad. There he saw the bonder army spread out all around; and there were so great numbers that people were going on every footpath and great crowds were collected far and near. They also saw there a troop which came down from Værdal, and had been out to spy. They came so close to the king's people that they knew each other. It was Rut of Viggia, with thirty men. The king ordered his pursuivants to go out against Rut, and make an end of him, to which his men were instantly ready. The king said to the Icelanders, " It is told

---

[1] *i.e.* the battle; a kenning from the name of the valkyrie Hildur.

[2] *Húskarlahvǫt*, " The Rousing of the Retainers." It is not clear whether this is an old alternative title for the *Bjarkamál*, or whether Olaf's men renamed it to please themselves.

me that in Iceland it is the custom that the bonders give their house-servants a sheep to slaughter; now I give you a ram to slaughter." [1] The Icelanders were easily incited to this, and went out immediately with a few men against Rut, and killed him and the troop that followed him. When the king came to Stiklestad he made a halt, and made the army stop, and told his people to alight from their horses, and get ready for battle; and the people did as the king ordered. Then he placed his army in battle array, and raised his banner. Dag was not yet arrived with his men, so that his wing of the battle array was wanting. Then the king said the Upland men should go forward in their place, and raise their banner there. "It appears to me advisable," says the king, "that Harald my brother should not be in the battle, for he is still in the years of childhood only." Harald replies, "Certainly I shall be in the battle, but if I am so weak that I cannot handle the sword, then I know a good plan, namely, of tying the sword-handle to my hand. None is more willing than I am to give the bonders a blow; so I shall go with my comrades." It is said that Harald made these lines:—

> " Our army's wing, where I shall stand,
> I will hold good with heart and hand;
> My mother's eye shall joy to see
> A battered, blood-stained shield from me.
> The brisk young scald should gaily go
> Into the fray, give blow for blow,
> Cheer on his men, gain inch by inch,
> And from the spear-point never flinch."

Harald got his will, and was allowed to be in the battle.

CHAPTER CCXXII. OF THORGILS HALMESON. — A bonder, by name Thorgils Halmeson, father to Grim the Good, dwelt in Stiklestad farm. Thorgils offered the king his assistance, and was ready to go into battle with him. The king thanked him for the offer. "I would rather," says the king, "thou shouldst not be in the fight. Do us rather the service to take care of the people who are wounded, and to bury those who may fall, when the battle is over. Should it happen, bonder, that I fall in this battle, bestow the care on my body that may be necessary, if that be not forbidden thee." Thorgils promised the king what he desired.

CHAPTER CCXXIII. OLAF'S SPEECH.—Now when King Olaf had drawn up his army in battle array he made a speech, in

[1] Rut means a young ram.

which he told the people to raise their spirit, and go boldly forward, if it came to a battle. " We have," says he, " many men, and good; and although the bonders may have a somewhat larger force than we, it is fate that rules over victory. This I will make known to you solemnly, that I shall not fly from this battle, but shall either be victorious over the bonders, or fall in the fight. I will pray to God that the lot of the two may befall me which will be most to my advantage. With this we may encourage ourselves, that we have a more just cause than the bonders; and likewise that God must either protect us and our cause in this battle, or give us a far higher recompense for what we may lose here in the world than what we ourselves could ask. Should it be my lot to have anything to say after the battle, then shall I reward each of you according to his service, and to the bravery he displays in the battle; and if we gain the victory, there must be land and movables enough to divide among you, and which are now in the hands of your enemies. Let us at the first make the hardest onset, for then the consequences are soon seen. There being a great difference in the numbers, we have to expect victory from a sharp assault only; and, on the other hand, it will be heavy work for us to fight until we are tired, and unable to fight longer; for we have fewer people to relieve with than they, who can come forward at one time and retreat and rest at another. But if we advance so hard at the first attack that those who are foremost in their ranks must turn round, then the one will fall over the other, and their destruction will be the greater the greater numbers there are together." When the king had ended his speech it was received with loud applause, and the one encouraged the other.

CHAPTER CCXXIV. OF THORD FOLASON.—Thord Folason carried King Olaf's banner. So says Sigvat the scald, in the death song which he composed about King Olaf, adding a refrain from the story of the Creation [1]:—

> " Thord, I have heard, by Olaf's side,
> Where raged the battle's wildest tide,
> Moved on, and, as by one accord,
> Moved with them every heart and sword.
> The banner of the king on high,
> Floating all splendid in the sky
> From golden shaft, aloft he bore,—
> The Norseman's rallying point of yore."

[1] Or " of Christ's Resurrection " (*Uppreistarsaga*).

CHAPTER CCXXV. OF KING OLAF'S ARMOUR.—King Olaf
was armed thus:—He had a gold-mounted helmet on his head,
and had in one hand a white shield, on which the holy cross was
inlaid in gold. In his other hand he had a lance, which to the
present day stands beside the altar in Christ Church. In his
belt he had a sword, which was called Neite, which was remarkably sharp, and of which the handle was worked with gold. He
had also a strong coat of ring-mail. Sigvat the scald speaks of
this:—

> " A greater victory to gain,
> Olaf the Stout strode o'er the plain
> In strong chain armour, aid to bring
> To his brave men on either wing.
> High rose the fight and battle-heat,—
> The clear blood ran beneath the feet
> Of Swedes, who from the East came there,
> In Olaf's gain or loss to share."

CHAPTER CCXXVI. KING OLAF'S DREAM.—Now when King
Olaf had drawn up his men the army of the bonders had not yet
come near upon any quarter, so the king said the people should
sit down and rest themselves. He sat down himself, and the
people sat around him in a wide-spread crowd. He leaned down,
and laid his head upon Finn Arneson's knee. There a slumber
came upon him, and he slept a little while; but at the same
time the bonders' army was seen advancing with raised banners,
and the multitude of these was very great.

Then Finn awakened the king, and said that the bonder-
army advanced against them.

The king awoke, and said, " Why did you awaken me, Finn,
and did not allow me to enjoy my dream? "

Finn, " Thou must not be dreaming; but rather thou shouldst
be awake, and preparing thyself against the host which is
coming down upon us; or, dost thou not see that the whole
bonder crowd is coming? "

The king replies, " They are not yet so near to us, and it
would have been better to have let me sleep."

Then said Finn, " What was the dream, sire, of which the
loss appears to thee so great that thou wouldst rather have
been left to waken of thyself? "

Now the king told his dream,—that he seemed to see a high
ladder, upon which he went so high in the air that heaven was
open; for so high reached the ladder. " And when you awoke
me, I was come to the highest step towards heaven."

Finn replied, " This dream does not appear to me so good as

it does to thee. I think it means that thou art fey; [1] unless it be the mere want of sleep that has worked upon thee."

CHAPTER CCXXVII. OF ARNLIOT GELLINE'S BAPTISM.— When King Olaf was arrived at Stiklestad, it happened, among other circumstances, that a man came to him; and although it was nowise wonderful that there came many men from the districts, yet this must be regarded as unusual, that this man did not appear like the other men who came to him. He was so tall that none stood higher than up to his shoulders: very handsome he was in countenance, and had beautiful fair hair. He was well armed; had a fine helmet, and ring armour; a red shield; a superb sword in his belt; and in his hand a gold-mounted spear, the shaft of it so thick that it was a handful to grasp. The man went before the king, saluted him, and asked if the king would accept his services.

The king asked his name and family, also what countryman he was.

He replies, "My family is in Jemteland and Helsingeland, and my name is Arnliot Gelline; but this I must not forget to tell you, that I came to the assistance of those men you sent to Jemteland to collect scatt, and I gave into their hands a silver dish, which I sent you as a token that I would be your friend." [2]

Then the king asked Arnliot if he was a Christian or not.

He replied, "My faith has been this, to rely upon my power and strength, and which faith hath hitherto given me satisfaction; but now I intend rather to put my faith, sire, in thee."

The king replies, "If thou wilt put faith in me, thou must also put faith in what I will teach thee. Thou must believe that Jesus Christ has made heaven and earth, and all mankind, and to him shall all those who are good and rightly believing go after death."

Arnliot answers, "I have indeed heard of the White Christ, but neither know what he proposes, nor what he rules over; but now I will believe all that thou sayest to me, and lay down my lot in your hands."

Thereupon Arnliot was baptized. The king taught him so much of the holy faith as appeared to him needful, and placed him in the front rank of the order of battle, in advance of his

[1] *i.e.* fated to die soon, and showing signs of this by dreams, premonitions, clairvoyance, abnormal recklessness, etc.

[2] *Vide* p. 297.

banner, where also Gauka-Thore and Afrafaste with their men were.

CHAPTER CCXXVIII. CONCERNING THE ARMY COLLECTED IN NORWAY.—Now shall we relate what we have left behind in our tale,—that the lendermen and bonders had collected a vast host as soon as it was reported that King Olaf was come from Russia, and had arrived in Sweden; but when they heard that he had come to Jemteland, and intended to proceed westwards over the keel-ridge to Værdal, they brought their forces into the Drontheim country, where they gathered together the whole people, free and unfree, and proceeded towards Værdal with so great a body of men, that there was nobody in Norway at that time who had seen so large a force assembled. But the force, as it usually happens in so great a multitude, consisted of many different sorts of people. There were many lendermen, and a great many powerful bonders; but the great mass consisted of labourers and cottars. The chief strength of this army lay in the Drontheim land, and it was the most warm in enmity and opposition to the king.

CHAPTER CCXXIX. OF BISHOP SIGURD.—When King Canute had, as before related,[1] laid all Norway under his power, he set Earl Hakon to manage it, and gave the earl a court-bishop, by name Sigurd, who was of Danish descent, and had been long with King Canute. This bishop was of a very hot temper, and particularly obstinate, and haughty in his speech; but supported King Canute all he could in conversation, and was a great enemy of King Olaf. He was now also in the bonders' army, spoke often before the people, and urged them much to insurrection against King Olaf.

CHAPTER CCXXX. BISHOP SIGURD'S SPEECH.—At a Housething, at which a great many people were assembled, the bishop desired to be heard, and made the following speech: "Here are now assembled a great many men, so that probably there will never be opportunity in this poor country of seeing so great a native army; but it would be desirable if this strength and multitude could be a protection: for it will all be needed, if this Olaf does not give over bringing war and strife upon you. From his very earliest youth he has been accustomed to plunder and kill: for which purposes he drove widely around through all

countries, until he turned at last against this, where he began
to show hostilities against the men who were the best and most
powerful; and even against King Canute, whom all are bound
to serve according to their ability, and in whose scatt-lands he
set himself down. He did the same to Olaf the Swedish king.
He drove the earls Swend and Hakon away from their heritages;
and was even most tyrannical towards his own connections, as
he drove all the kings out of the Uplands: although, indeed, it
was but just reward for having been false to their oaths of
fealty to King Canute, and having followed this King Olaf in
all the folly he could invent; so their friendship ended according
to their deserts, by this king mutilating some of them, taking
their kingdoms himself, and ruining every man in the country
who had an honourable name. Ye know yourselves how he has
treated the lendermen, of whom many of the worthiest have
been murdered, and many obliged to fly from their country;
and how he has roamed far and wide through the land with
robber bands, burning and plundering houses, and killing people.
Who is the man among us here of any consideration who has
not some great injury from him to avenge? Now he has come
hither with a foreign troop, consisting mostly of forest-men,
vagabonds, and such marauders. Do ye think he will now be
more merciful to you, when he is roaming about with such a
bad crew, after committing devastations which all who followed
him dissuaded him from? Therefore it is now my advice, that
ye remember King Canute's words when he told you, if King
Olaf attempted to return to the country ye should defend the
liberty King Canute had promised you, and should oppose and
drive away such a vile pack. Now the only thing to be done
is, to advance against them, and cast forth these malefactors
to the wolves and eagles, leaving their corpses on the spot they
cover, unless ye drag them aside to out-of-the-way corners in
the woods or rocks. No man would be so imprudent as to
remove them to churches, for they are all robbers and evil-doers."
When he had ended his speech it was hailed with the loudest
applause, and all unanimously agreed to act according to his
recommendation.

CHAPTER CCXXXI. OF THE LENDERMEN.—The lendermen
who had come together appointed meetings with each other, and
consulted together how they should draw up their troops, and
who should be their leader. Kalf Arneson said that Harek of
Thiotto was best fitted to be the chief of this army, for he was

descended from Harald Haarfager's race. " The king also is particularly enraged against him on account of the murder of Grankel, and therefore he would be exposed to the severest fate if Olaf recovered the kingdom: and Harek withal is a man experienced in battles, and a man who does much for honour alone."

Harek replied, that the men are best suited for this who are in the flower of their age. " I am now," says he, " an old and decaying man, not able to do much in battle: besides, there is near relationship between me and King Olaf; and although he seems not to put great value upon that tie, it would not beseem me to go as leader of the hostilities against him, before any other in this meeting. On the other hand, thou, Thore, art well suited to be our chief in this battle against King Olaf; and thou hast distinct grounds for being so, both because thou hast to avenge the death of thy relation, and also hast been driven by him as an outlaw from thy property. Thou hast also promised King Canute, as well as thy connections, to avenge the murder of thy relative Asbiorn; and dost thou suppose there ever will be a better opportunity than this of taking vengeance on Olaf for all these insults and injuries? "

Thore replies thus to his speech: " I do not confide in myself so much as to raise the banner against King Olaf, or, as chief, to lead on this army; for the people of Drontheim have the greatest part in this armament, and I know well their haughty spirit, and that they would not obey me, or any other Halogaland man, although I need not be reminded of my injuries to be roused to vengeance on King Olaf. I remember well my heavy loss when King Olaf slew four men, all distinguished both by birth and personal qualities; namely, my brother's son Asbiorn, my sister's sons Thore and Griotgard, and their father Olve; and it is my duty to take vengeance for each man of them. I will not conceal that I have selected eleven [1] of my house-servants for that purpose, and of those who are the most daring; and I do not think we shall be behind others in exchanging blows with King Olaf, should opportunity be given."

CHAPTER CCXXXII. KALF ARNESON'S SPEECH.—Then Kalf Arneson desired to speak. " It is highly necessary," says he, " that this business we have on hand do not turn out a mockery and childwork, now that an army is collected. Something else

[1] Thore and the eleven wore the coats made by Lapland sorcery, *vide* p. 349, also p. 375.

is needful, if we are to stand battle with King Olaf, than that each should shove the danger from himself; for we must recollect that although King Olaf has not many people compared to this army of ours, the leader of them is intrepid, and the whole body of them will be true to him, and obedient in the battle. But if we who should be the leaders of this army show any fear, and will not encourage the army and go at the head of it, it must happen that with the great body of our people the spirit will leave their hearts, and the next thing will be that each will seek his own safety. Although we have now a great force assembled, we shall find our destruction certain, when we meet King Olaf and his troops, if we the chiefs of the people are not confident in our cause, and have not the whole army confidently and bravely going along with us. If it cannot be so, we had better not risk a battle; and then it is easy to see that nothing would be left us but to shelter ourselves under King Olaf's mercy, however hard it might be, as then we would be less guilty than we now may appear to him to be. Yet I know there are men in his ranks who would secure my life and peace if I would seek it. Will ye now adopt my proposal—then shalt thou, friend Thore, and thou, Harek, go under the banner which we will all of us raise up, and then follow. Let us all be speedy and determined in the resolution we have taken, and put ourselves so at the head of the bonders' army that they see no distrust in us; for then will the common man advance with spirit when we go merrily to work in placing the army in battle-order and in encouraging the people to the strife."

When Kalf had ended they all concurred in what he proposed, and all would do what Kalf thought of advantage. All desired Kalf to be the leader of the army, and to give each what place in it he chose.

CHAPTER CCXXXIII. HOW THE BARONS SET UP THEIR BANNERS.—Kalf Arneson then raised his banner, and drew up his house-servants along with Harek of Thiotto and his men. Thore Hund, with his troop, was at the head of the order of battle in front of the banner; and on both sides of Thore was a chosen body of bonders, all of them the most active and best armed in the forces. This part of the array was long and thick, and in it were drawn up the Drontheim people and the Haloga-landers. On the right wing was another array; and on the left of the main array were drawn up the men from Rogaland,

Hordaland, the Fjord districts, and Sogn, and they had the third banner.

CHAPTER CCXXXIV. OF THORSTEIN KNARESMED.—There was a man called Thorstein Knaresmed,[1] who was a merchant and master ship-carpenter, stout and strong, very passionate, and a great manslayer. He had been in enmity against King Olaf, who had taken from him a new and large merchant vessel he had built, on account of some manslaughter-mulct, incurred in the course of his misdeeds, which he owed to the king. Thorstein, who was with the bonders' army, went forward in front of the line in which Thore Hund stood, and said, " Here I will be, Thore, in your ranks; for I think if I and King Olaf meet, to be the first to drive a weapon at him, if I can get so near, to repay him for the robbery of the ship he took from me, which was the best that ever went on merchant voyage." Thore and his men received Thorstein, and he went into their ranks.

CHAPTER CCXXXV. OF THE PREPARATIONS OF THE PEASANTS. —When the bonders' men and array were drawn up the lendermen addressed the men, and ordered them to take notice of the place to which each man belonged, under which banner each should be, who there were in front of the banner, who were his side-men, and that they should be brisk and quick in taking up their places in the array; for the army had still to go a long way, and the array might be broken in the course of march. Then they encouraged the people; and Kalf invited all the men who had any injury to avenge on King Olaf, to place themselves under the banner which was advancing against King Olaf's own banner. They should remember the distress he had brought upon them; and, he said, never was there a better opportunity to avenge their grievances, and to free themselves from the yoke and slavery he had imposed on them. " Let him," says he, " be held a useless coward who does not fight this day boldly: and they are not innocents who are opposed to you, but people who will not spare you if ye spare them."

Kalf's speech was received with loud applause, and shouts of encouragement were heard through the whole army.

CHAPTER CCXXXVI. OF THE KING'S AND THE PEASANTS' ARMIES.—Thereafter the bonders' army advanced to Stiklestad, where King Olaf was already with his people. Kalf and Harek

[1] i.e. " the shipbuilder "; from knǫrr, a type of merchant-ship.

went in front, at the head of the army under their banners. But the battle did not begin immediately on their meeting; for the bonders delayed the assault, because all their men were not come upon the plain, and they waited for those who came after them. Thore Hund had come up with his troop the last, for he had to take care that the men did not go off behind when the battle-cry was raised, or the armies were closing with each other; and therefore Kalf and Harek waited for Thore. For the encouragement of their men in the battle the bonders had the field-cry—" Forward, forward, bondermen! " King Olaf also made no attack, for he waited for Dag and the people who followed him. At last the king saw Dag and his men approaching. It is said that the army of the bonders was not less on this day than a hundred times a hundred men.[1] Sigvat the scald speaks thus of the numbers:—

> " I grieve to think the king had brought
> Too small a force for what he sought:
> Although the ever-noble lord
> Gripped fast the gold hilt of his sword.
> The foemen, more than two to one,
> The victory by numbers won;
> And this alone, as I've heard say,
> Against King Olaf turned the day."

CHAPTER CCXXXVII. MEETING OF THE KING AND THE PEASANTS.—As the armies on both sides stood so near that people knew each other, the king said, " Why art thou here, Kalf, for we parted good friends south in Möre? It beseems thee ill to fight against us, or to throw a spear into our army; for here are four of thy brothers."

Kalf replied, " Many things come to pass differently from what may appear seemly. You parted from us so that it was necessary to seek peace with those who were behind in the country. Now each must remain where he stands; but if I might advise, we should be reconciled."

Then Finn, his brother, answered, " This is to be observed of Kalf, that when he speaks fairly he has it in his mind to do ill."

The king answered, " It may be, Kalf, that thou art inclined to reconciliation; but, methinks, the bonders do not appear so peaceful."

Then Thorgeir of Quiststad [2] said, " You shall now have such peace as many formerly have received at your hands, and which you shall now pay for."

---

[1] The big hundreds as usual; therefore 14,400 men.
[2] Now Kvistad in Inderöen.

The king replies, " Thou hast no occasion to hasten so much to meet us; for fate has not decreed to thee to-day a victory over me, who raised thee to power and dignity from a mean station."

CHAPTER CCXXXVIII. BEGINNING OF THE BATTLE OF STIKLESTAD.—Now came Thore Hund, went forward in front of the banner with his troop, and called out, " Forward, forward, bondermen! " Thereupon the bondermen raised the war-cry, and shot their arrows and spears. The king's men raised also a war-shout; and that done, encouraged each other to advance, crying out, " Forward, forward, Christ-men! cross-men! king's men! " When the bonders who stood outermost on the wings heard it, they repeated the same cry; but when the other bonders heard them they thought these were king's men, turned their arms against them, and they fought together, and many were slain before they knew each other. The weather was beautiful, and the sun shone clear; but when the battle began the heaven and the sun became red, and before the battle ended it became as dark as at night.[1] King Olaf had drawn up his army upon a rising ground, and it rushed down from thence upon the bonder-army with such a fierce assault, that the bonders' array bent before it; so that the breast of the king's array came to stand upon the ground on which the rear of the bonders' array had stood, and many of the bonders' army were on the way to fly, but the lendermen and their house-men stood fast, and the battle became very severe. So says Sigvat:—

> " Thundered the ground beneath their tread,
> As, iron-clad, thick-tramping, sped
> The men-at-arms, in row and rank,
> Past Stiklestad's sweet grassy bank.
> The clank of steel, the bowstrings' twang,
> The sounds of battle, loudly rang;
> And bowmen hurried on advancing,
> Their bright helms in the sunshine glancing."

The lendermen urged their men, and forced them to advance. Sigvat speaks of this:—

> " Midst in their line their banner flies,
> Thither the stoutest bonder hies:
> But many a bonder thinks of home,
> And many wish they ne'er had come."

[1] The earliest mention of this eclipse is in Sigvat's verse (p. 374); the oldest prose sources do not mention it, but the *Legendary Saga of St. Olaf* does, adds an earthquake, and draws an explicit parallel with the portents at Christ's death. The point is important to the dating of the battle; *vide* note, p. 381.

Then the bonder-army pushed on from all quarters. They who stood in front hewed down with their swords; they who stood next thrust with their spears; and they who stood hindmost shot arrows, cast spears, or threw stones, hand-axes, or sharp stakes. Soon there was a great fall of men in the battle. Many were down on both sides. In the first onset fell Arnliot Gelline, Gauka-Thore, and Afrafaste, with all their men, after each had killed a man or two, and some indeed more. Now the ranks in front of the king's banner began to be thinned, and the king ordered Thord to carry the banner forward, and the king himself followed it with the troop he had chosen to stand nearest to him in battle; and these were the best armed men in the field, and the most expert in the use of their weapons. Sigvat the scald tells of this:—

> " Loud was the battle-storm there,
>   Where the king's banner flamed in air.
>   The king beneath his banner stands,
>   And there the battle he commands."

Olaf came forth from behind the shield-bulwark, and put himself at the head of the array; and when the bonders looked him in the face they were frightened, and let their hands drop. So says Sigvat:—

> " I think I saw them shrink with fright
>   Who once had lavished gold fire-bright,
>   When Olaf's spear-sharp eye was cast
>   On them, and called up all the past.
>   Clear as the serpent's eye—his look
>   No Drontheim man could stand, but shook
>   Beneath its glance, and skulked away.
>   How fearsome Olaf seemed that day!"

The combat became fierce, and the king went forward in the fray. So says Sigvat:—

> " When on they came in fierce array,
>   And round the king arose the fray,
>   With shield on arm brave Olaf stood,
>   Dyeing his sword in their best blood.
>   For vengeance on his Drontheim foes,
>   On their best men he dealt his blows:
>   He who knew well death's iron play,
>   To his deep vengeance gave full sway."

CHAPTER CCXXXIX. THORGEIR OF QUISTSTAD'S FALL.— King Olaf fought most desperately. He struck the lenderman before mentioned (Thorgeir of Quiststad) across the face, cut off the nose-piece of his helmet, and clove his head down below the eyes so that they almost fell out. When he fell the king said, " Was it not true, Thorgeir, what I told thee, that thou shouldst not be victor in our meeting? " At the same instant Thord stuck the banner-pole so fast in the earth that it remained standing. Thord had got his death-wound, and fell beneath the banner. There also fell Thorfinn Mudr, and also Gissur Gulbraascald, who was attacked by two men, of whom he killed one, but only wounded the other before he fell. So says [p. 358] Hofgarde Refr:—

> " Bold in the iron-storm was he,
>   Firm and stout as forest tree,
>   The hero who, 'gainst two at once,
>   Made Odin's fire from sword-edge glance;
>   Dealing a death-blow to the one,
>   Known as a brave and generous man,
>   Wounding the other, ere he fell,—
>   His bloody sword his deeds showed well."

It happened then, as before related, that the sun, although the air was clear, withdrew from the sight, and it became dark. Of this Sigvat the scald speaks:—

> " No common wonder in the sky
>   Fell out that day—the sun on high,
>   And not a cloud to see around,
>   Shone not, nor warmed Norway's ground.
>   The day on which fell out this fight
>   Was marked by dismal dusky light.
>   This from the East I heard [1]—the end
>   Of our great king it did portend."

At the same time Dag Ringson came up with his people, and began to put his men in array, and to set up his banner; but on account of the darkness the onset could not go on so briskly, for they could not see exactly whom they had before them. They turned, however, to that quarter where the men of Hordaland and Rogaland stood. Many of these circumstances took place at the same time, and some happened a little earlier, and some a little later.

CHAPTER CCXL. KING OLAF'S FALL.—On the one side of Kalf Arneson stood his two relations, Olaf and Kalf, with many other brave and stout men. Kalf was a son of Arnfinn Armodson, and a brother's son of Arne Armodson. On the other side of Kalf Arneson stood Thore Hund. King Olaf hewed at Thore Hund, and struck him across the shoulders; but the sword

---

[1] i.e. from Norway; Sigvat, who was not at the battle himself, speaks from the point of view of someone in Iceland.

would not cut, and it was as if dust flew from his reindeer-skin coat. So says Sigvat:—

> " The king himself now proved the power
> Of Finn-folk's craft in magic hour,
> The mighty power of magic song
> Protected well Thore the strong.
> Our generous and noble lord
> Struck out with his gold-hilted sword
> At Thore's shoulders; but the blade
> Was blunted, and no wound it made."

Thore struck at the king, and they exchanged some blows; but the king's sword would not cut where it met the reindeer skin, although Thore was wounded in the hands. Sigvat sang thus of it:—

> " To challenge Thore—that is bold;
> Why never yet have I been told
> Of one who did a bolder thing
> Than to change blows with his true king.
> Against his king his sword to wield,
> Leaping across the shield on shield
> Such was the Dog's [1] deed in the fight—
> Who ever saw a fiercer sight? "

The king said to Biorn the marshal, " Do thou beat the dog on whom steel will not bite." Biorn turned round the axe in his hands, and gave Thore a blow with the hammer of it on the shoulder so hard that he tottered. The king at the same moment turned against Kalf's relation Olaf, and gave him his death-wound. Thore Hund struck his spear right through the body of Marshal Biorn, and killed him outright; and Thore said, " It is thus we hunt the bear." [2] Thorstein Knaresmed struck at King Olaf with his axe, and the blow hit his left leg above the knee. Finn Arneson instantly killed Thorstein. The king after the wound staggered towards a stone, threw down his sword, and prayed God to help him. Then Thore Hund struck at him with his spear and the stroke went in under his mail-coat and into his belly. Then Kalf struck at him on the left side of the neck. But all are not agreed which of the Kalfs [3] had been the man who gave the wound in the neck. These three wounds were King Olaf's death; and after the king's death the greater part of the forces which had advanced with

---

[1] Thore's nickname was Hund—the Dog.

[2] Biorn, the marshal's name, signifies a bear.

[3] Kalf Arneson or Kalf Arnfinnsson. Theodoricus, writing *c.* 1180, says men disagree on how many wounds Olaf had and who dealt them.

him fell with the king. Biorn Gulbraascald sang these verses about Kalf Arneson:—

> " Warrior! who Olaf dared withstand,
>   Who against Olaf held the land,
>   Thou hast withstood the bravest, best,
>   Who e'er has gone to his long rest.
>   At Stiklestad thou wast the head;
>   With flying banners onwards led
>   Thy bonder troops, and still fought on,
>   Until he fell—the much-mourned one."

Sigvat also made these verses on Biorn:—

> " The marshal Biorn, too, I find,
>   A great example leaves behind,
>   How steady courage should stand proof,
>   Though other servants stand aloof.
>   To battle first his steps he bent,
>   To serve his master still intent;
>   And now beside his king he fell,—
>   A noble death for scalds to tell."

CHAPTER CCXLI. BEGINNING OF DAG RINGSON'S ATTACK.—
Dag Ringson still kept up the battle, and made in the beginning so fierce an assault that the bonders gave way, and some betook themselves to flight. There a great number of the bonders fell, and these lendermen, Erlend of Gerde and Aslak of Finnö; and the banner also which they had stood under was cut down. This onset was particularly hot, and was called Dag's storm. But now Kalf Arneson, Harek of Thiotto, and Thore Hund turned against Dag, with the array which had followed them, and then Dag was overwhelmed with numbers; so he betook himself to flight with the men still left him. There was a valley through which the main body of the fugitives fled, and men lay scattered in heaps on both sides; and many were severely wounded, and many so fatigued that they were fit for nothing. The bonders pursued only a short way; for their leaders soon returned back to the field of battle, where they had their friends and relations to look after.

CHAPTER CCXLII. KING OLAF'S MIRACLE SHOWN TO THORE HUND.—Thore Hund went to where King Olaf's body lay, took care of it, laid it straight out on the ground, and spread a cloak over it. He told since that when he wiped the blood from the face it was very beautiful; and there was red in the cheeks, as if he only slept, and even much clearer than when he was in life. The king's blood came on Thore's hand, and ran up between his fingers to where he had been wounded, and the wound grew up so speedily that it did not require to be bound up. This circumstance was testified by Thore himself when King Olaf's holiness came to be generally known among the people; and Thore Hund was among the first of the king's powerful opponents who endeavoured to spread abroad the king's sanctity.

CHAPTER CCXLIII. OF KALF ARNESON'S BROTHERS.—Kalf Arneson searched for his brothers who had fallen, and found Thorberg and Finn. It is related that Finn threw his dagger at him, and wanted to kill him, giving him hard words, and calling him a faithless villain, and a traitor to his king. Kalf did not regard it, but ordered Finn and Thorberg to be carried away from the field. When their wounds were examined they were found not to be deadly, and they had fallen from fatigue, and under the weight of their weapons. Thereafter Kalf tried to bring his brothers down to a ship, and went himself with them. As soon as he was gone the whole bonder-army, having their homes in the neighbourhood, went off also, excepting those who had friends or relations to look after, or the bodies of the slain to take care of. The wounded were taken home to the farms, so that every house was full of them; and tents were erected over some. But wonderful as was the number collected in the bonder-army, no less wonderful was the haste with which this vast body dispersed when it was once free; and the cause of this was, that the most of the people gathered together from the country places were longing for their homes.

CHAPTER CCXLIV. OF THE PEASANTS OF VÆRDAL.—The bonders who had their homes in Værdal went to the chiefs Harek and Thore, and complained of their distress, saying, "The fugitives who have escaped from the battle have proceeded up over the valley of Værdal, and are destroying our habitations, and there is no safety for us to travel home so long as they are in the valley. Go after them with war-force, and let no mother's son of them escape with life; for that is what they intended for us if they had got the upper hand in the battle, and the same they would do now if they met us hereafter, and had better luck than we. It may also be that they will linger in the valley if they have nothing to be frightened for, and then they would not proceed very gently in the inhabited country." The bonders made many words about this, urging the chiefs to advance directly, and kill those who had escaped. Now when the chiefs talked over this matter among themselves, they thought there was much truth in what the bonders said. They resolved, therefore, that Thore Hund should undertake this expedition through Værdal, with 600 men of his own troops. Then, towards evening, he set out with his men; and Thore continued his march without halt until he came in the night to Suul, where he heard the news that Dag Ringson had come there in the evening, with many other flocks of the king's men, and had halted there until they took supper, but were afterwards gone up to the mountains. Then Thore said he did not care to pursue them up through the mountains, and he returned down the valley again, and they did not kill many of them this time. The bonders then returned to their homes, and the following day Thore, with his people, went to their ships. The part of the king's men who were still on their legs concealed themselves in the forests, and some got help from the people.

CHAPTER CCXLV. OF THE KING'S BROTHER, HARALD SIGURDSSON.—Harald Sigurdsson was severely wounded; but Ragnvald Brusesson brought him to a bonder's the night after the battle, and the bonder took in Harald, and healed his wound in secret, and afterwards gave him his son to attend him. They went secretly over the fjelds, and through the waste forests, and came out in Jemteland. Harald Sigurdsson was fifteen years old when King Olaf fell. In Jemteland, Harald found Ragnvald Brusesson; and they went both east to King Jarisleif in Russia, as is related in the Saga of Harald Sigurdsson.[2]

CHAPTER CCXLVI.[1] OF THORMOD KOLBRUNARSCALD.—Thormod Kolbrunarscald was under King Olaf's banner in the battle; but when the king had fallen, the battle was raging so that of the king's men the one fell by the side of the other, and the most of those who stood on their legs were wounded. Thormod was also severely wounded, and retired, as all the others did, back from where there was most danger of life, and some even fled. Now when the onset began which is called Dag's storm, all of the king's men who were able to combat went there; but Thormod did not come into that combat, being unable to fight, both from his wound and from weariness, but he stood by the side of his comrade in the ranks, although he could do nothing. There he was struck by an arrow in the left side; but he broke off the shaft of the arrow, went out of the battle, and up towards the houses, where he came to a barn which was a large building. Thormod had his drawn sword in his hand; and as he went in a man met him, coming out, and said, "It is very bad there with howling and screaming; and a great shame it is that brisk young fellows cannot bear their wounds: it may be that the king's men have done bravely to-day, but they certainly bear their wounds very ill."

Thormod asks, "What is thy name?"

He called himself Kimbe.

Thormod: "Wast thou in the battle too?"

"I was with the bonders, which was the best side," says he.

"And art thou wounded any way?" says Thormod.

"A little," said Kimbe. "And hast thou been in the battle too?"

Thormod replied, "I was with them who had the best."

"Art thou wounded?" says Kimbe.

"Not much to signify," replies Thormod.

As Kimbe saw that Thormod had a gold ring on his arm, he said, "Thou art certainly a king's man. Give me thy gold ring, and I will hide thee. The bonders will kill thee if thou fallest in their way."

Thormod says, "Take the ring if thou canst get it: I have lost that which is more worth."

Kimbe stretched out his hand, and wanted to take the ring, but Thormod, swinging his sword, cut off his hand: and it is related that Kimbe behaved himself no better under his wound than those he had been blaming just before. Kimbe went off, and Thormod sat down in the barn, and listened to what people were saying. The conversation was mostly about what each had seen in the battle, and about the valour of the combatants. Some praised most King Olaf's courage, and some named others who stood nowise behind him in bravery. Then Thormod sang these verses:—

> "Olaf was brave beyond all doubt,—
> At Stiklestad was none so stout;
> Spattered with blood, the king, unsparing,
> Cheered on his men with deed and daring.
> But I have heard that some were there
> Who in the fight themselves would spare;
> Though, in the arrow-storm, the most
> Had perils quite enough to boast."

CHAPTER CCXLVII. THORMOD'S DEATH. — Thormod went out, and entered into a chamber apart, in which there were many

wounded men, and with them a woman binding their wounds.
There was fire upon the floor, at which she warmed water to
wash and clean their wounds. Thormod sat himself down beside
the door, and one came in, and another went out, of those who
were busy about the wounded men. One of them turned to
Thormod, looked at him, and said, "Why art thou so dead-
pale? Art thou wounded? Why dost thou not call for the
help of the wound-healers?" Thormod then sang these verses:—

> " I am not blooming, and the fair
> And slender girl loves to care
> For blooming youths—few care for me;
> Yet Fenja's meal [1] I scattered free.
> The reason is that now I feel
> The slash and thrust of Danish steel;
> And pale and faint, and bent with pain,
> Return from yonder battle-plain."

Then Thormod stood up and went in towards the fire, and
stood there awhile. The nurse woman said to him, "Go out,
man, and bring in some of the split fire-wood which lies close
beside the door." He went out and brought in an armful of
wood, which he threw down upon the floor. Then the nurse-
girl looked him in the face, and said, "Dreadfully pale is this
man—why art thou so?" Then Thormod sang:—

> " Thou wonderest, sweet sprig, at me,
> A man so hideous to see:
> Deep wounds but rarely mend the face,
> The crippling blow gives little grace.
> The arrow-drift o'ertook me, girl,—
> A fine-ground arrow in the whirl
> Went through me, and I feel the dart
> Sits, lovely girl, too near my heart."

The girl said, "Let me see thy wound, and I will bind it."
Thereupon Thormod sat down, cast off his clothes, and the girl
saw his wounds, and examined that which was in his side, and
felt that a piece of iron was in it, but could not find where the
iron had gone in. In a stone pot she had stirred together leeks
and other herbs, and boiled them, and gave the wounded men
of it to eat, by which she discovered if the wounds had pene-
trated into the belly; for if the wound had gone so deep, it
would smell of leek. She brought some of this now to Thormod,
and told him to eat of it. He replied, "Take it away, I have
no appetite for broth." Then she took a large pair of tongs,
and tried to pull out the iron; but it sat too fast, and would in
no way come, and as the wound was swelled, little of it stood out

[1] Gold; Fenja was an ogress whose handmill ground out gold (see *The
Prose Edda*, trans. J. Young, p. 118).

to lay hold of. Now said Thormod, " Cut so deep in that thou
canst get at the iron with the tongs, and give me the tongs and
let me pull." She did as he said. Then Thormod took a gold
ring from his hand, gave it to the nurse-woman, and told her to
do with it what she liked. " It is a good man's gift," said he:
" King Olaf gave me the ring this morning." Then Thormod
took the tongs, and pulled the iron out; but on the iron there
was a hook, at which there hung some morsels of flesh from the
heart,—some white, some red. When he saw that, he said,
" The king has fed us well. I am fat even at the heart-roots: "
and so saying he leant back, and was dead. And with this ends
what we have to say about Thormod.

CHAPTER CCXLVIII. OF SOME CIRCUMSTANCES OF THE
BATTLE.—King Olaf fell on Wednesday, the 29th of July.[1] It
was near mid-day when the two armies met, and the battle
began before half-past one, and before three the king fell. The
darkness continued from about half-past one to three also.[2]
Sigvat the scald speaks thus of the result of the battle:—

> " The loss was great to England's foes,
>   When their chief fell beneath the blows
>   By his own thoughtless people given,—
>   When the king's shield in two was riven.
>   The people's sovereign took the field,
>   The people clove the sovereign's shield.
>   Of all the chiefs, that bloody day,
>   Dag only came out of the fray."

And he composed these:—

> " Such mighty bonder-power, I ween,
>   With chiefs or rulers ne'er was seen.
>   It was the people's mighty power
>   That struck the king that fatal hour.
>   When such a king, in such a strife,
>   By his own people lost his life,
>   Full many a gallant man must feel
>   The death-wound from the people's steel."

[1] The same date is given by Theodoricus and Eystein, and is that on
which the Feast of St. Olaf was held. Yet there is room for doubt. The
tradition of an eclipse goes back to Sigvat (p. 372), and in fact a total
eclipse visible at Stiklestad did occur on 31st August 1030. So either the
battle was in July and the eclipse is a fiction suggested by the real one in
August; or the battle was in August and the July date is a misreckoning.
This could arise from a text reading: " when 1029 years and two hundred
and nine days had passed since Christ's birth." Reckoning in long hundreds
(249 days) from 25th December, this gives 31st August; reckoning in
continental hundreds (209 days) from 1st January, this gives 29th July.
No extant text does use this precise formula, but the *Legendary Saga*
comes very close to it.

[2] It has been calculated that the eclipse of 31st August began at 1.40,
was total at 2.53, and was over by 4.0.

The bonders did not spoil the slain upon the field of battle, for immediately after the battle there came upon many of them who had been against the king a kind of dread as it were; yet they held by their evil inclination, for they resolved among themselves that all who had fallen with the king should not receive the interment which belongs to good men, but reckoned them all robbers and outlaws. But the men who had power, and had relations on the field, cared little for this, but removed their remains to the churches, and took care of their burial.

CHAPTER CCXLIX. A MIRACLE ON A BLIND MAN.—Thorgils Halmeson and his son Grim went to the field of battle towards evening when it was dusk, took King Olaf's corpse up, and bore it to a little empty houseman's hut which stood on the other side of their farm. They had light and water with them. Then they took the clothes off the body, swathed it in a linen cloth, laid it down in the house, and concealed it under some fire-wood so that nobody could see it, even if people came into the hut. Thereafter they went home again to the farm-house. A great many beggars and poor people had followed both armies, who begged for meat; and the evening after the battle many remained there, and sought lodging round about in all the houses, great or small. It is told of a blind man who was poor, that a boy attended him and led him. They went out around the farm to seek a lodging, and came to the same empty house, of which the door was so low that they had almost to creep in. Now when the blind man had come in, he fumbled about the floor seeking a place where he could lay himself down. He had a hat on his head, which fell down over his face when he stooped down. He felt with his hands that there was moisture on the floor, and he put up his wet hand to raise his hat, and in doing so put his fingers on his eyes. There came immediately such an itching in his eyelids, that he wiped the water with his fingers from his eyes, and went out of the hut, saying nobody could lie there it was so wet. When he came out of the hut he could distinguish his hands, and all that was near him, as far as things can be distinguished by sight in the darkness of night; and he went immediately to the farm-house into the room, and told all the people he had got his sight again, and could see everything, although many knew he had been blind for a long time, for he had been there before going about among the houses of the neighbourhood. He said he first got his sight when he was coming out of a little ruinous hut which was all wet inside. " I groped in the water," said he, " and rubbed my eyes with my wet hands." He told where the hut stood. The people who heard him wondered much at this event, and spoke among themselves of what it could be that produced it: but Thorgils the peasant and his son Grim thought they knew how this came to pass; and as they were much afraid the king's enemies might go there and search the hut, they went and took the body out of it, and removed it to a garden, where they concealed it, and then returned to the farm, and slept there all night.

CHAPTER CCL. OF THORE HUND.—On the fifth day following after this, Thore Hund came down the valley of Værdal to Stiklestad; and many people, both chiefs and bonders, accompanied him. The field of battle was still being cleared, and people were carrying away the bodies of their friends and relations, and were giving the necessary help to such of the wounded as they wished to save; but many had died since the battle. Thore Hund went to where the king had fallen, and searched for his body; but not finding it, he inquired if any one could tell him what had become of the corpse, but nobody could tell him where it was. Then he asked the bonder Thorgils, who said, " I was not in the battle, and knew little of what took place there; but many reports are abroad, and among others that King Olaf has been seen in the night up at Staf [p. 355], and a troop of people with him: but if he fell in the battle, your men must have concealed him in some hole, or under some stone-heap." Now although Thore Hund knew for certain that the king had fallen, many allowed themselves to believe, and to spread abroad the report, that the king had escaped from the battle, and would in a short time come again upon them with an army. Then Thore went to his ships, and sailed down the fjord, and the bonder-army dispersed, carrying with them all the wounded men who could bear to be removed.

CHAPTER CCLI. OF KING OLAF'S BODY.—Thorgils Halmeson and his son Grim had King Olaf's body, and were anxious about preserving it from falling into the hands of the king's enemies, and being ill-treated; for they heard the bonders speaking about burning it, or sinking it in the sea. The father and son had seen a clear light burning at night over the spot on the battle-field where King Olaf's body lay, and since, while they concealed it, they had always seen at night a light burning over the corpse; therefore they were afraid the king's enemies might seek the body where this signal was visible. They hastened, therefore, to take the body to a place where it would be safe. Thorgils and his son accordingly made a coffin, which they adorned as well as they could, and laid the king's body in it; and afterwards made another coffin, in which they laid stones and straw, about as much as the weight of a man, and carefully closed the coffins. As soon as the whole bonder-army had left Stiklestad, Thorgils and his son made themselves ready, got a large rowing boat, and took with them seven or eight men, who were all Thorgils' relations or friends, and privately took the coffin with the king's body down to the boat, and set it under the foot-boards. They had also with them the coffin containing the stones, and placed it in the boat where all could see it; and then went down the fjord with a good opportunity of wind and weather, and arrived in the dusk of the evening at Nidaros, where they brought up at the king's pier. Then Thorgils sent some of his men up to the town to Bishop Sigurd, to say that they were come with the king's body. As soon as the bishop heard this news, he sent his men down to the pier, and they took a small rowing boat, came alongside of Thorgils' ship, and demanded the king's body. Thorgils and his people then took the coffin which stood in view, and bore it into the boat; and the bishop's men rowed out into the fjord, and sank the coffin in the sea. It was now quite dark. Thorgils and his people now rowed up into the river past the town, and landed at a place called Saurlid, above the town. Then they carried the king's body to an empty house standing at a distance from other houses, and watched over it for the night, while Thorgils went down to the town, where he spoke with some of the best friends of King Olaf, and asked them if they would take charge of the king's body; but none of them dared to do so. Then Thorgils and his men went with the body higher up the river, buried it in a sand-hill on the banks, and levelled all around it so that no one could observe that people had been at work there. They were ready with all this before break of day, when they returned to their vessel, went immediately out of the river, and proceeded on their way home to Stiklestad.

CHAPTER CCLII. OF THE BEGINNING OF KING SWEND ALFIVA-SON'S GOVERNMENT.—Swend, a son of King Canute, and of Alfiva, a daughter of Earl Alfrin, had been appointed to govern Jomsborg in Vendland. There came a message to him from his father King Canute, that he should come to Denmark; and likewise that afterwards he should proceed to Norway, and take that kingdom under his charge, and assume, at the same time, the title of king of Norway. Swend repaired to Denmark, and took many people with him from thence, and also Earl Harald[1] and many other people of consequence attended him. Thorarin Loftunge speaks of this in the song he composed about King Swend, called the Glelogn song:— [2]

> " 'Tis told by fame,
> How grandly came
> The Danes to tend
> Their young king Swend.
> Grandest was he,
> That all could see;
> Then, one by one,
> Each following man
> More splendour wore
> Than him before."

Then Swend proceeded to Norway, and his mother Alfiva was with him; and he was taken to be king at every Law-thing in the country. He had already come as far as Viken at the time the battle was fought at Stiklestad, and King Olaf fell. Swend continued his journey until he came north, in autumn, to the Drontheim country; and there, as elsewhere, he was received as king.

CHAPTER CCLIII. OF KING SWEND'S LAWS.—King Swend introduced new laws in many respects into the country, partly after those which were in Denmark, and in part much more severe. No man must leave the country without the king's permission; or if he did, his property fell to the king. Whoever killed a man outright, should forfeit all his land and movables. If any one was banished the country, and an heritage fell to him, the king took his inheritance. At Yule every man should pay the king a meal[3] of malt from every harvest steading, and a leg of a three-year-old ox, which was called the meadow gift, together with a spand[4] of butter; and every housewife a rock[5] full of unspun lint, as thick as one could span with the fingers of the longest hand.[6] The bonders were bound to build all the houses the king required upon his farms. Of every seven males

---

[1] Son of Thorkel the Tall, *vide* p. 342.   [2] *Vide* note, p. 390.
[3] *Mælir* (maling) is a measure of grain of a size varying in different districts; it is still used in the Orkneys and Shetland.
[4] *Spann*, another variable measure, here equal to 36 lb.
[5] *Rykkjartó* is not connected with English " rock "=" distaff," but with *rýgr*, " housewife." It means a skein of undressed flax or wool.
[6] More accurately: " between the thumb and the longest finger."

one should be taken for the service of war, and reckoning from the fifth year of age; and the outfit of ships should be reckoned in the same proportion.[1] Every man who rowed upon the sea to fish should pay the king five fish as a tax, on coming into land, wherever he might come from. Every ship that went out of the country should have stowage reserved open for the king in the middle of the ship. Every man, foreigner or native, who went to Iceland, should pay a tax to the king. And to all this was added, that Danes should enjoy so much consideration in Norway, that one witness of them should invalidate ten of Northmen.[2]

When these laws were promulgated the minds of the people were instantly raised against them, and murmurs were heard among them. They who had not taken part against King Olaf said, " Now take your reward and friendship from the Canute race, ye men of the Drontheim inner district who fought against King Olaf, and deprived him of his kingdom. Ye were promised peace and justice, and now ye have got oppression and slavery for your great treachery and crime." Nor was it very easy to contradict them, as all men saw how miserable the change had been. But people had not the boldness to make an insurrection against King Swend, principally because many had given King Canute their sons or other near relations as hostages; and also because no one appeared as leader of an insurrection. They very soon, however, complained of King Swend; and his mother Alfiva got much of the blame of all that was against their desire. Then the truth, with regard to Olaf, became evident to many.

CHAPTER CCLIV. OF KING OLAF'S SANCTITY.—This winter many in the Drontheim land began to declare that Olaf was in reality a holy man, and his sanctity was confirmed by many miracles. Many began to make promises and prayers to King Olaf in the matters in which they thought they required help, and many found great benefit from these invocations; some in respect of health, others of a journey, or other circumstances in which such help seemed needful.

CHAPTER CCLV. OF EINAR TAMBARSKELVE.—Einar Tambar-

---

[1] *i.e.* that in the same way one man in seven must contribute to the building and fitting out of the king's warships.

[2] This may probably have referred not to witnesses of an act, but to the class of witnesses in the jurisprudence of the middle ages called compurgators who testified not the fact, but their confidence in the statements of the accused.

skelve was come home from England to his farm, and had the fiefs which King Canute had given him when they met in Drontheim, and which were almost an earldom. Einar had not been in the strife against King Olaf, and congratulated himself upon it. He remembered that King Canute had promised him the earldom over Norway, and at the same time remembered that King Canute had not kept his promise. He was accordingly the first great person who looked upon King Olaf as a saint.[1]

CHAPTER CCLVI. OF THE SONS OF ARNE.—Finn Arneson remained but a short time at Egge with his brother Kalf; for he was in the highest degree ill-pleased that Kalf had been in the battle against King Olaf, and always made his brother the bitterest reproaches on this account. Thorberg Arneson was much more temperate in his discourse than Finn; but yet he hastened away, and went home to his farm. Kalf gave the two brothers a good long-ship, with full rigging and other necessaries, and a good retinue. Therefore they went home to their farms, and sat quietly at home. Arne Arneson lay long ill of his wounds, but got well at last without injury of any limb, and in winter he proceeded south to his farm. All the brothers made their peace with King Swend, and sat themselves quietly down in their homes.

CHAPTER CCLVII. BISHOP SIGURD'S FLIGHT [1031].—The summer after there was much talk about King Olaf's sanctity, and there was a great alteration in the expressions of all people concerning him. There were many who now believed that King Olaf must be a saint, even among those who had persecuted him with the greatest animosity, and would never in their conversation allow truth or justice in his favour. People began then to turn their reproaches against the men who had principally excited opposition to the king; and on this account Bishop Sigurd in particular was accused. He got so many enemies, that he found it most advisable to go over to England to King Canute. Then the Drontheim people sent men with a verbal message to the Uplands, to Bishop Grimkel, desiring him to come north to Drontheim. King Olaf had sent Bishop Grimkel back to Norway when he went east into Russia, and since that time Grimkel had been in the Uplands. When the message

---

[1] It has also been suggested that the eclipse and the failure of crops during Swend's reign were seen as marks of God's anger at Olaf's death and contributed to the sudden change in attitude towards him.

came to the bishop he made ready to go, and it contributed much to this journey that the bishop considered it as true what was told of King Olaf's miracles and sanctity.

CHAPTER CCLVIII. KING OLAF THE SAINT'S REMAINS DISINTERRED.—Bishop Grimkel went to Einar Tambarskelve, who received him joyfully. They talked over many things, and, among others, of the important events which had taken place in the country; and concerning these they were perfectly agreed. Then the bishop proceeded to the town (Nidaros), and was well received by all the community. He inquired particularly concerning the miracles of King Olaf that were reported, and received satisfactory accounts of them. Thereupon the bishop sent a verbal message to Stiklestad to Thorgils and his son Grim, inviting them to come to the town to him. They did not decline the invitation, but set out on the road immediately, and came to the town and to the bishop. They related to him all the signs that had presented themselves to them, and also where they had deposited the king's body. The bishop sent a message to Einar Tambarskelve, who came to the town. Then the bishop and Einar had an audience of the king and Alfiva, in which they asked the king's leave to have King Olaf's body taken up out of the earth. The king gave his permission, and told the bishop to do as he pleased in the matter. At that time there were a great many people in the town. The bishop, Einar, and some men with them, went to the place where the king's body was buried, and had the place dug; but the coffin had already raised itself almost to the surface of the earth. It was then the opinion of many that the bishop should proceed to have the king buried in the earth at Clement's church; and it was so done. Twelve months and five days after King Olaf's death his holy remains were dug up (3rd August 1031), and the coffin had raised itself almost entirely to the surface of the earth; and the coffin appeared quite new, as if it had but lately been made. When Bishop Grimkel came to King Olaf's opened coffin, there was a delightful and fresh smell. Thereupon the bishop uncovered the king's face, and his appearance was in no respect altered, and his cheeks were as red as if he had but just fallen asleep. The men who had seen King Olaf when he fell remarked, also, that his hair and nails had grown as much as if he had lived on the earth all the time that had passed since his fall. Thereupon King Swend, and all the chiefs who were at the place, went out to see King Olaf's body. Then said Alfiva, " People buried

in sand rot very slowly, and it would not have been so if he had
been buried in earth." Afterwards the bishop took scissors,
clipped the king's hair, and arranged his beard; for he had a long
beard, according to the fashion of that time. Then said the
bishop to the king and Alfiva, " Now the king's hair and beard
are such as when he gave up the ghost, and it has grown as much
as ye see has been cut off." Alfiva answers, " I will believe in
the sanctity of his hair, if it will not burn in the fire; but I have
often seen men's hair whole and undamaged after lying longer
in the earth than this man's." Then the bishop had live coals
put into a pan, blessed it, cast incense upon it, and then laid
King Olaf's hair on the fire. When all the incense was burnt the
bishop took the hair out of the fire, and showed the king and the
other chiefs that it was not consumed. Now Alfiva asked that
the hair should be laid upon unconsecrated fire; but Einar
Tambarskelve told her to be silent, and gave her many severe
reproaches for her unbelief. After the bishop's recognition,
with the king's approbation and the decision of the Thing, it was
determined that King Olaf should be considered a man truly
holy; whereupon his body was transported into Clement's
church, and a place was prepared for it near the high altar. The
coffin was covered with costly cloth, and stood under a gold
embroidered tent. Many kinds of miracles were soon wrought
by King Olaf's holy remains.

CHAPTER CCLIX. OF KING OLAF'S MIRACLES.—In the sand-
hill where King Olaf's body had lain on the ground a beautiful
spring of water came up, and many human ailments and infirmi-
ties were cured by its waters. Things were put in order around
it, and the water ever since has been carefully preserved.[1] There
was first a chapel built, and an altar consecrated, where the king's
body had lain; but now Christ's church stands upon the spot.
Archbishop Eystein [2] had a high altar raised upon the spot where
the king's grave had been, when he erected the great minster
which now stands there; and it is the same spot on which the
altar of the old Christ church [3] had stood. It is said that Olaf's
church [4] stands on the spot on which the empty house had stood

[1] Harald the Stern had this spring covered in, and built over it the church
called Maria Kirke (see *Sagas of the Norse Kings*, pp. 189–90).
[2] Eystein Erlendsson was the second Archbishop of Nidaros (1161–88):
c. 1170 he wrote the *Passio et Miracula Beati Olavi* (*vide* p. xxv).
[3] The one which was built by Olaf Kyrre (1066–93). See *Sagas of the
Norse Kings*, p. 245.
[4] The one built by Magnus the Good (1035–47). See *Sagas of the Norse
Kings*, p. 189.

in which King Olaf's body had been laid for the night. The place over which the holy remains of King Olaf were carried up from the vessel is now called Olaf's Road, and is now in the middle of the town. The bishop adorned King Olaf's holy remains, and cut his nails and hair; for both grew as if he had still been alive. So says Sigvat the scald:—

> " I lie not, when I say the king
> Seemed as alive in every thing:
> His nails, his yellow hair still grew,
> (My verse extols his servants true);
> For once beneath far Russian skies
> He gave a man with blinded eyes
> A lock of his own golden hair,
> And thus he cured him then and there."

Thorarin Loftunge also composed a song upon Swend Alfivason, called the Glelogn [1] Song, in which are these verses:—

> " Swend, king of all,
> In Olaf's hall
> His throne doth raise—
> Through all his days
> May our gold-giver
> Live here for ever!
> Here Olaf the king
> Had his dwelling
> Until he went
> As a glorious saint
> (All men know this)
> Into Heaven's bliss.

> " King Olaf there
> To hold a share
> On earth prepared,
> Nor labour spared
> A sea to win
> From heaven's great King;
> Which he has won
> Next God's own Son.

> " His holy form,
> Untouched by worm,
> Lies at this day
> Where good men pray,
> And nails and hair
> Grow fresh and fair;
> His cheek is red,
> His flesh not dead.

> " Around his bier,
> Good people hear
> The small bells ring
> Over the king,
> By their own power;
> Yea, every hour
> All men can hear
> The bells ring clear.

[1] *Glælogn* apparently means " Calm Sea." The poem must date from *c*. 1032, and is valuable evidence of the early growth of the Olaf cult.

" Tapers up there,
(Which Christ holds dear,)
By day and night
The altar light:
Olaf, I know,
While on earth below,
Quite free from sin,
Did salvation win.

" And crowds do come,
The deaf and dumb,
Cripple and blind,
Sick of all kind,
Cured to be
On bended knee;
And off the ground
Rise whole and sound.

" To Olaf pray
To eke thy day,
To save thy land
From spoiler's hand.
God's man is he
To deal to thee
Good crops and peace;
Let not prayer cease.

" When thou dost pray,
Thy prayers be heard
Before the King-Post
Of the Holy Word." [1]

Thorarin Loftunge was himself with King Swend, and heard these great testimonials of King Olaf's holiness, that people, by the heavenly power, could hear a sound over his holy remains as if bells were ringing, and that candles were lighted of themselves upon the altar, as by a heavenly fire. But when Thorarin says that a multitude of lame, and blind, and other sick, who came to the holy Olaf, went back cured, he means nothing else than that there were a vast many persons who at the beginning of King Olaf's miraculous working regained their health. King Olaf's first miracles are clearly written down, although they occurred somewhat later.

CHAPTER CCLX. OF KING OLAF'S AGE AND REIGN.—It is reckoned, by those who have kept an exact account, that Olaf the Saint was king of Norway for fifteen years from the time

[1] Literally: " When you offer up your prayers before the mighty nails of book-speech " (*fyr reginnagla bókamáls*). The last phrase must be a metaphor for Olaf, though its terms are obscure. According to *Eyrbyggja saga*, *reginnaglar* were driven in posts at the entrance to heathen temples; *bókamál* means Latin, language of the Bible and of Christian culture. Olaf is viewed as the noblest timber upholding the fabric of Christianity.

Earl Swend left the country; but he had received the title of king from the people of the Uplands the winter before. Sigvat the scald tells this:—

> " For fifteen winters o'er the land
> King Olaf held the chief command,
> Before he fell up in the North:
> His fall made known to us his worth.
> No worthier prince before his day
> In our North land e'er held the sway.
> Too short he held it for our good:
> All men wish now that he had stood."

Saint Olaf was thirty-five years old when he fell according to what Are the Learned the priest says, and he had been in twenty pitched battles. So says Sigvat the scald:—

> " Some warriors trusted in God, some not,
> In Olaf's troop; but well I wot
> God-fearing Olaf fought and won
> Twenty pitched battles, one by one,
> And always placed upon his right
> His Christian men in a hard fight.
> May God be merciful, I pray,
> To him—for he ne'er shunned the fray."

We have now related a part of King Olaf's story, namely, the events which took place while he ruled over Norway; also his death, and how his sainthood was manifested. Now shall we not neglect to mention what it was that most advanced his honour. This was his miracles; but these will come to be treated of afterwards in this book.[1]

CHAPTER CCLXI. OF THE DRONTHEIM PEOPLE. — King Swend, the son of Canute the Great, ruled over Norway for some years; but was a child both in age and understanding. His mother Alfiva had most sway in the country; and the people of the country were her great enemies, both then and ever since. Danish people had a great superiority given them within the country, to the great dissatisfaction of the people; and when conversation turned that way, the people of the rest of Norway accused the Drontheim people of having principally occasioned King Olaf the Saint's fall, and also that the men of Norway were subject, through them, to the ill government by which oppression and slavery had come upon all the people, both great and small; indeed upon the whole community. They insisted

---

[1] Snorri's *Separate Saga of St. Olaf* ends with eight chapters containing stories of miracles ascribed to him; these miracles, and others also, he inserted in later parts of *Heimskringla* (see *Sagas of the Norse Kings*).

that it was the duty of the Drontheim people to attempt opposition and insurrection, and thus relieve the country from such tyranny; and, in the opinion of the common people, Drontheim was also the chief seat of the strength of Norway at that time, both on account of the chiefs and of the population of that quarter. When the Drontheim people heard these remarks of their countrymen, they could not deny that there was much truth in them, and that in depriving King Olaf of life and land they had committed a great crime, and at the same time the misdeed had been ill paid. The chiefs began to hold consultations and conferences with each other, and the leader of these was Einar Tambarskelve. It was likewise the case with Kalf Arneson, who began to find into what errors he had been drawn by King Canute's persuasion. All the promises which King Canute had made to Kalf had been broken; for he had promised him the earldom and the highest authority in Norway: and although Kalf had been the leader in the battle against King Olaf, and had deprived him of his life and kingdom, Kalf had not got any higher dignity than he had before. He felt that he had been deceived, and therefore messages passed between the brothers Kalf, Finn, Thorberg, and Arne, and they renewed their family friendship.

CHAPTER CCLXII. OF KING SWEND'S LEVY [1033].—When King Swend had been three years in Norway the news was received that a force was assembled in the western countries, under a chief who called himself Trygve, and gave out that he was a son of Olaf Trygvesson and Queen Gyda [1] of England. Now when King Swend heard that foreign troops had come to the country, he ordered out the people on a levy in the north, and the most of the lendermen hastened to him; but Einar Tambarskelve remained at home, and would not go out with King Swend. When King Swend's order came to Kalf Arneson at Egge, that he should go out on a levy with King Swend, he took a twenty-benched ship which he owned, went on board with his house-servants, and in all haste proceeded out of the fjord, without waiting for King Swend, sailed southwards to Möre, and continued his voyage south until he came to Giske to his brother Thorberg. Then all the brothers, the sons of Arne, held a meeting, and consulted with each other. After this Kalf returned to the north again; but when he came to Frekösund [p. 333] King Swend was lying in the sound before

[1] *Vide* p. 31.

him. When Kalf came rowing from the south into the sound they hailed each other, and the king's men ordered Kalf to bring up with his vessel, and follow the king for the defence of the country. Kalf replies, " I have done enough, if not too much, when I fought against my own countrymen to increase the power of the Canute family." Thereupon Kalf rowed away to the north until he came home to Egge. None of these Arnesons appeared at this levy to accompany the king. He steered with his fleet southwards along the land; but as he could not hear the least news of any fleet having come from the west, he steered south to Rogaland, and all the way to Agder: for many guessed that Trygve would first make his attempt on Viken, because his forefathers had been there, and had most of their strength from that quarter, and he had himself great strength by family connection there.

CHAPTER CCLXIII. KING TRYGVE OLAFSSON'S FALL.—When Trygve came from the west he landed first on the coast of Hordaland, and when he heard King Swend had gone south he went the same way to Rogaland. As soon as Swend got the intelligence that Trygve had come from the west he returned, and steered north with his fleet; and both fleets met within Bokn in Soknasund, not far from the place where Erling Skialgsson fell. The battle, which took place on a Sunday, was great and severe. People tell that Trygve threw spears with both hands at once. " So my father," said he, " taught me to celebrate mass." [1] His enemies had said that he was the son of a priest; but he made much boast of the fact that he showed himself more like a son of King Olaf Trygvesson, for this Trygve was a most doughty man. In this battle King Trygve fell, and many of his men with him; but some fled, and some received quarter and their lives. It is thus related in the ballad of Trygve:—

> " Trygve comes from the northern coast,
> King Swend turns round with all his host;
> To meet and fight they both prepare,
> And where they met grim death was there.
> From the sharp strife I was not far,—
> I heard the din and the clang of war;
> And the Hordaland men at last gave way,
> And their leader fell, and they lost the day."

This battle is also told of in the ballad about King Swend, thus:—

[1] This mode of spear-throwing was used by Olaf Tryggvason (*vide* p. 75).

" My girl! it was no Sunday morn,
    And many a man ne'er saw its eve,
Though ale and leeks by old wives borne
    The bruised and wounded did relieve.
Then Swend to valiant men calls out:
    ' Stem to stem your vessels bind';
The raven a mid-day feast smells out,
    And he comes croaking up the wind."

After this battle King Swend ruled the country for some time, and there was peace in the land. The winter after it he passed in the south parts of the country.

CHAPTER CCLXIV. OF THE COUNSELS OF EINAR TAMBARSKELVE AND KALF ARNESON.—Einar Tambarskelve and Kalf Arneson had this winter meetings and consultations between themselves in the merchant town.[1] Then there came a messenger from King Canute to Kalf Arneson, with a message to send him three dozen axes, which must be chosen and good. Kalf replies, " I will send no axes to King Canute. Tell him I will bring his son Swend so many, that he shall not think he is in want of any."

CHAPTER CCLXV. OF EINAR TAMBARSKELVE AND KALF ARNESON'S JOURNEY OUT OF THE COUNTRY [1034].—Early in spring Einar Tambarskelve and Kalf Arneson made themselves ready for a journey, with a great retinue of the best and most select men that could be found in the Drontheim country. They went in spring eastward over the ridge of the country to Jemteland, from thence to Helsi geland, and came to Sweden, where they procured ships, with which in summer they proceeded east to Russia, and came in autumn to Ladoga. They sent men up to Novgorod to King Jarisleif, with the errand that they offered Magnus, the son of King Olaf the Saint, to take him with them, follow him to Norway, and give him assistance to attain his father's heritage and be made king over the country. When this message came to King Jarisleif he held a consultation with the queen and some chiefs, and they all resolved unanimously to send a message to the Northmen, and ask them to come to King Jarisleif and Magnus; for which journey safe conduct was given them. When they came to Novgorod it was settled among them that the Northmen who had come there should become Magnus's men, and be his subjects; and to this Kalf and the other men who had been against King Olaf at Stiklestad were solemnly bound by oath. On the other

[1] *Kaupang*, another name for Trondhjem (Nidaros).

hand, King Magnus promised them, under oath, secure peace and full reconciliation; and that he would be true and faithful to them all when he got the dominions and kingdom of Norway. He was to become Kalf Arneson's foster-son; and Kalf should be bound to do all that Magnus might think necessary for extending his dominion, and making it more independent than formerly.

APPENDIX I

CORRECTIONS TO THE TRANSLATED TEXT

IN THE following a more accurate translation of the text of the *Heimskringla* is given after the bracket mark (*small figures denote line numbers*):

5^9 went] had herself rowed out. 5^{13} was ... land] made ready to leave. 10^2 was much beloved] was very loving towards him. 10^{24} to them] back to his kingdom. 10^{25-6} accordingly ... feast] as has been written. 11^{21} and tells him] and they begin their talk. The king tells the earl of. 12^9 your ... left it] this kingdom which your father held and which you inherited from him. 13^{15} his mother] Gunhild. 15^3 Frode] Thorgil's son. 18^{15} It ... certain] It is said. 32^{17} which showed] then they knew for certain. 32^{17-18} and was very] the dog seemed to them amazingly. 32^{18} sell] give. 32^{19} " I ... you "] " Willingly." 37^{37} earl was] earls were (*i.e.* Hakon and Eric). 44^{26} Rane] they. 44^{27} he] they (twice). 48^{25} the same ... to him] he had seen the same man come back down. 53^{21} the proclaiming] that he wished to proclaim. 64^{27-8} As soon ... asleep] But when on the first night they were lying together, then as soon as the king was asleep. 71^{14} witches] trolls. 74^2 as ... commands] that thou mayest not do a thing which I could not on any account tolerate. 75^{16-20} that one ... ground] that he helped one of his bodyguard who had climbed the peak in such a way that he could get neither up nor down; but the king went to him and carried him down to level ground in his arms. $102^{27,37}$ snow-mountains, snowy mountains] glaciers. $104^{5,\,6}$ snowy mountains, snowy ridges] glaciers. 106^{11} snow-covered mountain ranges] glaciers. 108^{1-2} mixed ... words] and this scream said. 109^{36-7} Our goodwife is wonderful] There is something very strange about our goodwife. 121^{18} they] he. 129^{23-4} and of Hild] as was written before. 164^{10-12} but he ... bonders] Eilif had thirty men, those of his company. He was in the upland parts of the inhabited districts, up near the forests, and he had gathered some bonders there. 172^{12-13} so long as ... this mission] until such times as I think might make it more likely that this mission could be successfully carried out. 201³⁴⁻⁵ in high spirits . . . king came] Then the king's daughter was glad; and she was just coming out from her own quarters, but when she saw the king come. 214⁶ descendants] beloved friends. 214⁴²⁻³ Who is . . . and me?] What men are taking the lead in stealing my country away from me? 218¹ sire, . . . Almighty] for my Lord and God. 234² the same accusations] this accusation. 234¹⁵⁻¹⁶ in such . . . contradict it] will not acknowledge. 235⁹⁻¹⁰ for a good winter] and welcome winter in. 245¹ one] Thore Sel. 247³⁸ we do here] we Rogalanders do. 247⁴⁰ my friend] kinsman. 250¹⁴ in which . . . truth] and it seemed to Asbiorn that he was evidently twisting the truth. 250¹⁵ Among other things] Then. 251¹⁹ was there] was coming in such haste. 252¹⁰ must take care then] shalt have thy way in this, in so far. 258³⁶⁻⁹ And I knew . . . God's also.] And the second reason was that I knew that even if you were angry with me, my life was the utmost that would be at stake; and if you wish that I should lose it for this fault, then I can expect that I too will be God's. 263¹³ some will be] they will be unequal, some being. 270⁶ and cold . . . him] for henceforth cold counsel will come to him from under every rib (*i.e.* henceforth every plan formed in my heart will be aimed against him). 275⁴ although] even if he thinks nothing of the fact that. 276²⁰ proceeded . . . at first] lay very low at first, took to small boats, travelled by night. 277⁹ and a man]; all these foster-sons of Thrand's were men. 296²⁴,³³ witch, witch-wife] she-troll. 313¹⁰⁻¹⁴ housething . . . set in] King Olaf spoke out and said that things had gone according to his guess, for King Canute had not stayed long in Helge river. " I now expect that the rest of our dealings with him will go according to my guess. He now has only a small host compared with what he had in the summer, and he will later have even less, for it is no pleasanter for them than for us to live out on board ship in late autumn; and victory is fated to be ours, if we do not lack perseverance and boldness. This summer things went in such a way that it was we who had the smaller force, yet they who lost men and wealth to us." Then the Swedes began to speak, and said it was not wise to wait there for winter and frost—" although the Norwegians press for it. They do not know so well how the ice can form here, how the whole place has often frozen over in winter. We wish to go home now, and not stay here any longer." Then the Swedes began to grumble loudly, and all to talk at once. 383³⁸ a clear light] something as if it were candle-light. 385³⁶⁻⁷ with . . . hand] between the thickest finger (*i.e.* the thumb) and the longest finger.   385²³ harvest steading] hearth.   391³⁸⁻⁹ King Olaf's . . . although they] As for the greatest of King Olaf's miracles, they are mostly written down and accounts given of them, and so are those which.

APPENDIX II

INTERPOLATIONS IN THE TRANSLATED TEXT

The following passages are to be dismissed as interpolations in the text of *Heimskringla* (*small figures denote line numbers*):

5^{10} or small island. 9^{21} for the first. 11^2 of it. 11^5 as usual. 12^{12} kind of. 13^{32} in Jutland. 15^{14} no doubt. 18^6 at his mercy. 20^4 Earl Hakon's son. 21^{20-8} So says Hallarstein . . . ships sweep. 31^{21} called Gyda. and am. 34^{8-9} that . . . waste. 36^2 without . . . consent. 41^9 in . . . which. 42^{15} Halkelson. 42^{27} young. to the gods. 46^{32} at that tide. 48^{27-8} or slave. 50^3 or council. 52^1 and again. 52^{40} Ingerid and Ingigerd. 53^4 Urguthriot and Brimiskjar. 53^{24} in . . . work. 57^4 in Drontheim. 58^{30-1} an old . . . and. 59^{27-8} with . . . men. 60^2 upon the island. 69^7 Vige. 72^{13-43} They carried . . . many thanks. 73^{21-2} wherever . . . distinction. 75^{23-4} could walk . . . rails. 75^{24} and cut. 76^{37-8} the length . . . ells. 82^5 queen. 82^{37} Bollason. 84^{13}-85^{36} CHAPTER CV. Earl Rognvald . . . about him. 85^{39-41} and past . . . sister. 86^{6-28} with all . . . fine men. 87^{32} to Sweden. 98^{44} and Earl Eric's brother. 104^{36} they thought the. 122^{31} The king . . . England. 129^{16-19} During . . . son of Swend. 130^{15-21} When Olaf . . . Swedish King. 133^5 came to . . . died, and. 138^3 to procure . . . was needed. 144^{38} as a token. 145^1 north, south, east, west. 147^{23-4} and had . . . single house. 148^7 in Iceland. 154^{26} in prison. 154^{27} and. on board a ship. 161^{17-25} Sigvat tells . . . heads hung high. 212^{36} and a day. 235^{31} by his men-at-arms. 238^{18} when. 238^{19} they heard of the king. 239^{30-1} at a farm called Lidstad. 240^{34} is so powerful and. 242^{39-40} the king . . . journey. 243^8 the scald. 249^{19} and people. 250^{28} when in anger. 268^{38} and reduce . . . desert. 270^{11-12} and . . . favour. 301^{27-9} and gave . . . vengeance (the chief manuscript is here defective). 301^{29-30} to king . . . relations (the chief manuscript is here defective). 324^{7-8} advising . . . cause of it. 326^9 or . . . refrain. 326^{11} or long poem. 339^{9-11} and even . . . law. 378^{16-25} CHAPTER CCXLV. Of the . . . Sigurdsson. 394^{23} which . . . Sunday.

APPENDIX III

OMISSIONS IN THE TRANSLATED TEXT

In this list a passage following the sign + is in the original text of the *Heimskringla* and should be inserted after the word given before the bracket mark (*small figures denote line numbers*):

6^{10} Hakon] + as has been written already. 9^2 cloak] + or cape. 12^2 now] + once again. 12^{12} can] + rightfully. 27^{16} fire to] + all. 31^{25} married] + and I am called Gyda. 32^{33} standing] + unburnt in Sogn. 37^{38} waste] + wherever they went. 41^7 seems] + to me. 41^8 an] + large. 42^2 Valders] + a lenderman (see p. 150, n. 2). 42^{31} taking] + Vogn. 43^7 foster-brother] + Harald Grænske. 44^{18} coming] + from other lands. 46^4 Ireland] + to Dublin. 48^{13} Brynjolf] + that deed had aroused great displeasure. 50^{22} good] + just as it had been before. 51^1 body] + and dragged it away and burned it. 53^{39} Christianity] + which Olaf was preaching. 55^{42} match "] + And they dropped the discussion for the time being. 56^{36} king] + to conclude the matter. 58^{34} off] + north. 58^{34} queen] + east. 59^{29} for him] + He had nearly three hundred (*i.e.* 360) men. 60^{30} stones] + which are still standing there. 64^{34} king's] + Olaf's. 69^1 story] + of Raud's revenge. 73^2 king] + and ordered that it should be solemnly celebrated. 76^{25} relations] + the brothers. 81^{14} story] + of their journey. 81^{39} they] + all. 82^8 own] + than you are now. 86^{30} Sound, and] + in this expedition the king went. 94^{40} arrow] + came so close to the earl that it. 95^{22} gently] + that I see. 99^9 districts] + and Fjalir. 108^{21} Crossness] + ever afterwards. 121^{33} land] + then again, as so often. 121^{36} to sea] + But the host of the Finlanders was coming down by the inland path just as the king sailed away by sea. 130^{10} Einar] + She was a woman of most outstanding character. 137^{21} Olaf] + the Thick. 138^8 set with] + enamelling and. 155^9 as] + it seemed to him that. 158^9 Biorn] + the Thick. 159^{32} answer] + from the bonders. 160^{16} rather than] + to submit. 161^5 Asgaut] + and eleven others with him. 165^{17} bonders] + of the district. 191^{20} and said] + as was true. 202^5 this man] + this thick fellow. 208^{33} court] + they laid before the earl the tokens which the earl

and Sigvat had exchanged at parting; also. 224¹³ ambushes] +
and armed men. 235¹⁰ summer] + and they then welcome summer
in. 237¹⁴ or] + do battle with him and. 247³⁹ conversation] + and
in that you take after kinsmen not distant from you. 251⁴⁰
locked up] + alone. 254³⁸ guest-quarters] + which had been
prepared for him. 260³⁰ use] + —. It was a spear. 261²⁸
sent a] + large. 263¹² hereafter] + as it has been till now.
265¹¹ way] + when they were ready. 287¹⁶ you] + refuse this
and. 290⁴ casks] + which seemed to them very extraordinary.
318¹⁸ hell.] + And again Sigvat spoke this verse: "It will be a
sad exchange for Heaven when they plunge into Hell's deep
fires—these men who showed hateful treachery to their lord."
332³ could] + "We will not plunder their bodies," he said.
"Each man is to keep only what he has already won." Then
the men went back on board their ship, and made ready as fast
as they could. 338² race] + if things go as my words indicate.
341¹⁰ sword "] + Then Jokul died. 354⁸ days;] + and equally
clearly I saw places I have not seen before. 370²³ array] +
when the horns sounded and the battle-note was blown, and then
go forward in their array. 391³⁵ means] + or mentions.
394¹⁷ *add* King *before* Trygve.

INTRODUCTION TO INDEXES

(i) ICELANDIC *á* is represented by *aa* and *a*; Icelandic *ö* normally by *o*, sometimes by *ö*; Icelandic final *i* or *ir* as *e*. Medial and final *f* in Icelandic usually appears as *f*, but sometimes as *v*; medial *j* usually appears as *i* but sometimes is omitted entirely; initial *Hl-*, *Hr-* usually appear as *L-*, *R-* (thus *Hlaðir* is rendered as *Lade*, *Hrani* as *Rane*). Icelandic *þ* (=*th* as in *thin*) is represented by *th*; Icelandic *ð* (=*th* as in *then*) by *d*.

In the alphabetical order *æ* is included as if it were *ae*, *œ* as if it were *oe*, and *ö* is found under *o*.

(ii) Under each separate name are first listed those individuals who are not denoted as somebody's son or daughter, and the alphabetical order here depends on their description (nickname, place-name, relationship to some other person). Then come the individuals whose father's or mother's name is given, arranged in alphabetical order according to the parent's name.

(iii) The following abbreviations are used: Abp., archbishop; Bp., bishop; d., daughter; D., Denmark, Danish; E., earl; Emp., emperor; Eng., England, English; f. father; F., Faroes, Faroese; G., Greenland; Gt., Great; I., Iceland, Icelandic; Ir., Ireland, Irish; K., king; m., mother; N., Norway, Norwegian; O., Orkney; O.T., King Olaf Trygvesson; Q., queen; R., Russia; s., son; S., Sweden, Swedish; St., Saint; St. O., King Olaf Haraldsson the Saint; w., wife.

Names of Norwegians and of places in Norway and well-known place-names outside Scandinavia are not normally distinguished by any sign in the Indexes.

INDEX

PERSONS

405

PLACES

GROUP NAMES

THINGS

TAXES, LAWS, ETC.

MYTHICAL AND ANTIQUARIAN

ANIMALS, WEAPONS, SHIPS, ETC.

CHURCHES

LITERARY REFERENCES

BIOGRAPHY

ESSAYS AND CRITICISM

FICTION

HISTORY

LEGENDS AND SAGAS

POETRY AND DRAMA

REFERENCE

RELIGION AND PHILOSOPHY

7

SCIENCE

TRAVEL AND TOPOGRAPHY

EVERYMAN'S LIBRARY was founded in 1906, and the series stands without rival today as the world's most comprehensive low-priced collection of books of classic measure. It was conceived as a library covering the whole field of English literature, including translations of the ancient classics and outstanding foreign works; a series to make widely available those great books which appeal to every kind of reader, and which in essence form the basis of western culture. The aim and scope of the series was crystallized in the title Everyman's Library, justified by world sales totalling (by 1963) some forty-six millions.

There were, of course, already in being in 1906 other popular series of reprints, but none on the scale proposed for Everyman. One hundred and fifty-five volumes were published in three batches in the Library's first year; they comprised a balanced selection from many branches of literature and set the standard on which the Library has been built up. By the outbreak of the First World War the Library was moving towards its 750th volume; and, in spite of the interruptions of two world wars, the aim of the founder-publisher, a library of a thousand volumes, was achieved by the jubilee in 1956, with Aristotle's *Metaphysics*, translated by John Warrington.

In March 1953 a fresh development of the Library began: new volumes and all new issues of established volumes in Everyman's Library were now made in a larger size. The larger volumes have new title-pages, bindings and wrappers, and the text pages have generous margins. Four hundred and twenty-two volumes in this improved format had been issued by 1960. In that year new pictorial wrappers appeared and they have provided the volumes with a surprisingly contemporary 'look'.

Editorially the Library is under constant survey; volumes are examined and brought up to date, with new introductions, annotations and additional matter; often a completely new translation or a newly edited text is substituted when transferring an old volume to the new format. New editions of Demosthenes' *Public Orations*, Harvey's *The Circulation of the Blood and Other Writings*, Aristotle's *Ethics* and Professor T. M. Raysor's reorganization of Coleridge's *Shakespearean Criticism* are examples of this type of revision.

The new larger volumes are in keeping with the original 'home-library' plan but are also in a suitable size for the shelves of all institutional libraries, more so since many important works in Everyman's Library are unobtainable in any other edition. This development entails no break in the continuity of the Library; and fresh titles and verified editions are being constantly added.

A Classified Annotated Catalogue of the library is available free, the annotations giving the year of birth and death of the author, the date of first publication of the work and in many instances descriptive notes on the contents of the last revised Everyman's Library edition. Also available is A. J. Hoppé's *The Reader's Guide to Everyman's Library*, revised and reissued in 1962 as an Everyman Paperback. It gives in one alphabetical sequence references and cross-references of a comprehensive kind, including all authors and all works, even works included in anthologies, and a factual annotation of each work. Running to more than 400 pages, and referring to 1,260 authors, it is virtually a guide to all books of classic standing in the English language.